Stygg Havn

D1308114

BRUCE CASWELL

Copyright © 2020 by Bruce Caswell
All rights reserved. This book or any portion thereof
may not be reproduced or used in any manner
whatsoever without the express written permission
of the publisher except for the use of brief
quotations in a book review.

Printed in the United States of America

First Printing, 2020

ISBN 979-8-56-214978-7

Big Pine Publishing
18045 Berry Lane
Wayzata, MN 55391

www.brucecaswell.com

1 NEW BEGINNINGS

Having lived most of my life on the farm outside of Aitkin, Minnesota, I knew nothing of the wilderness and barren coastline that lay ahead. The only other great adventure in my life had ended in disaster—fighting Germans in the Argonne Forest and losing part of my face to one of Kaiser's sharpshooters. The bullet entered my right eye socket, tore through the bone across my temple, and exited just above my ear. An inch to the left and I would have been dead. An inch to the right and it would have missed me altogether. Funny how fate swings so wildly on such a narrow margin.

Since then, every human interaction had been painful, overshadowed by the insecurity caused by a facial deformity, only partially covered by my eye patch. I'd given up on love and friendship, convinced that solitude would be my only option. That was why the new Assistant Lighthouse Keeper job, deep in the wilderness of Lake Superior's north shore, had so much appeal.

Having left the Aitkin train station a half-hour earlier, the passengers were now settled. The man ahead of me read his newspaper. The mother behind focused on quieting her three excited children. The couple across the aisle had all the youthful excitement and loving mannerisms of newlyweds. Next to me sat a man who appeared wealthy enough to own the whole railroad and every city along the way. His dark gray gabardine suit fit perfectly, complemented by a heavily starched shirt, as bright as a whitewashed wall on a hot summer day. He opened a small monogrammed case, took out two cigarettes, and offered one to me.

"Thanks," I said, impressed. "We're used to rolling our own back in Aitkin. Never had one from a silver case before."

He laughed. His glance bounced from my uniform to my eye patch, then back to my uniform, as if these accoutrements revealed everything he needed to know about me. He pulled from his pocket a sterling contraption with an engraved geometric pattern, matching the one on his cigarette case.

"You a lighthouse keep?" he asked. "In Duluth?"

He withdrew the metal igniter stick from the monogrammed lighter and gave us both a light.

"Assistant, at Stony Point," I answered. "Fifty miles north of Duluth. They say it's really wild up there."

"I know it well," he said. "It is wild, but in ways that might surprise you."

He slipped the lighter into his vest pocket, then brushed a small smudge of ash off of his lapels.

"My name's Gus."

"I'm Jonah," I replied.

"You're a vet?"

I could tell he already knew the answer by the way he asked the question.

"I don't mean to pry," he continued. "My brother Franklin's a vet. Lost a leg in the war. Been working ever since to get his life back together."

"Must not be working all that hard," I said. "The war's been over for six years."

Gus gave a bitter look, making me rethink the insensitivity of my comment. I took a long drag on the cigarette, then blew a line of smoke up toward the ceiling.

"What I meant to say was that Franklin and I have lots in common. Both of us pissed away the last six years of our lives. It's easy to do when your life's been ripped apart by the war."

I wanted to leave it at that; I always tried to avoid conversations about my army years.

"That's why you're going to Stony Point?" he asked. "To start anew?"

"You might say that."

Truth was, I was getting away, not just starting anew. In the first months of my return from the war, the whole city of Aitkin rallied to help. My initial plan was to return to the family farm. But over the months and then years, the neighborly support melted into a sickly sweet perpetuity of pity that I couldn't escape from.

"Travelling alone then?" Gus asked. "Not married?"

"Yeah. I'm alone. Not married."

I saw no good reason to elaborate about an ex-wife who insisted we get married before I shipped off to war, then couldn't stand the sight of me once I returned. After we split, she went on to date every available man in Aitkin County. Some new guy every weekend. I pretended not to care, but it was hard to let go. She still had the train-stopping beauty of a movie star. Jenny finally married Fred, a man much older, but with lots of money from his banking business. They moved into the old mansion in Aitkin, right off Main Street. That's when I knew I had to leave.

"Strange to think how different life would have been if not for the war," I said. "Maybe I'd still be on the family farm. Now I just want to live my own life, far away from all those people. The solitude of Stony Point should suit me well."

"Solitude?" Gus asked, looking confused. He started to talk but took a long drag off his cigarette instead.

"So, how's Franklin?"

The question yanked Gus out of his deep thought. He wiped his hair back and surveyed the passengers nearby.

"Franklin? Oh, he'll be ok."

I grimaced. "He's an amputee. His leg's buried in some French battlefield. And you think he's ok?"

Gus pulled another cigarette out of his case for me and gave me a light.

"Maybe he's not ok," he said. "He sits on the porch all day, counting the ships that go in and out of Duluth Harbor. That's all he does."

Gus watched the trees fly by as we sped through a tamarack bog, which stretched east to west as far as we could see. Scrubby clumps of trees poked from thickets of speckled alder, willow, and swamp holly. I'd hunted deer around the edges of these swamps but never ventured very deep into them. They're tough to get into and even worse to get out of.

"Everything you said rings true," Gus said. "Franklin doesn't think he belongs. He doesn't want to be around people anymore. All his friends are off living their own lives, running their businesses, and socializing at their clubs. He has a law degree and practiced for over a year before the war, but now he doesn't want to work. The gals that used to flock to him never come around anymore."

I adjusted my eye patch, making sure it covered as much of the empty socket and scars across my temple as possible.

"How did you get the job?" Gus asked.

"My uncle. He works for the Lighthouse Service in Detroit."

Dad begged him to find me a job. Luckily they were having a hard time filling the position at Stony Point. Uncle Amos applied for me, conveniently omitting a few important facts. My new boss will be surprised to find an unmarried one-eyed assistant. Hopefully they can't just send me back once I'm up there.

I closed my eyes, hoping for a moment of silence. For me, a full day of physical work is energizing, while a half-hour of conversation sucks the life right out of me. Listening to the rhythm of the rails, I imagined a lighthouse high above the waters of Lake Superior, the waves lapping against the rocky shoreline below. Water as far as the eye could see to the southeast, and nothing but dense forests and craggy rock formations to the northwest. It gave me hope. Made me almost optimistic.

"You should stop by the house and meet Franklin. Stay with us for a couple of days. You could always take the next ship to the lighthouse."

"My orders are to arrive today, May 15. I need to board the steamer as soon as I get to Duluth."

Gus took a drag off his cigarette, flicked the ash into the tray, and watched the swamp roll by.

"I should tell you, though. Stony Point isn't all wilderness. Not anymore. There's a completely different kind of wild up there now."

#

Scanning the ships docked along the piers of Duluth Harbor, I lowered my expectations for the steamer from Duluth to Stony Point. Rust-bucket freighters of all kinds and shapes filled the harbor, their bulkheads scarred by bubbled and peeling paint, crisscrossed with veins of rust. Decks were lumpy and dull from years of accumulated grime and varnish. Coal-fired boilers belched lung-burning black smoke from their stacks. Coarse men from unfamiliar shores packed the piers and ships, none of them as friendly or upstanding as the Germans and Scandinavians that filled the streets and churches of Aitkin.

Yet my steamer, the SS America, stood out like a petunia in a potato patch. Its crew busily scrubbed teak decks, cleaned windows, and polished fixtures, preparing for her departure. Its freshly painted white bulkheads glowed against the pier. Just above the waterline, rows of portholes ran the length of the ship. The main deck featured curved glass windows looking out across the bow, followed by a stretch of large windows to midship. Beyond that, a line of lifeboats was tied up against the railings. Sitting at the top of it all was a glass-enclosed room, which must have been the pilothouse, perched like the final tier of a wedding cake.

Before boarding, I worried that my cleaned and pressed keeper's uniform might be too haughty. I was told the boat hauled trout and herring from all the fishing villages along the north shore, to be processed and marketed by the factories in Duluth. But there were none of the roustabout fishermen, miners, and lumberjacks that I'd expected to be making this trip.

The decks overflowed with the swankiest bunch of young men I'd ever seen, straight from the society pages of Harper's Magazine. They wore suit jackets over pleated pants, topped with straw boater hats or an occasional fedora. The less formal sported two-tone shoes, knickers, colorful Fair Isle sweaters, and tweed flatcaps like the golfers wear. They hobnobbed among themselves, shaking hands and slapping backs as one might at a college fraternity reunion. It made no sense; these sheiks heading up into the wilderness aboard a ship made for hauling fish. They packed the decks tighter than the hordes at the Aitkin County Fair on a Friday night.

I'd never cared for crowds. Bumping through the multitude of dandies brought back the terrors and shell shock from the war. The thick smoke from the freighters and the commotion of the stevedores felt oddly similar to the danger of the trenches. The loud hum of the steamship engines reminded me of machine guns firing from the German lines. It all brought back the jitters, shortness of breath, and claustrophobia that haunted me and took me at inopportune times. My anxiety turned into panic as the ship's horn blew three ear-piercing blasts, signaling its backing away from the pier. I forced my way through the crowd toward the port side, hoping to find it less crowded.

Whether polite or perturbed, most of the dandies let me through—all except for the largest among the crowd. He blocked my passage, standing next to a ladder up to the pilothouse. Wearing a golf cardigan two sizes too small, the crescent-shaped bulge of his belly flopped out between his belt and sweater. His face was round and puffy, like an overripe tomato. He lifted me a foot off the ground with a monstrous bear hug that squeezed the jiffy out of me. The corners of his smile curled up way too high, pushing pencil-thin lips deep into the fatty jowls bulging from the sides of his face. I thrashed to loosen his grip, but he held tight, laughing as I struggled to pull my arms loose.

"Patchy!" he said, making fun of my eye covering. "A one-eyed pushy-patchy. Looks like someone needs to teach you manners."

Having pulled my right arm out from his grasp, I grabbed the metal ladder leading up to the pilothouse and swung my leg around, hooking my foot on one of the rungs.

"Time for Patchy to get tossed overboard!"

He let loose an almost girl-like screeching laugh, an octave higher than might have been expected from a guy his size. As he tried to pull me away from the ladder, my left arm came free. Without a thought, I boxed his right ear, bringing my cupped hand hard against the side of his head, knowing it would rupture his eardrum and hurt like a hammer-smashed finger. His crazy smile turned to shock as he dropped me and grabbed the side of his head before falling to his knees. I scrambled up the ladder to the platform outside of the pilothouse, crawled through the open doorway, and slid into the chair next to the binnacle. Unable to catch my breath, I completely ignored the captain at the helm. My chest heaved, my head bobbed up and down between my knees, and my lungs labored, starved for oxygen.

"Some nerve," he said. "Comin' in here after picking fights with my passengers."

I tried to control my breathing but couldn't, huffing like a dog left too long in the hot sun.

"You havin' a heart attack?"

I couldn't talk, stand, or sit up straight. The captain reached into the cupboard and pulled out an old greasy paper bag.

"Breathe into this before you pass out."

It took a while, but the bag and the relative calm of the pilothouse helped me settle, and my breathing came under control. By now, we'd steamed out of the canal and past the city, the mansions of Duluth's richest families spreading out in front of us along the lakeshore. The young men crowded the portside deck to catch the best view of the shoreline. The captain steered with one hand and made entries to the ship's log with the other. His eyes bounced back and forth from the rocky coast to the logbook. He looked as tough as the wilderness with a chiseled face framed by a nest of curly white hair and a tangle of a beard. But his uniform conveyed authority. The brightness of the white twill cloth and the crispness of the creases spoke of his professionalism.

"His name's Lenny. A real dunce. Always tormenting someone on board. He's a keg of dynamite looking for a match."

He glanced my way, then did a double take, having only now noticed my eye patch.

"What's wrong with your face?"

"Jonah Franken. New keeper. Stony Point."

"That's not what I asked. What happened to your face?"

"Great War. Argonne Forest. Got shot."

After a couple of deep breaths, I pulled my face out of the bag, sat up, and adjusted the patch over my eye socket. I searched for Lenny in the crowd but couldn't find him.

"Where'd all these dandies come from?" I asked. "They look straight out of some high society magazine."

"Oh, they're high society, all right. Some of the richest young men ever."

The captain scanned the deck like a chaperone at a school dance.

"The sons of Duluth's finest. Their daddies made millions in lumber, shipping, and mining. Those boys are hell-bent on spending their family's money as fast as they can."

I wiped my hair back and took a tug at my coat sleeves. The bow ahead of us sliced through the wave crests, blowing up a curl of foam that cascaded back down along the hull.

"What are they doing up here?"

The captain appeared confused by the question, obviously thinking everyone knew what these men were up to.

"You don't know? They're going to Stony Point Lodge. Right next to the lighthouse. Didn't they tell you about the lodge?"

My dream of a reclusive existence at an isolated outpost on the unpopulated fringe of the wilderness burned off like the morning fog. I picked up the greasy bag and put it back up to my mouth.

"The swankiest place west of Chicago," he continued. "Mr. Gates built it. Just finished it last year. Got its own electric light power plant. Heck, the lighthouse doesn't even have electric lights. At night, the lodge shines like heaven. A regular playland for the rich. All summer long, this steamer will be filled, bringing young men back and forth from Duluth to Stony Point. Can't say for a fact, but I'm told the men's steamer trunks are empty on the ride up and full of Canadian whisky on the ride back. Great way to thumb your nose at prohibition."

"Any women?"

The captain smiled as if we'd stumbled upon his favorite topic.

"No wives or girlfriends if that's what you mean. Gates says Stony Point is a gentlemen's lodge. A place to hunt and fish. Says it's no place for a bunch of wives who would just spoil all the fun."

"So, no women?"

The captain struck a smile and held it longer than what was comfortable. After two friendly slaps to my knee, he took a deep breath.

"Oh, there're women all right. Dozens of them with the beauty of movie stars. Gates calls them his Dainty Dollies. Each one as young, fresh, and easy to look at as anyone you'd find in the big cities."

"What do they do?" I asked.

"Gates swears that they're waitresses, cigarette girls, dancers, or singers. I say they're the sprinkles on the cake, the thrill that makes a trip to Stony Point worth the effort. Gates says there's no heavy petting, but one can only imagine what happens when the hotsy-totsies and the stinking rich get together miles away from prying eyes."

"Right next to the lighthouse?"

"All summer long. The women stay in a dorm just past the lodge, and there's a fresh new batch of rich young men every week. It all happens right across the harbor from the lighthouse, on the hill above the little fishing village."

The captain closed his logbook and set it on the shelf where the greasy bag had been.

"Everyone likes Gates. He's as swanky as they come. You

like parties?"

"Not really," I said. "I'd rather have my teeth pulled."

He took a long look at my face, first the normal left profile and then the mangled right side.

"Well, if the lodge doesn't pan out, there's always the fishing village. A real craphole. Nothing but a pier, a handful of tar-paper shacks, and a small warehouse. Living there must be as painful as having your teeth pulled."

The captain went back to his work. The young men on the deck below talked and laughed in small groups along the railing as the mansions slowly gave way to the rocks and forests of the wilderness. Lenny had one of the ship's crew in a headlock, leaning him over the edge, threatening to throw him over. His antics came as no surprise to the captain.

I focused on the wilderness gliding by. The rugged shoreline stretched endlessly, showing only an occasional scar from years of logging or mining in the area. We journeyed past granite outcroppings mixed with stands of white pine, aspen, and birch. Rivers and creeks wove jagged paths through the rock, cascading to the great lake from the rugged forests above. The air off Superior prickled with an icy clean crispness that took your breath away.

It'd been six years since coming home from the Great War with nothing but fields of corn to fill up my landscapes. Nothing like the exhilaration of primordial waters and the ruggedness of the wilderness. The bow slicing through the waves offered a pleasant rhythm that settled my nerves and took my mind off the Dainty Dollies and wealthy socialites.

#

The engines throttled down to a soft purr as we made our way around Tollefson Island into Stony Point Harbor. It wasn't that large as harbors go—about the size of a horse pasture back home. And the island was more of a peninsula, connected to the southwest side of the harbor, then running up to the northeast, providing protection for half of the bay.

"Without that island, Stony Point would be as godforsaken as the rest of the shoreline up here," the captain said. "It keeps the storms and ice from tearing the whole damn place apart."

The sights captivated me. The main lodge stretched across the hillside, larger and more imposing than any of the lakeside mansions north of Duluth. On the other side of the harbor, the lighthouse stood as a venerable fortress upon a tall granite outcropping, surrounded by a little hamlet of well-maintained buildings.

Across from the pier laid the junky, cluttered, and disheveled village. Against the grandeur of the lighthouse and the lodge, the fishing camp was a dump. Tar-paper shacks, a broken-down warehouse, dilapidated storage buildings, and drying reels for the nets littered the shore. It reminded me of the ravine on the farm where we dumped anything no longer useful, leaving a tangled pile of rusting rubbish. The fishing village could easily have been mistaken for the lodge's trash pile.

As we docked, two open-air busses and two trucks belched smoke, idling along the shore, positioned strategically to block the filthy fishing village from view. The young guests disembarked, heading straight for a flock of ladies along the shore, as if they were old friends. The women were flirtatious but not sexual, familiar, but not intimate. Each was outfitted identically as if in uniform—yellow dresses with above-the-knee hems, blue sashes across the hips, long strings of pearls, and a blue hat with a shape similar to the Keystone Cops helmets. Each had a tray of drinks or finger food for the new arrivals. Not the typical welcome party for a wilderness hunting and fishing camp.

Some guests and greeters paired up right away. Others formed into friendly and chatty small groups. Impressively, not a single guest appeared to be alone, each quickly pulled in with amiable smiles and engaging conversations.

Among them, a tall, blond-haired gentleman drew as much attention as the women. Dressed in a cream-colored suit with a red carnation boutonniere, he approached each of the new arrivals as a close friend might, making a point of shaking hands and joking with guests as they piled onto the bus. As the busses rumbled up the dirt road to the lodge, he stayed behind, overseeing the steamer crew and lodge attendants, who busily unloaded the luggage, supplies, and cargo destined for the lodge, then loaded boxes of trout and herring from the fishing village into the lower holds. Once finished, the SS America backed away from the dock with three loud horn blasts.

I walked along the pier to find my luggage, rightly assuming I'd get no help from the lodge attendants. Everything lay organized along the edge of the dock according to its use or intended destination. Steamer trunks lined one side. The cartons of food, bushels of vegetables, and boxes of baked goods were stacked across the other side, along with the linens, floral arrangements, and operational supplies for the lodge. A small, half-crushed box set apart from the rest of the goods. I opened the box and found six red carnation boutonnieres, all smashed flat. A casualty in what had otherwise been a very orderly unloading.

"Hey, fella! What do you have there?"

The man in the cream-colored suit charged across the pier toward me. I held the flowers out with a stunned, guilty look, like a kid caught with Mutt & Jeff comics at Sunday school.

"Those my boutonnieres?"

He took the box from my hand, inspecting the damage with great disappointment, sorting through them like broken fine china.

"Are you Mr. Gates?" I asked.

"Humph," he answered. "A real mess. All ruined. What happened here?"

"I found them this way. They must have . . ."

I didn't know what to say that wouldn't sound like a sad excuse. He poked at the boutonnieres, inspecting each one.

"Well, they're no good. Can't wear smashed carnations now, can I?"

Gates glanced at my uniform and my face, then chuckled.

"You the new keep?"

"Yes, sir."

"Have you met Cephas or Polly yet?" he asked.

"Who are they?"

"Cephas is the head keeper, and Polly is his other assistant. They'll pop a rivet when they see you."

It was strange how people reacted. Most looked away, not wishing to be rude. Some flushed with pity. Gates was amused by my disfigurement. I guess some people are so far removed from affliction that they're entertained by it. He turned toward the lodge, laughing and poking at his smashed carnations.

#

The lighthouse had a dock too, but not one deep enough for the steamer. With both hands behind my back, holding tight to the leather strap of my footlocker, I dragged my luggage across the harbor, from the village to the lighthouse. From the shore, I watched as the busses and trucks rolled up along the southwest side of the lawns above, before unloading guests and supplies onto the large patios that surrounded the lodge. Being careful not to slip and fall, my concentration shifted back and forth, from the sights and sounds of the festivities above to the shoreline of smooth stones ahead of me, avoiding any of the larger rocks that might cause me to trip.

The lodge dwarfed everything in sight, including the lighthouse. The center of the building featured tall sweeps of leaded glass rising four stories to a peaked green tiled roof. Stone columns separated the window panels, stretching from the patios below, all the way upward to the eaves. Wings spread out from either side of the main room, built of timbers and stone. Dormers jutted out from the rafters on the fourth floor, and green awnings shaded the windows on the first three floors. It all had a solid rustic quality while at the same time feeling open and airy—a very tasteful combination of north shore wilderness mixed with opulence and style.

Captivated by the grandeur of the lodge, I failed to notice the large rock straight in front of me until it was too late. My face hit the ground, and the luggage landed across my legs. I rolled out from under the trunk, picked myself up off the shore, wiped the dirt from my coat, and resumed the dragging.

These blunders and hardships drew neither ridicule nor sympathy from two men who watched me from the lighthouse dock. Both wore their official keeper uniforms. The older one had the sober appearance of Ulysses Grant with his piercing eyes, slicked-back hair, and graying beard. I assumed him to be Cephas, the head keep. The other was short and round with intelligent eyes and a grin that looked either mischievous or malicious, depending on which way he faced.

Cephas didn't look at me as I approached, but the stumpy guy stared sharply, like a painter studies his subject, peering deep inside, capturing every aspect of human essence. It felt invasive. I reached the edge of the dock drenched in sweat, my hair flopping across my face and my eye patch covering only half of the socket.

"You in the right place?" Cephas asked.

The short guy snorted, choking back a laugh. Cephas glanced away, then back. He scanned the harbor—his eyes bouncing from the pier, to the lodge, to the lighthouse, and back to the pier, focusing on anything and everything but me. I straightened out my eye patch, wiped my forehead, and pushed my hair back under my cap. The short guy chimed in before I could answer.

"Can I see your eyeball?"

"Shut up, Polly."

Undeterred, Polly reached up toward my eye patch. Cephas grabbed his arm, pulling it back with the intensity and impatience one might show to an unruly teenager after a lifelong history of disobedience. If I could take any solace from my bad first impression, it was knowing that Cephas was equally dissatisfied with Polly.

"Jonah Franken," I said. "Your new assistant."

"Franken?" Polly asked, trying to keep a straight face. "Like Frankenstein?"

Polly had a way of capturing attention. A natural tenor with a scratchy voice, he talked like a preteen who had smoked too many cigarettes. On the surface, one could disregard his verbal jabs as no more than sarcastic entertainment, but he had something sinister in his eyes and a smile that suggested malice. Cephas took his cap off, combed his oily hair back, and then replaced the cap, looking irritated.

"Where's your wife?" Cephas asked. "Your application said you were married. And what happened to your eye?"

"Lost it in the war. That must have been mentioned on my application."

I knew I'd have some explaining to do upon my arrival, knowing darned well that my application made no mention of missing eyes or nonexistent wives. My uncle, who had submitted the paperwork, had done whatever needed to be done to get me off the farm and out of Aitkin.

" . . . and when it came to leaving our hometown, my wife couldn't bear to leave her family back home," I said, lying again.

I kept talking as long as Cephas would allow—about my time in the war, serving in the Signal Corps, being shot just before Armistice, and then coming back home to live on the farm. I talked about Jenny as if she'd been a perfect angel, standing by me through all the trials of my injury, right up to her crying into her handkerchief as the train left the station for Duluth.

"I got a wife," Polly said. "Round as a harbor buoy. She just might have that baby any day now."

"Enough," Cephas said. "I've heard way too much blather from both of you gobwaggers. Grab your stuff and get it up to the cottage."

A long staircase rose from the shore to the right and a tramway to the left—both leading up to the lighthouse. The tram rode along a raised railbed, lifted by a gasoline-powered winch at the top. Polly slapped me on the back in a superior sort of way as I dragged my steamer trunk onto the trolley.

"Lucky for trams," he said. "Or Frankenstein would be hauling that luggage up that cliff by hisself."

Polly liked to talk. I didn't trust him and found his idle chatter nerve-racking. On the tram ride up, his blathering about old girlfriends, communism, and prohibition, went largely ignored. My attention was fixed on the tan-colored brick lighthouse ahead of us, trimmed in white and topped with a large lantern peering out across the great lake. Six other buildings surrounded the tower, all aligned as if by some strict military code. Built of brick and tile, everything looked overbuilt, even with the fury of Lake Superior taken into account. The site had a dignity, scale, and sheer weight that, like the lodge, seemed out of place so deep in the wilderness.

Once my gear was stowed, Polly introduced me to the lighthouse with an authority that would lead one to believe he had built the whole darn thing himself.

"A real feat of engineering," he said. "Has a third-order, bivalve Fresnel lens made in France. The lamp is one of those Heap air-pressure pneumatic lamps. Some fine technology, yes, sir."

Polly's wife, Elsie, came out to meet us. She was a short woman, whose pregnancy made her as round as she was tall. Side by side, the two had the profiles of Tweedledee and Tweedledum. She had an earthy inelegance like her husband, but hers came from simplicity, not heartlessness.

"What happened to your face?" she asked.

"Had it blowed off!" Polly said. "Blown apart by a kraut during the war. Looks like hell, don't it?"

Elsie nodded in agreement, curling her lip up as if the nature of my deformity finally made sense. She rubbed her belly with one hand and twirled one of her reddish-brown curls with the other.

"You married?" she asked.

"Left her back home," Polly answered. "His wife didn't want to come. Probably making time with some other man back home, don't ya think?"

Elsie laughed nervously, slightly embarrassed.

#

Elsie spent the afternoon cooking dinner for us. By six o'clock, we were all gathered around the stove in Polly and Elsie's cottage, each holding a large bowl, waiting for our helpings of venison stew. After filling our bowls, we moved on to grab fresh-baked biscuits from a plate next to the stove. Cephas and I each took two. Polly took five. We sat at the table, and Cephas said grace before we all dug in.

"Why all the buildings?" I asked. "There's room up here for two or three platoons of men."

"If you're complaining, we can find a tent for you to sleep in," Cephas said.

"Not complaining. Just never lived in a place so big. I figured I'd be sleeping in some cozy corner of the lighthouse."

"The Lighthouse Service designed the cottages for large families," he said.

"They figure a wife and kids are extra hands for all the chores that need to be done. That's why I was curious as to the whereabouts of your wife."

"Yes! Your wife must come and stay," Elsie said. "I need someone to help with cooking and chores. I need a friend to have coffee with. We need more women and children up here."

"Well, I have no kids, and my wife's not here. So, where do I stay?" I asked.

"My cottage is the one closest to the lighthouse," Cephas said. "Polly and Elsie get this one right in the middle. Yours is the one furthest from the lighthouse."

Polly sat across from me, paying no attention to our conversation. Three of his biscuits were already gone. He crumbled his fourth into the bowl of stew.

"What about the two barns in back?" I asked. "You keep horses?"

"No horses. Those are workshops. Full of all the tools, hardware, and lumber you might ever need up here. There'll be no excuses for not getting chores done."

"There's a foghorn building too," Elsie said. "Heavens, those horns make a horrible sound. I nearly wet my pants every time they go off. Sounds like the bellowing of some nasty sea creature."

Cephas wiped the corners of his mouth with his napkin before pushing his chair away from the table.

"You'll have plenty of time to learn all about your job up here," he said. "The first thing you need to know is we each have four-hour shifts every night. Polly starts at eight o'clock, I start at midnight, and your shift starts at four in the morning. That means it's time for us all to catch some sleep."

He didn't have to ask me twice.

#

I jolted up from bed with the ear-splitting ring of the alarm clock, which I'd set for three o'clock. I lit the kerosene lantern on the nightstand next to my bed and went to the bathroom to pee. The party at the lodge was in full swing, and in the still of the night, the screams, laughs, and curses could be heard over the distance. Polly's scratchy tenor voice rose above it all, punctuated with laughter and jeers from the guests. I couldn't understand all the words but recognized the raspy pitch of his voice and the way he emphasized his syllables, ranging from sharp staccato outbursts to broad, flowing lyrics. I could only guess how entertaining it would have been to hear all the words.

Earlier in the evening, I had organized everything for my first shift. My cleaned and pressed shirt, trousers, and coat hung on the valet stand. The polished shoes sat next to the bed. My folded undershorts, undershirt, and socks sat in a neat stack on my dresser, along with my pocket watch, carving knife, wallet, and eye patch. This was my first real job off the farm. I wanted to be on time and make a good impression. Before going to bed, I had taken inventory of what would be needed and double-checked to make sure everything would go according to plan.

As I got dressed, I noted that my carving knife, pocket watch, and wallet were still sitting on my folded undershirt, but the eye patch was nowhere to be found. It had been right where it was supposed to be, twice confirmed the night before. Nothing of mine had much value, and the eye patch would have been worthless to anyone else. No other man within five hundred miles would have a need for that small circle of cloth. I turned the building upside down looking for it. The sheets were pulled off the bed and shaken. Everything was emptied from my steamer trunk. I moved the dresser away from the wall, checked all the drawers, and swept the floor. I covered every inch of the cottage, still unable to find my eye patch.

Retracing my steps, I recalled all my activities from the night before, making a mental note of any place I might have left it. The more I searched, the more I considered it stolen.

I tried unsuccessfully to make a replacement with a leather shoelace and a hankie. The flimsy materials and my poor sewing skills resulted in something more similar to a shepherd's sling. It hid neither the socket nor the scars and made me look like a kid all costumed up for Halloween. If anything else was missing, it wouldn't have bothered me so. My watch, knife, and even my underwear seemed unnecessary by comparison. I needed the eye patch.

I searched the cottage one more time before dressing, then climbed the outside stairs to the cleaning room adjacent to the lighthouse tower, already fifteen minutes late for my first shift.

"Britches!" Cephas said. "Your eye!"

By now, I'd given up hope for a positive first impression with Cephas. His pipe hung from the side of his mouth, his Bible laid in his lap, and piles of lighthouse logbooks were haphazardly stacked next to him. He stared as I sat down in the chair, waiting for some explanation.

"The patch is gone. Someone stole it."

Cephas stood with his arms outstretched like a preacher on Sunday morning. The pipe hung loosely from his lip as his Bible fell to the floor. He waved his hands up and down three times, as if only one or two waves wouldn't fully capture the magnitude of his displeasure.

"Who on this side of Hades would give a rip 'n fizzle about your blasted eye patch?"

Cephas's hand shook as he pulled the pipe out of his mouth. I'd noticed his tremor earlier in the day as he lit the tobacco, but he trembled more now. He stared through me, both mad and repulsed as he reached down and picked up his Bible.

"I had it on my dresser, now it's gone."

Cephas raised his Bible, appearing ready to call upon the holy powers to intercede, then he melted back into his chair, the book in one hand and the pipe in the other. He set the Bible down on the stack of logbooks, grabbed the old coffee can from under the seat, and tapped the ashes from the pipe into the can.

"One more year," he said. "Lord, help me survive one more year so I can retire. Retirement with a full pension. That's all I ask."

He put his hand on the Bible, giving his prayer a little more emphasis.

"Lord, save me from these dunderheaded flapjacks who don't have a lick of sense. Help me survive just one more year."

Cephas stuffed the pipe into his coat pocket, slowly rose, and then walked through a small passageway to the tower, a spiral staircase running from the base to the watch room up above.

"You coming?" he called back. "Think I'm bound to do all the work myself?"

When I reached the top of the spiral lighthouse staircase, Cephas was already leaning over a complex contraption with gears the size of wagon wheels and a crank as long as a man's arm.

"'Bout time you earn your keep. Here's the clockwork mechanism. It turns the lantern above. Wind it every two hours. No exceptions."

He stood with his hands on his hips until I realized he wanted me to do the cranking. I cranked as he continued his lecture.

"The light rotates with a flashing sequence of ten seconds. Not nine, not eleven, but ten. A half-second on, and nine and a half seconds off. This is real important. Each lighthouse has a different sequence, so a ship captain will know which lighthouse they're viewing. We don't want boat captains to be confused."

The cranking was hard. I figured I could handle any physical requirements at least as well as Polly or Cephas. Still, my arms ached after the required cranks. From Polly's earlier tour, I had learned the glass and steel lens structure that the clockwork turned weighed a full four tons and floated on a frictionless bed of mercury.

"You get used to it," he said. "Be sure to check the ten-second flash sequence regularly. Lock the mechanism in the morning once you extinguish the light."

He turned to a brass tank hanging on the wall with a little hand pump on its side. "This is the kerosene for the light. Takes two gallons. Fill it up every morning, and pressurize it every two hours with this little pump. In the morning, use this petcock here to extinguish the lamp."

He led me up the ladder to the lantern room half encased in glass, the giant lens contraption smoothly rotating in a clockwise direction, shooting out the beam of light.

"Every morning, start by inspecting the lantern and trimming the wick. Then put on a pair of clean white linen gloves, and use a feather duster or one of the white cleaning cloths to polish the soot off each lens. It should take you at least an hour and a half. Once everything is spotless, lower the lens bag over the whole mechanism, and close the curtains in the lantern room. Otherwise, the sunlight discolors the lenses."

He opened the glass door and led me out to the lantern gallery, the outside catwalk at the top of the lighthouse that surrounded the lantern room. I had been doing my best to keep a mental note of each task as we went through the tour, but the sights and sounds from the metal balcony filled my head, overriding everything I'd learned up until that point. The beam reached infinitely, sweeping out across the glassy expanse of Superior. Every puff of breeze gave me goose bumps as the wind rose and fell. The noises from across the harbor were amplified. Laughing and joking from the lodge rang through as if it came from the cottage next door. Smells of pine forests and burning kerosene were refreshing compared to the years of manure stench on the farm.

We stood on the dark side of the gallery to avoid the bright light. To the southeast, only a rough outline of the fishing village resting against the shore was visible in the moonlight. The boats were pulled up along the water's edge, nets drying on their reels. Above the shacks, the lodge shone as bright as day, the windows of the great room glowing with a honey-amber hue. Lights along the walkways illuminated the patios and gardens leading down to the expansive lawn, and even the lawn shimmered with its own electric lamps. Guests gathered outside, still buzzing with plenty of energy at this late hour.

"Are you paying attention?"

"Yes, sir," I replied, hoping to reassure him, even though everything he'd said dissolved among the incredible sights, sounds, and smells.

As we stood out on the gallery, a ship came into view, crossing the beam of light, looking like a speck out on the water near the horizon. Cephas checked the time, then grabbed a telescope for a closer look. From there, he headed back down to the cleaning room and entered the sighting into the logbook.

"Ore boat out of Two Harbors," he said. "You don't have to, but I like to keep track of the boats. It helps me appreciate the work we're doing."

Cephas closed the book and set it back down on top of the pile. He pulled the pipe from his pocket and scraped the bowl with his knife, then tapped the few remaining ashes into the coffee can on the floor. He slipped the pipe through his tobacco pouch, packed the shag with his thumb, and then lit it with those trembling fingers. With a series of sharp breaths, the flame sucked down into the bowl at each inhale.

"This is a holy place," Cephas said. "Look at that beam out there. On a clear dark night, they can see this light from as far away as Grand Marais. Like the eye of the Lord, bringing safety and salvation for those mariners."

With his pipe clenched in his teeth, he picked up his well-worn Bible and opened it to a dog-eared page.

"For the eyes of the Lord run to and fro throughout the whole earth, to give strong support to those whose heart is blameless toward him," he quoted. "Second Chronicles, chapter 16. You remember that, Jonah. A holy place. The eye of the Lord."

We both watched as the beam swept from left to right, methodically making its full pass. Every ten seconds.

"Polly in bed?" I asked.

"Doubt it. He's up at the lodge. The guests all think he's a hoot. Gates says he's cheap entertainment for the boys."

He closed his Bible and set it back on the stack of logbooks. "Quite the storyteller," Cephas said. "All Polly needs is a thread of truth. Next thing you know, he weaves it into a web of intrigue, suspense, horror, and comedy that keeps everyone on the edges of their seats. Certainly gives the men and the Dainty Dollies something to talk about."

He crossed his legs and puffed on his pipe with long draws, looking much more relaxed than he had earlier. "Polly puts all his body into those stories. He waves his arms to punctuate words, moves his feet to set a tempo, and mugs it up with crazy facial contortions to emphasize a galaxy of emotions. He goes on and on about his war years, his hometown shenanigans, old romances, and loony relatives."

Cephas lit another match and circled it around the pipe bowl to relight, even though most of the tobacco was ash by now.

"Polly doesn't do much work up here and hardly listens to me anymore. He figures as long as Gates is happy, he doesn't really care what I think. Says if he loses the job at the lighthouse, he'll just go work at the lodge. I shouldn't let him get away with it, but sometimes it's easier when that big blob is gone."

The tobacco burned out again. He tapped the ash into the can, cleaned the bowl, stuck the pipe in his coat pocket, and stood to leave.

"You a Christian?" Cephas asked.

"Used to be," I answered. "Haven't been to church since before the war."

"That's a long time," he said. "A man like you could use some religion. Make sure you find that eye patch."

#

Cephas went back to his cottage. I pulled my knife and a piece of basswood out of my pocket and sat down to carve. Carving settled my nerves. Even as a little boy, while everyone else played stickball or cops and robbers, my joy came from finding a quiet place to whittle. After the Great War, I had plenty of time to hone my skills, leaving the house full of little knickknacks and figurines.

As the wood chips fell to the floor, a rough figurine began to reveal itself. A round blob for a head, followed by a roughed-out torso, shoulders, and legs. With the figure blocked out, I whittled a boot for each foot and shaped the legs. Above the knee, I carved out the rain slicker and added detail to both arms. Within an hour, the body came to completion, finished off with a storm cap that covered his head and sloped down over his shoulders. Carving the face was always the most enjoyable part. I added a scowling sneer, an exaggerated nose, and huge bushy eyebrows that peeked out from under the cap.

With the carving complete, the knife and the old fisherman carved of basswood went back in my pocket. I climbed the spiral staircase to the watch room to check the lantern clockwork and the kerosene tank pressurization. By now, the wind had grown from a light breeze to a strong blow out of the southeast. Whitecaps crashed against the granite promontory below, making the whole lighthouse shake.

Moving away from the farm scared the dickens out of me, and worried Mom and Dad even more. After six years of festering, we all knew I couldn't stay at home. Having left, the thought of failure was too hard to bear. With Aitkin in my past, the lighthouse had to be my future. Cephas considered the place to be his "eye of the Lord." I needed it to be my hermitage, my retreat, my place of solitude for thinking, dreaming, and surviving.

Stony Point was originally described to me as nothing but jagged rocks and treacherous waters. A place of rough seas, fierce storms, freezing winds, and steep cliffs. That would've been fine by me. Even better would have been a place without Polly, Cephas, Gates, or partying guests. I hoped for solitude, a wilderness where a man can run around naked if he wanted to, with no one to notice or care.

Aside from all the people, Stony Point was a dream come true. In the letter of reassurance to my parents, I focused on the positive attributes—the blessed serenity in the watch room, high above the rest of the world. The peace that came from within the steel and brick fortress. The tower's strength, even as the winds whipped and the waves crashed outside. I wrote of the beam shining infinitely out across the waters, with a light that hypnotized as it swept from left to right, erasing layer after layer of trouble and trepidation. How the crisp, clear air filled my lungs, making me feel healthier than I'd been since before the war.

In the midst of my editorial optimism, a group of men gathered along the lighthouse dock below. The strong winds muffled their voices while they excitedly flailed their arms, chasing in and out among the waves like children. I folded my near-finished letter, slipped it into my pocket, and checked the ten-second time interval of the beam. Looking back out the window, I saw that the group of men were on their way up the stairs from shore, pushing, shoving, and falling as they raced to the top, soon congregating along the walkway near Polly's cottage. As they moved closer, Polly's high scratchy voice could be heard above the heavy weather, growling like a monster, then screaming as if in pain.

I ran down the circular stairs as the voices grew louder, worried that someone might have been hurt along the shore or while climbing the stairs. Polly continued to howl like a wolf caught in a steel trap as the rest of the crowd yelled and screamed along with him. A gust of wind startled me when I swung the lighthouse door open. Waves crashed around us, spray reaching all the way up to the lighthouse walkway. Polly stood two steps in front of the small band of lodge guests, staring at me in disbelief. Each of them looked drunk to the gills.

"Frankenstein!" Polly shouted. "Just like I said. A monster! Look at his face!"

Polly wore a red neckerchief, a tan vest, a blousy shirt that probably belonged to Elsie, and striped swimming shorts. Rounding out his eclectic costume was my eye patch, covering his right eye. He stepped back as I reached through the crowd, grabbing him with both hands around his collar. He fell backward, and I landed on top of him. The two of us wrestled on the wet gravel walkway, me fighting for my eye patch, and him wriggling to get free. He ripped the patch from his face, then tossed it away from the lighthouse, the wind carrying it out across the lake.

"Monster! He's got me! Help!"

Polly's hair stuck out in all different directions, shining with hair oil. His words slurred, and he beamed like a man possessed, waving his arms back and forth to fend me off. I lunged, grabbing a handful of his hair as he tried to crawl through the small group that surrounded us.

"Bastard's got me," he cried. "Help!"

The men grew more agitated as they watched us through shifting shadows, heavy winds, and crashing waves. Most stood and stared. From their midst, a hand the size of a catcher's mitt grabbed my coat, pulling me away from Polly and to my feet. It was Lenny, the same lodge guest from the steamer who'd wanted to toss me overboard. He threw me against the lighthouse, my head slamming on the bricks. In his right hand, he held a whisky bottle, swinging it in lazy circles above his head. As I tried to grab his arm, the bottle briefly whizzed past my face. On the backswing, it smashed into the bony ridge above my good eye, knocking me to the ground.

#

I didn't pass out. At least not for long. A flash of white light punctuated the physical blow of the whisky bottle as it hit my face. I fell, but instantly jumped up and ran, fueled by some primitive response. Like a dog chasing rabbits, I felt no right or wrong, no good or bad, just intense concentration as we rounded the lighthouse toward the stairs.

I pressed a hankie against the cut above my eye, barely able to see through the blood. Cast in a red hue, only general shapes were visible. Spotting the white blob of men a third of the way down the stairway, I drove myself, taking two steps at a time, picking up speed. Drunk as they were, they stumbled and tripped their way down, both hands holding tight to the railing.

I knew the slowest of them could be caught. There were no screams or yells, only the sounds of chaos—the cadence of our feet, the huffing of our breathing, and the pounding surf to the left of us. The cold spray off the lake added to the fervor, soaking us with each crashing wave.

Lunging forward, I grabbed the shirt of the man in front of me, pulling him close in with my right arm, throwing my left over his shoulder. That's when my foolishness became apparent. His shoulder was thick as an Easter ham. Rather than slowing down, he picked up the pace, carrying me like a flimsy knapsack. I tried to pull loose, but he held my arm tight, letting out his unmistakable high-pitched screeching laugh that I remembered from the steamer. Lenny lumbered as we hit the water, neither speeding up nor slowing down. Before the crashing of a wave, he reached back with his free hand and grabbed my belt. Using both hands, he flung me over his head into the ice-cold crashing surf.

I struggled to stand and catch a breath as the rough seas pulled me under. Unable to see with my good eye swollen shut, I lost my bearings, unsure if the shoreline lay ahead, behind, left, or right. The numbness from the icy waters crept through my muscles, sapping away my strength. As I labored to keep my head up, my mouth and nose filled with water, causing fits of coughing and gasps for air. My last thought was of Jenny, hoping she'd be sick with guilt upon hearing of my death, her unfaithfulness having driven me from the safety of the farm.

2 FOES & FRIENDS

I awoke, confused, with an uncontrollable shiver, believing myself to be at the old family farmhouse on a frosty winter morning. Naked under the covers, I had a cloth draped across my head, covering my eyes. A natural light filtered into the room and through the bandages. Someone held a rag full of crushed ice against the cut above my eye. The stinging pain of the ice pack and the throbbing of the wound were my first indications that this wasn't Aitkin. I reached up to push the cold compress away.

"Stop. Lie down!"

The memories of bottle-smashing, stair-chasing, and lake-drowning activities came back to mind.

"You need stitches. Six at least."

Scandinavian, I guessed, comparing her accent to the Norwegian farmers back home.

"Nurse?"

"Better than any nurse you'll find this side of Duluth. Keep that eye covered. It's the only good one you have."

The bed was as hard and cold as a slab of granite. The waxy canvas blanket covering me smelled of linseed oil, an improvement over the pungent swampy smell of the room—the smell of rotted fish.

"Where's Cephas?"

"Went to get dry clothes," she said. "I'm cleaning the wound now with iodine. Dette vil svi . . . This will sting."

The whole side of my face lit up with an intense burning pain as she swabbed back and forth with an iodine-soaked rag. I bit the inside of my cheek to fight the pain, throttling a full-blown scream down to a whimpering whine.

"Sit still."

She worked in silence, stitching up the wound. The rusty taste of blood from biting my cheek grew stronger as I clamped my teeth down with each puncture from the needle or knotting of the thread. My eye still covered, I focused on nothing but the pain. My injuries were much more severe during the war, but somehow this pain felt worse. Maybe because the poking and knotting were never-ending. What was supposed to be six stitches felt like sixty. Once finished, she cleaned the wound with iodine again.

"Where are my clothes?" I asked, still shivering.

"I'll go see what's taking him."

She threw a second tarp-like blanket over me and lifted me into a reclining position, then propped me up with more canvas behind my shoulders and head.

"Drink some coffee. It'll make you feel better."

The metal cup warmed my hands, and a few sips took the edge off the chills. The coffee smell was a welcome change from the fish, linseed oil, and iodine. Without being too obvious, I lifted the cloth from my eye and saw that I was in a small room no bigger than my eight-foot square bedroom back home. The bed sat in a corner. A small wood stove rested against the opposite wall, close enough for me to reach out and touch. To the left of the stove, shelves held a smattering of pots and pans, and a sparse collection of canned food items. To the right of the stove, the door to the outside stood ajar.

\#

Cephas eventually arrived with a dry set of clothes. He

helped me dress, then guided me back to the lighthouse. With my head wrapped in gauze, I held a rag full of crushed ice against the newly sutured wound.

Once back at my cottage, he took the bandage off to assess the damage. "Someone punched you?" he asked.

"No. Lenny hit me with a whisky bottle."

"Who's Lenny? Why'd he hit you?"

"I tried to get my eye patch back."

"Lenny took your eye patch?"

"No, Polly took it."

"Polly took your eye patch? Then threw you in the lake?"

"No. Lenny threw me in the lake."

Cephas sat at the table, took his hat off, and rubbed his face with both hands.

"You know how slap dragin' stupid you sound?" he asked.

By now, my head throbbed along with the pain from the wound.

"Anyone find my eye patch? Who pulled me out of the water?"

"Don't know and don't care. Polly says you attacked them for no reason. Says the lodge guests hit you in self-defense. Says he never saw your eye patch."

"That so? Where is he? I saw him wearing it. He has the brass balls to steal my eye patch, bring his buddies up to harass me, and then blame it all on me?"

I stood and headed for the door, still holding the towel filled with crushed ice against my head. "I'll go get him, and we can talk this over if I don't kill him first."

"He's not here."

"Where is he?"

"Up at the lodge."

His right hand trembled back and forth on the table as if erasing imaginary logbook entries. When he noticed me watching, he pulled his hands into his lap.

"Spends lots of time at the lodge?" I asked.

"Don't get started with me," Cephas said. "As far as I'm concerned, you're both as worthless as a piss pot."

He looked broken as he rubbed his right hand with his left, watching his fingers tremble.

"He's like the court jester up there, isn't he?" I asked.

"Shut your trap."

Cephas grabbed his cap from the table, started to stand, and then settled back down. I didn't mean to agitate him but had no intention of accepting the blame.

"So, the court jester played up at the lodge all night, wearing his costume with my eye patch, making fun of me, pretending I am a monster."

Cephas stared across the table at nothing in particular.

"Then he brought his buddies to the lighthouse to hassle me. That's what happened."

He stood and walked to the door, looking out at the harbor below.

"Why do you keep him around?" I asked.

"What's that leave me with? A one-eyed assistant whose wife didn't even bother to come with him?"

He reached in his pockets and pulled out his pipe, tobacco pouch, and matches. He stuck the pipe in between his teeth as he opened the door.

"You still have morning chores. See to it they get done."

My rage only grew, watching Cephas walk back to his cottage. Now alone, everything replayed in my head. I struggled to think of what could have been said or done differently. Polly was the perpetrator, and Cephas should have known that.

I reached into my wallet to count my money. Instead of cash, my unfinished letter home fell to the floor. Less than twelve hours ago, my optimism and fresh perspective gushed with sentiments of tranquility; now, it sounded so naïve. Mom might've treasured my description of the peace, serenity, and majesty of Lake Superior. Dad would have taken a special interest in lighthouse technology. Both would've been thrilled by my humor and satisfaction—something they hadn't seen in their son since before the war. The nearly finished letter would have left them believing things were fine.

I tore up the letter and threw the little scraps of paper in the wood stove. Those reassurances would have to wait.

#

By the next morning, I'd finished my shift without any major mishaps. If Polly was around, he kept himself well hidden. Elsie dropped off a plateful of freshly made doughnuts, going out of her way to be extra friendly. Cephas acted as if nothing had happened, which helped us get back to normal. The lake was calm with a light warm breeze out of the south. I had no interest in hanging around the lighthouse, so I went fishing.

Inside the boathouse, the two sixteen-foot rowboats sat high and dry on their skids. Officially, they were to be used for the weekly trips to Beaver Creek to get supplies. Stout and seaworthy, each had oars stored neatly across the bench seats, and a sail rolled up around the mast, stowed against the gunwale. The boats had a fresh coat of spar varnish inside and out, trimmed with white enamel across the gunwales.

A soft sneeze sputtered from outside the boathouse. A little girl, not more than five years old, watched me from behind the heavy wooden door, her head cocked to one side. She wore a simple dress and overcoat, with a pair of black buckle boots, far too big for her feet. Reaching into my coat pocket, I found the old fisherman I'd carved the night before and carried it out to give to her. My damaged face didn't scare her, and the fascination with the figurine kept her attention. She glanced back and forth from my face to the old fisherman.

"For you," I said.

She cautiously took the carving from my hand, running her fingers over the soft wood, and giggling at its features before embracing it with both arms. I slipped back into the boathouse to look for tackle, wondering why such a young girl would be out there all by herself.

Inside, I found three baitcaster rods and reels, a fishing net, a bait bucket, and a rusty and disorganized tackle box, with lures and hooks all jumbled together among the bobbers and weights. Two of the three reels had backlash bird nests the size of baseballs. It took me over ten minutes to untangle the two reels and clean up the rods before putting them and the net and bait bucket into the boat. I took the tackle box with me, intending to sort it out onshore.

As I came from the boathouse, a woman sat along the shore with the little girl. In her early twenties, she wore a plain dress with an overcoat, both relatively clean considering the surroundings. She stood and gathered the little girl in her arms as the breeze blew her dark hair back into her face.

"You look much better," she said.

"Better than what?"

"Better than you did yesterday."

I never would have guessed it was her—the one who had stitched me up. The one with the hot coffee and the waxy blankets. Much younger and more attractive than I expected, in spite of the old clothes. There was none of the glitz and glamour of the lodge's Dainty Dollies, but she had a warmth that welcomed and comforted. Her smile and the glint in her eye made her distinctively approachable. She took the figurine from the little girl and offered it back to me.

"No, it's for the girl."

Turning the carving back and forth, she inspected it closely.

"This is really good," she said.

"It's nothing. Just a fisherman. I carve them all the time."

She laughed, letting the little girl down while still holding the figurine.

"Veldig bra . . . really good. Not Norsk, though. Too fat to be Norwegian. Too big a nose. Maybe a Swedish fisherman."

Her smile reminded me of the nurses at the field hospital in France—friendly and approachable, not blubbering and full of pity like all the Aitkin church women.

"You stitched me up?"

"Ja," she said. I'm Mae. Dette er min daughter, Rose."

Mae put her left hand on top of my head, then poked, pinched, and pried at the wound with her right. She appeared genuinely interested, like she had both a personal and professional stake in my recovery. I hardly moved a muscle, not used to any kind of physical attention from a woman since the war.

"Still looks sore, but it'll heal up nice. Not too much of a scar."

She took my chin in her hand and moved my head from side to side, as a doctor might during a patient examination.

"You need a patch for that other eye, though."

"I had one, but it's gone. I tried to make one, but it didn't turn out."

She had the confidence and wisdom of a person twice her age, taking charge as if an expert at nursing people back to health. She made me nervous. It had been a long time since I had been this close to a young woman.

"Keep ice on that eye," she said. "See you tomorrow?"

My mind thought yes, but my lips stammered, too surprised to answer.

"Be here tomorrow," she said.

Mae gathered Rose in her arms and walked back to the village. Rose watched me from over her mom's shoulder, dangling the carved fisherman in her left hand and giving me a little wave with the right as she went.

I grabbed my bait from the minnow trap at the edge of the dock, pushed the boat out into the water, and rowed across the harbor to the northeast side of the island. The winds off the lake slowly pushed me back closer to shore. I raised and lowered the anchor, looking for a drop-off that might hold fish. Finding a steep gradient from five to thirty-five feet, I anchored on the deep side. With a chub on the hook, I twisted a half-ounce weight onto the line before casting out across the starboard side of the boat. The line spun off the reel as the weight took the bait down to the bottom. I leaned back against the gunnel with the rod across my lap, my hand resting on the reel.

Closing my eyes, I thought about Mae, Rose, and Jenny. Memories of Jenny brought back the loneliness and alienation of my days in Aitkin. During the painful post-war years, I'd had to witness her ascent, how she courted with more than her share of men before settling on Fred, the richest man in town. That whole time I languished, with no prospects for work, friends, or romance, spending more of my time alone on the farm.

Now, after only a few minutes with Mae and Rose, I could forget all of that. They both showed an acceptance for my injuries that Jenny had found repulsive. It felt so comfortable to be around them. Incredibly, Mae had actually ordered me to come see her again. What a treat to have something so wonderful to look forward to.

Yet I knew nothing about her. Mae had a daughter, so maybe she also had a husband. Maybe a giant jealous one with arms the size of pier posts and a temper as hot as a stovepipe. I didn't need more heartbreak, enemies, or fights. A woman like her could twist my head into knots, leaving me plain stupid, not knowing up from down or right from left. The lighthouse was my new beginning, an opportunity to rise above the pain of lingering lost relationships. Even if she was single, there was no sense getting all worked up over her now. Still, it was a joy to think about her. I couldn't wait to see her again.

The line tugged, almost pulling the rod into the lake. The hook set, the weight of the fish bent the rod into a semicircle as it ran, stripping line off the reel. As I slowly reeled her in, I reset the drag, only to have her take two more runs before she could be coaxed up to the side of the boat. A nice lake trout for lunch.

#

"Smells tasty," Cephas said. "Always liked fresh fish."

Elsie labored next to the stove, hardly able to reach the skillet full of fillets, diced potatoes, and onions, as she had to bend way over that sizeable tummy. I mixed a can of evaporated milk with a few cans of cold water for us to drink, and Cephas opened a can of peaches. Polly stared at the tabletop like a little boy forced to eat while his friends played stickball.

"You're quite the cook, Elsie," Cephas said. "Don't you agree, boys?"

I smiled and nodded, happy to find my boss looser and more lighthearted. Elsie dished a plate up for each of us, and we all sat to eat. Polly hunched over his food, shoveling it in with his right hand. His left curled around his dish as if to protect it.

"Don't know why I have to eat here," he complained. "Could be up at the lodge eatin' real cuisine."

Resting her hands on the edge of the table, Elsie labored to catch her breath and hold her temper.

"You spend more time up there than you do with me," she said. "Why don't you get one of those Dainty Dollies to bear your child?"

"I just might. At least they don't nag me all the time."

Elsie grabbed her plate and went to the bedroom to eat alone. Cephas ate slowly, his hands shaking with each mouthful. The tremor didn't interfere with his eating but shook enough to be noticeable. For his age, he looked fit and strong. His chiseled face gave him a healthy appearance, and he had the strength to lift whatever needed to be lifted. Yet somehow, the shaking made him look old.

That afternoon, Cephas led me around the lighthouse grounds, teaching me the routine for keeping everything properly maintained. We started in the barns behind the cottage. He watched as I inspected the tools, checking the sharpness of the knives, saws, and bits. I rummaged through the cans and jars of hardware, taking a mental inventory of the supplies. I always enjoyed the daily chores and routine maintenance on the farm.

"I'll be fuddled," Cephas said. "Looks like I got an assistant who knows his way around the shop. Polly wouldn't know which end of the shovel goes in the ground."

"I don't mean to brag, but I'm a darned good carpenter and mechanic," I said, inspecting the planes and draw knives. "And I'm not too proud to paint, shovel, or rake. I'll be more than happy to fill my days with honest hard work up here."

I imagined Cephas to be well organized. We would get along fine when it came to upkeep and order.

By late afternoon, Cephas retired to his cottage to sleep before his shift. He handed me a can of paint and a brush, with orders to paint the back of the barn. It didn't really need painting. He likely wanted to test my skills, to see if I could cut an edge around the eaves without messing up the trim. Grabbing the ladder, I gladly went to work, finishing the job in short order. I cleaned the brushes and put all the supplies away well before sunset.

The late-night shift at the lighthouse had become the favorite part of my day. After a few hours' sleep, I walked into the cleaning room fifteen minutes early, the moon just starting to set. The night was cool and crisp, with a stiff wind off the lake.

Scraping the ash out of his pipe into the old coffee can, Cephas sat in his chair, a pile of logbooks and his Bible stacked beside him.

"Finish the barn?"

He had already checked my work. I had noticed him behind the barn as I washed the brushes. By the tone of his voice, I assumed he approved of the results.

"It's all painted, the brushes are cleaned, and everything is put away," I answered. "The side facing the lake is starting to peel. I'll paint that tomorrow if you'd like."

Cephas nodded. If he appreciated my initiative and ambition, he did his best not to show it.

"Where's Polly?" I asked.

"At the lodge. Likely telling stories and raising Cain."

He pulled the tobacco pouch out of his coat pocket, filled the bowl, lit a match, and rotated the flame until he had an even burn.

"When might you get another eye patch?" he asked.

"Tried to make one. It turned out way too flimsy. I can't find the right material."

I slid my chair to the right of him, watching the beam of light as it skimmed across the water, measuring the ten-second intervals between flashes with my pocket watch.

"I know lots about Polly," he said. "Don't know that much about you, though."

"Not much to say," I said. "I grew up an only child. Served in the Signal Corps during the war, got injured, and spent the last six years back at the farm."

"And your parents?"

"They're good, hard-working people. Dad's worked the farm all his life. He takes care of the crops and cows. Mom handles the chickens and the garden."

"Don't they need you back home?"

"They get by without me. They knew I couldn't stay in Aitkin. They were glad to see me leave."

Cephas showed no emotion as he puffed on his pipe, regularly exhaling a wisp of smoke out the side of his mouth. I'd always liked the smell of pipe tobacco. The blend he smoked had an earthy vanilla aroma, with enough of a bite to make it interesting. Not too fruity like some tobaccos and not the stench of burning cow dung like the brands sold at the Aitkin Corner Store.

"What about your wife?" he asked.

I pulled the knife out of my pocket and thought before answering. I'd already told him she was waiting for me back home.

"Don't have one," I said, starting to carve. I didn't feel like holding that secret in any longer.

"You said she . . ."

"Yeah. The truth is she divorced me right after the war. She couldn't handle my disfigurement. Now you know."

Cephas stood up and walked to the glass windows, watching the beam skim across the water. Glancing back at me, he checked out the wound above my eye, then focused in on my mangled side. I kept looking out at the finger of light spreading across the lake.

"Ever read the Bible?" he asked.

I didn't answer. He reached down next to his chair and pulled the book into his lap, then paged through it. "In the sermon on the mount, Jesus told us how to live as Christians. He taught us how to pray and told us how to behave."

Cephas found the passage he wanted and held its place with his finger.

"Jesus said, 'The eye is the lamp of the body; so then if your eye is clear, your whole body will be full of light. But if your eye is bad, your whole body will be full of darkness.' Matthew 6:22."

I rubbed my eyes, feeling the hot swelling on my right side, still tender from being hit by the whisky bottle. The hollow of my empty socket itched from damaged nerves that might never heal.

"Did you hear me? About the body being filled with darkness?"

"Sir, I don't cause trouble, and I'm not filled with darkness if that's what you're saying."

"You work hard," Cephas said. "But you lied about your wife. You've been in fights with Polly and the lodge guests, almost drowned, and you run around here with your disfigurement for all to see. Misfortune follows you."

"It's not my fault."

"I don't care whose fault it is. Trouble is trouble. Maybe you need to move back to the farm."

His words weighed heavy and hung there. I stared at him in disbelief. He stared back, puffing on his pipe, not wanting to be the first to break eye contact.

"Ever think they might need you back on the farm?" he asked.

I kept staring, thinking of Mom and Dad, all worn from worry over the last six years. They'd be heartbroken to have their son return with a smashed-up face, broken spirit, and no prospects. Even worse would be facing Jenny—her living like a millionaire, and me unable to hold a miserable job as an assistant lighthouse keeper.

"I'm not going back."

"Why not?"

He clenched the pipe in his teeth and pulled the watch out of his pocket, checking the time before putting it back. After a couple of long draws, the pipe had a steady burn going again. I'd lost all interest in discussing my parents, my ex-wife, or my miserable circumstances.

"Fire Polly. He steals my eye patch and leads a bunch of drunks up to the lighthouse to cause trouble, and you want to blame me?"

I rolled my carving knife back and forth in my right hand,

holding the chunk of basswood in my left. He glanced at the knife and the piece of wood, then pulled his watch out to check the time again, as if he had a pressing appointment that he couldn't miss.

"Ever spend time around sailors?" he asked. "They're a superstitious bunch, fearing all sorts of things. They fear Fridays 'cause that's the day Jesus was crucified. They fear Thursdays, or 'Thor's Day,' 'cause he's the God of thunder and storms. Whistling or killing an albatross on the ship is bad luck, as is having a banana or a woman on board."

Cephas pulled the pipe out of his mouth, pointing the mouthpiece toward me as he spoke.

"But what they fear most of all is a 'Jonah,' just like in the Bible story. A bad-luck person who brings a curse from God with him wherever he goes. Bad weather, breakdowns, or sickness—they're all indications of having what they call a 'Jonah' on board. So now, here I am with an assistant keeper named Jonah, who's divorced and has two damaged eyes! It's enough to bring evil on anybody. I'm not sayin' you're bad. Just sayin', you're cursed. Definitely a Jonah."

He tapped the ash from his pipe into the can, scraped the bowl out with his knife, and put the pipe in his pocket.

"You don't believe that crap, do you?"

"Watch your mouth! The Lord rewards the faithful and punishes the unfaithful. The good book tells us not to test the Lord. I can't think of a greater test than letting some divorced one-eyed Jonah run amok in this holy place."

Cephas stood and picked up his Bible.

"I don't know what to believe. I'm stuck with a gobwagger like Polly and a real-life Jonah like you. The Lord must be testing me. Never had a year like this before. A few more months and then please, Lord, let me retire."

He checked his watch again.

"Gates invited us all to the lodge tomorrow, around three o'clock."

"Me too?"

"You too. And there will be some visitors tonight. A couple

of boats will arrive at the pier. Leave them be, ok?"

I knew better than to question who they were, what they would be doing, or why they were coming so late at night.

"Yes, sir."

"Just mind your own business about these boats. It's nothing that concerns you or anybody else, understand?"

His stare spoke as clearly as his words. His eyes drilled through me, searching for the slightest hint that I might not fully appreciate what he expected of me.

"Yes, sir, I'll leave it be."

After lingering for a few uncomfortable minutes, Cephas headed back to his cottage, leaving me to sort through the jumble of confusion he had left behind. After my first-rate painting job, I'd expected commendations, not condemnations. One minute I'm being fired, the next minute he's inviting me up to the lodge to meet Gates. If he were to fire anyone, Polly would be the rational choice, yet it was me who struck fear in his heart, with Bible verses supporting all his fears. He considered me the bad omen, the black cat crossing his path, his broken mirror.

Polly's scratchy tenor voice rose up at the lodge, singing an old drinking song inappropriate for anything but troopships and army barracks. I remembered the ditty from my war years, about the "Highland Tinker" and all his sexual exploits, each verse bawdier than the one before it, followed by raucous jeers from the guests. And to think that Cephas blamed me for defiling his holy place.

With Cephas gone, I carved. Tonight, it was a taller, more slender figurine than the previous night's fisherman. The legs were slim and graceful with shoes, not boots. The overcoat ended a bit below the knees, and the arms flowed along the side with the hands clasped at the waist. Instead of a rain hood, I carved hair cascading over the shoulders. The nose, mouth, and eyes were soft and elegant, not comical. I spent extra time making every detail just so and shaping the arms and legs with a grace that had to be smoothed gently from the wood. A pretty young woman.

A rumbling sound arose from the northeast of the lighthouse as I put the finishing touches on the figurine. At first, I assumed it was thunder, but the growling noise steadily grew louder as the boats approached without lights. They finally came into view as they entered the harbor, engines throttled down to a low rumble.

The fifty-foot speedboats had a cabin toward the bow and a cavernous cargo area aft. Trucks from the lodge drove alongside the village pier as white-shirt attendants gathered for the unloading. In short order, the boats tied up along the dock, their crews removing boxes from the holds and stacking them along the pier. Once the holds were empty, the boats slipped out into the darkness, in the same direction from which they had come. It took over an hour for the attendants to load the cases onto the trucks for the trip up to the lodge.

#

The sun rose bright over a clear sky as I finished the morning chores, filling the tank with kerosene, trimming the lantern wick, cleaning the lenses, and lowering the curtains in the lantern room. When everything was done, I wasn't sure what to do. Going back to the cottage to sleep was one option. Instead, I found myself heading down the stairs toward the waterfront. Ring-billed gulls crowded the beach, all facing into the wind. As I walked through the flock, the nearest gulls took flight, circled and squawked, only to land and reorient themselves in the same spots after I passed.

Rose played with her fisherman figurine among the smooth stones in front of the boathouse, her mom next to her, watching the sea birds along the shore. Mae had a bright, lingering smile, and watched intently as I walked over to sit next to her. Rose saw the head of the carved woman sticking out of my pocket and pulled it out, gathering it up in her arms, rocking it back and forth on her way back to where she played. Mae watched my every move.

"What?" I asked.

"You're a talented carver," she said, still beaming her bright smile.

"It helps pass the time up at the lighthouse. I thought Rose might like it. I'll carve some farm animals for her next."

"That's sweet. She's never seen a farm animal. Wouldn't know a pig from a goat."

"Why are you smiling like that?"

"Your eye's getting much better. A little puffy still, but much better."

"Well, thanks, I guess."

Mae reached for my head to do more poking and prodding. I pulled away gently, trying not to be rude. We sat watching Rose with little else to talk about.

"What does Cephas think about your eye?"

"He thinks I started the fight. Thinks the whole thing is all my fault. Says I'm some sort of curse on his holy place. Can you imagine?"

Mae didn't answer. We both watched Rose as she played, holding the fisherman in one hand and the carved woman in the other, wiggling them each in turn as if they were speaking to each other.

"And he wants me to go up to the lodge tomorrow. I'd rather clean toilets. Especially now that I don't have my eye patch."

Mae fumbled in her apron and pulled out a piece of black leather.

"I made you this."

She held up a dark leather eye patch with a suede headband. The patch was sewn into the shape of a contoured cup to fit tightly over the eye. The cup featured an overcast stitch all the way around the edge, giving it a clean, professional appearance. The strap passed through a channel in the patch, making it easy to adjust, to keep everything in its place. She had stitched elastic into the strap for a snug fit around my head.

She took my keeper's cap off and stretched the band over my head, then pulled the patch to fit perfectly over the socket. After a couple of minor tweaks, she combed my hair back with her fingers, put the cap back on my head, and pushed the band up against the cap to conceal it.

"Handsome."

Oh, to have a mirror. I reached up and felt the patch over my eye. Mae seemed pleased with her work as she grabbed my chin and moved my face from left to right to see it from different angles. This time, I didn't stop her.

"You look distinguished. Like that famous author."

"Joyce?"

"James Joyce. You look intelligent and sophisticated."

"How'd you know James Joyce?" I asked.

"From Anna and Nora, the two other ladies from the village. They work up at the lodge and sometimes bring magazines back. I saw his picture in an article. You look better than he does."

Mae brushed small wood shavings off the front of my coat, remnants from my carving the night before.

"So, I look like a famous author?"

"Right now, you look like a messy lighthouse keeper."

Funny how Cephas's Christianity foretold darkness and misfortune from the loss of my eye, while Mae saw an intelligence, comparing me to a famous author. How things change based on one's point of view. She kept brushing specks of wood shavings off my coat with a tender attentiveness that reminded me of Jenny during our courtship before the war.

"Mama! Mama!" Rose said, trying to recapture some of her mom's attention. We both watched as she played make-believe with the figurines, prancing them along the rocks as if running on the beach. She crashed both carvings headfirst into the stones, laughing.

"Ouch! Som gjør vondt!" Rose said.

"What did she say?"

"She says they're both clumsy. Can't you make your dolls more graceful?"

"I'll carve crutches," I said. "They'll come in handy when she breaks their legs."

Mae kept one hand over her knees to keep her dress in place and casually brushed the hair out of her face with her fingers time and time again, as the wind blew it right back. Her clothes were old but clean and flattering, in a way very different from the Dainty Dollies up at the lodge. They left more to the imagination, accentuating general shapes without being too revealing. Her eyes shone bright, and she had a glow in her cheeks without the rouge that some women wore. She flicked her head back, again trying to keep the hair out of her face. As she did, she noticed me watching her.

"Never seen a woman before?"

Embarrassed, I stood, having been caught gawking. Women were too darned complicated. The last thing I needed was another messed up romance and a broken heart.

"Thank you for the eye patch," I stammered. "Couldn't think of a nicer gift."

Mae reached her hand up to mine and pulled me back down next to her. "Glad you like it."

We sat and watched as Rose ran back and forth through a flock of gulls, scaring them up from the waterfront, leaving a thin line of birdless shoreline behind her. Once the gulls settled back onshore and repositioned themselves into the wind, she ran through the flock again, laughing as she went. The comic relief helped lighten the moment.

"Did you catch any fish yesterday?" Mae asked.

"A nice lake trout. Right on the other side of the island. Plenty to feed us all."

"One trout?" She smiled. "Nybegynner! . . . Rookie! I suppose it took you all day long to catch it?"

Even her sarcasm came out soft and comfortable. I lightly pushed her on the shoulder. She leaned back in, giving me a pat on my back. Rose ran up laughing, piling on top of her. After a little wrestling with her momma, Rose went back to chasing seagulls.

Mae asked me about the lighthouse. I described Cephas as moralistic and Polly as irresponsible. She told me about the village, how Anna and Nora cleaned and cooked at the lodge every day, while the fishermen tended nets and cleaned fish.

"Who pulled me out of the lake?" I asked.

"Gunnar and his son Hans. Hans finally dragged you out.

Gunnar would've left you to drown because you fought so hard. At least, that's what he said. Said he never knew anyone so close to death who fought so hard."

As we talked, the flock of gulls formed and reformed. Birds took flight then landed, always facing into the wind. Eventually, Rose grew tired of playing along the shore and lay in Mae's lap.

"Are you married?" she asked.

"Used to be. Got hitched before the war. She left me shortly after I returned. Thought she could do better, I guess."

Mae lightly grabbed my chin, adjusted my eye patch, and then put her hand on my cheek. "Her loss," she said.

I'd long forgotten the joys of being in the company of a young woman, and in spite of my bumbling mannerisms, Mae made me feel comfortable. She smoothed the wrinkles from Rose's dress and ran her fingers through her hair to loosen the tangles.

"Rose's papa died last year. Out on the lake. She misses him."

Mae wiped her eyes, and Rose stopped her play. She laid the figurine down, then wrapped her arms around Mae's waist. We watched the gulls until she had to get back to her chores.

"Will you come tomorrow?" she asked.

I nodded yes, once again feeling tongue-tied.

#

After lunch, Polly, Cephas, and I took the well-worn path running along the hillside between the lighthouse and the lodge. Polly led the way with more energy and enthusiasm than I'd ever seen from him around the lighthouse. The pathway opened onto a soft emerald-green lawn. The yard spread out as wide as the Aitkin Catholic Church Cemetery, sloping gently from the main building to the bluff above the shoreline, and stretching well past the lodge on both sides. Men gathered at sporting contest locations around the lawn. To the right stood shooting stations, including skeet, and target for rifles, pistols, and archery. To the left, a driving range stretched out into a rough of taller grass. Next to the range were places for chipping and putting, and interspersed throughout the middle of the lawn stood stations for lawn bowling and croquet. Up against the patios, buffets and bars ran the length of the lodge for the guests.

Polly attracted a crowd of both young men and Dainty Dollies as we crossed the lawn to the buffets. He spun a thread about one of his old girlfriends as he walked. The girls roared with laughter as he sashayed back and forth, swinging his hips as he went, wearing a coquettish grin, a finger daintily resting under his chin. I couldn't hear all the words that went along with the antics, but the raucous guffaws from the crowd led me to believe it to be both entertaining and off-color.

"I swear Polly should be a movie star," Cephas said. "Not like Douglas Fairbanks or Rudolph Valentino. More like a Fatty Arbuckle."

"Sure knows lots of the guests," I said.

"Up here every night. Should've put an end to it long ago."

"Why'd I have to come? Gates looking for another comic?"

Cephas scowled. "Got a big chip on your shoulder? Gates invites you up for food and drink, and all you can do is complain."

"I'm serious. Why would he want me here? We didn't exactly hit it off when we first met over his crushed boutonnieres."

As we approached the buffet, Cephas put his arm around my shoulders, like a father giving advice to his son.

"He wants to be neighborly. Wants you to be happy. Or he needs you to stop fighting with his guests. Whatever. Just get something to eat, have a drink or two, and don't do anything stupid."

A spread of fried chicken, pork chops, carved beef, sandwiches, roasted potatoes, and onions laid before us on a large white linen tablecloth, the food arranged around a sculptured ice swan. At the table on the other side of the stairs, four attendants filled glasses with drinks and ice for the guests.

"No booze in those drinks," Cephas said. "Gates says he doesn't serve booze. Then again, the Dainty Dollies seem to have enough booze for everyone. You just gotta be nice when you ask them."

As I looked across the lawn, the same lovely young ladies that welcomed the men off the steamer were now busy spiking drinks. Each had a silver flask slipped in to a garter under the hem of her dress. Upon finding a thirsty guest, the flask would flash, along with plenty of leg, and the drink was topped off. After a flirtatious exchange, the flask returned to the garter, and the young woman floated off across the lawn to find another thirsty guest.

"That's illegal," I said.

"Can't think of a single man up here who would complain," Cephas answered. "And as far as Gates is concerned, he doesn't serve any booze."

Polly stood in the drink line, telling the tale of his high school prom when his date's dress caught on a nail.

"Ripped all the way down the back!" he said.

He grabbed a light post in a rather lewd fashion to demonstrate how he saved her from baring it all, with him hugging tightly from behind. The crowd erupted in laughter, attracting the attention of Gates, who made his way through the crowd to greet Cephas with a big bear hug.

"Your boys doing burlesque?" Gates asked, causing Polly to redouble his entertainment efforts. Polly humped the light pole with all the more enthusiasm as the crowd cheered him on.

Gates dressed at least as well as Gus, the man I'd met on the train, but while Gus preferred conservative clothes, Gates came across as flamboyant. As before, a fresh red carnation boutonniere adorned his cream-colored formal jacket. The stiff, rounded collar of his white shirt perfectly framed his peach-colored silk tie, adorned with a ruby stickpin, its stone larger than a raspberry. He stepped right next to Cephas with his back facing me. Not that he was mad or displeased. To him, I didn't exist or fit into his plans. At least not yet. If he was snubbing me, I didn't care. It gave me time to eat and reflect.

Returning from the war, I'd had a layover in the Minneapolis station, waiting for my train home. The returning soldiers all had a swagger. Most of them hadn't slept in days, but it didn't matter. They had the energy of an overheated boiler, ready to burst if they didn't let it all out. They collected in groups with other men they didn't even know, laughing, telling stories, and bragging about the gals waiting back home for them. They talked about their hopes and dreams now that the war was over. Plans for starting businesses, running farms, and raising a family. Being tall, short, skinny, or portly didn't matter. Everyone joined in—except for me.

These survivors had all escaped death and serious injury. I was the one with half my face shot off. I stood as a grim reminder of their worst fears. I didn't have new possibilities to look forward to, and I'd had no idea if my gal back home wanted me anymore. They didn't intend to be rude, but I knew I didn't belong. Just as I didn't fit among these rich young men and the Dainty Dollies of Stony Point Lodge. I was the oddity, the discomfort in their midst.

Having finished my lunch, I picked up a slice of rhubarb pie with whipped cream on the top. Polly entertained on the other side of the lawn, looking skyward with his arms outstretched, balancing a croquet mallet from the tip of his nose. Weaving back and forth to keep it from falling, he kept running into the guests, which only added to the fun. Polly didn't belong either, but at least he knew how to entertain.

"Need a little something in that drink?"

The young woman looked to be straight from a McCall's magazine cover with her bob haircut, wispy dress, and perfectly done makeup. Before I could answer, the flask flashed, leaning toward my glass.

"You're from the lighthouse," she said, starting to pour. "You must know Polly!"

I slowly pulled my glass away, but she kept following it with her flask, concentrating on the pour, committed to making sure I had enough liquor in my drink.

"Polly's the cat's pajamas. He makes me blush, but he's so funny. I just have to listen."

I stuck my hand on top of my glass, gently pushing the flask away. She looked up with a puzzled smirk, as if no one had ever refused alcohol.

"Is that a real eye patch?" she asked. "Because Polly had one the other night. I don't think it was real, though."

She capped the flask and slipped it into the garter, not at all concerned about the amount of leg exposed. She scanned the crowd, looking for the next glass that needed a little nip. Before she left, she flashed a beautiful smile.

"A pleasure to meet you," she said. "And don't forget—at five o'clock there'll be boxing in the ring set up on the far side of the lawn. It's always a crowd favorite. If there's anything you need, just let me know."

She sashayed off to a nearby table of thirsty men. By now, queues had formed around the gaming stations, men eager to take their turns. Polly delighted the crowd at the putting station, a putter sticking straight out from his pants while he chased one of the Dollies across the green.

I headed to the main building, relieved to find it quiet, uncrowded, and comfortable. My footsteps echoed through the main hall as I walked past the rows of tables with their formal place settings and fresh flower arrangements. The leaded windows facing Superior filled the room with color and light, and the stone columns that separated the glass added a verticality that made the room feel as spacious as a cathedral.

Across from the leaded windows, an ornate humidor sat on a side table, with a selection of cigars unlike any I might find at the general store back home. These were moist and pliable, with no additives overpowering the aroma of the fine leaf tobacco they were made of. Above the humidor hung an architectural drawing of the lodge and grounds, showing the lawn, the formal gardens, and the outbuildings. I picked out a Cuban cigar from the humidor and lit it as I pored over the drawing's details.

Highway One, the soon to be completed highway from Duluth, ran across the top of the map. From the highway, a curved road led through woods to the main lodge. Nestled in the woods, a considerable structure labeled Warehouse sat off on its own with a separate entrance to the main road. Nearby, there was another large building labeled Dormitory, likely where all the Dollies lived. Both buildings appeared the same size as one of the main building's wings. From the drawing, I now had a much better understanding of just how large the Stony Point Lodge complex was.

Lake Superior ran across the bottom of the drawing with the lighthouse in the lower right corner of the map. Interestingly, there was no fishing village on it. No tar-paper shacks or reels for drying nets. In their place was a marina that would make any resort proud, featuring a band shell, beach huts, and a trolley running up the hill next to the existing stairway.

I took six more smokes for later, stuffing them into my coat pocket. From the windows facing Superior, the view across the gardens and lawns was spectacular. The steep hillside leading down to the lake blocked most of the shoreline, hiding the dingy fishing village from view as if it never existed.

I watched the fishermen as they came into the harbor, having finished their hard day's work of tending nets. Meanwhile, the guests putted, shot skeet, and bowled on the lawn. Dollies moved from guest to guest, spiking drinks and flirting. Workers set up the boxing ring to the left of the stairway heading down to the shore, and gentlemen gathered early to get a ringside view of the matches to come.

In a few hours, the young lodge guests would be sitting down to a formal dinner, followed by card games and dancing with the Dollies well into the night. In the village, the fishermen would be cleaning their catch, packing the fillets on ice, and getting the boxes ready for transport back to Duluth. The blessed and the oppressed, only a few hundred feet apart.

#

The bell rang out loudly on the lawn next to the boxing ring as I left the lodge. All the other games were finished for the day, and the whisky-eyed men now circled the ring, watching Gates glide around like Dempsey himself. His sophisticated combinations of jabs and uppercuts could even be appreciated by a rookie. He had a narrow stance, his weight square above his feet, keeping him balanced and solid while his core moved fluidly and independently. He took small steps, pivoting and shifting quickly with the grace of a dancer, always on the balls of his feet. As the men gathered, Gates held his gloves up to quiet the crowd.

"You boys know the rules. I take on all comers. If you survive one round against the Great Gates, you'll win the admiration of your peers and get to pick a flask from your favorite Dainty Dolly."

The men roared. A few up front removed their jackets, ready to jump into the ring.

"Who's man enough to face The Great Gates?"

The crowd cheered again. Attendants had already laced up the first challenger who jumped up to the canvas, his hands waving in the air.

When the bell rang, the challenger rushed the champ, swinging wildly. Gates deftly stepped out of the way, pulling his head back just in time to avoid blow after blow. The opponent tripped over his feet, lost his balance, and stumbled into the turnbuckle while the crowd roared their approval.

"Gates! Gates! Gates!"

To someone who appreciated boxing, the fight was nothing but a silly lampoon. I used to be a great boxer, one of the best in my battalion at Fort Jackson while we prepared to deploy overseas. I fought up a weight class and still remained unbeaten. I recognized quality footwork when I saw it and could anticipate punches based on a fighter's stance and favorite boxing combinations. But this wasn't boxing. Not even fighting. Nothing but Gates indulging his guests.

The Champ landed a few soft jabs, then allowed a few light punches from his opponent. With great footwork and form, he clearly had much more experience and talent than the competitor, but he held back, giving the appearance of an even match for the crowd. It made sense that Gates didn't want to hurt or embarrass any of his guests, so he mugged his way around the ring like a cat playing with a toy mouse.

After three minutes, the bell rang. The challenger jumped around like he had just knocked out Dempsey. He jumped out of the ring, running to the closest Dolly to claim his prize.

And so the fights went. Contender after contender, each hoping to land a real blow against the Great Gates, who showed no sign of tiring. Each contestant picked their own flask from the garter of their favorite Dolly, some doing so more politely than others. There were no losers, only winners.

After seven guests had sparred with Gates, Polly took a turn. He struggled to get a leg up on the canvas, then scooted himself under the ropes like a toddler learning to crawl. Short and plump in his trousers and undershirt, he began parading around, playing to the crowd, looking to be on the verge of a heart attack.

The bell rang, and the Champ stood relatively still, letting Polly flail wildly, throwing haymakers at Gates's midsection, causing no discernible harm. Laughing, Gates dropped to his knees, Polly still flailing away, the men roaring their approval. Even crouched down, the Champ easily deflected Polly's swings. Polly tired quickly, each punch slower and less precise than the previous one until he just put his gloves on his thighs and leaned over to catch his breath.

Showboating, the Champ let loose a couple of weak bolo punches, pretending to have swung with all his might. Polly restarted his wild haymakers with both fists flying while Gates reached out and put his right glove on Polly's head, holding him off at a distance. The crowd loved it, and they shouted their encouragement.

"Polly, Polly, Polly . . ."

Gates let up, giving Polly a chance to connect with a few punches, then wheeled back with such exaggeration that you would have thought he was truly knocked out. Gates hit the canvas with a thud, like a sack of potatoes. The crowd roared out the count.

"One! Two! Three!"

Polly stood, alternating between holding his gloves up to celebrate his win, and leaning over with his hands on his knees to catch his breath. Gates laid there, pretending to be knocked out.

" . . . Eight! Nine! Ten!"

The men erupted. Gates rolled over and pulled himself up, pretending to be barely conscious. He lifted Polly's hand and held it up, declaring him the winner.

"Two flasks! Polly gets two!"

Polly rolled out of the ring and headed into the wildly cheering crowd of guests. In a flash, the Dollies surrounded him, offering their flasks. Polly took four and would have taken more if he could've carried them.

I'd had enough. I pushed my way through the throng of inebriates, their arms outstretched as they chanted. Whisky splashed from their glasses as they cheered and jeered. Across the crowd, Polly stood on a chair, holding up his flasks, an attendant on either side to keep him from falling.

"Help me get him back to the lighthouse," Cephas said.

"He can go to hell."

"I can't leave him here. No telling what he'll do."

We pulled Polly down from his chair, still in his undershirt, cradling his flasks like a mother with quadruplets. Sweating profusely, he struggled to catch his breath from the day's festivities. We found his shirt and coat rumpled up in a ball. I pulled him to his feet, and Cephas helped him get dressed.

"Did ya see me? I came out shwinging! Like a wildcat. Hitting him right on the whishkers. Right where I wanted him. That corkscrew knocked him out. Me, the main event! I should go pro!"

Cephas corralled the reckless swinging of Polly's arms, slipping them one at a time into the wrinkled shirt and coat. I wondered if Polly truly believed the words he said. Like a little kid dreaming of his sports heroes, Polly couldn't distinguish between make-believe and reality. What a happy world he must have lived in.

Holding the flasks tightly in his hands, he began swinging at me to prove his point. "Don't crossh me, Jonah, you don't know what theesh meat hooks are capable of. Crossh me and you'll get a crap-load of both!"

As he swung, his legs crossed. He would have tumbled if not for my reaching out to catch him. He shuffled his feet to regain his balance, still swinging. Cephas grabbed Polly around the collar to settle him down.

"Too much fun, Polly. Remember, you have a shift to work tonight."

By the time we returned to the lighthouse, Polly's adrenaline had worn off, and he didn't have the strength to stand. Cephas took his flasks. I walked him back to his cottage to get him into bed. Elsie helped him undress. He continued throwing those roundhouses even though his arms could barely move.

"Wishkers . . . hit 'em right on the wishkers and d-d-down he goezzz."

We laid him down on the bed and covered him with the blanket.

"Right on the wishkers . . ."

#

A small ribbon of yellow-orange peaked along the eastern horizon as I left the lighthouse, a half-hour before sunrise. Cephas wouldn't approve of my leaving so early, but I needed to catch the villagers before they left for their fishing grounds. With the lighthouse lantern still lit and my morning chores undone, I took the stairs down to the lake and walked the shoreline to the fishing village. The fishermen stopped working and watched me approach. They weren't used to having visitors. Upon reaching the two men at the first boat, I extended my hand.

"I'm Jonah. The new keeper."

Neither looked impressed. They stood with hands on hips in dead silence. Awkwardly, I pulled my hand back, rubbing them together as if to hide the original welcoming gesture.

"One of you saved me from drowning the other day. I wanted to thank him."

The men hardly twitched, offering nothing but blank stares. Men from the other boats began to gather as if fearing an altercation. Mae, Rose, and the other women watched from the shacks. I reached into my coat pocket and pulled out a handful of cigars from the lodge, holding them out toward the group of men. In a flash, the disagreeable attitudes turned warm as they jostled among themselves, each hoping to get their own. I lit match after match, lighting cigars as the men stood in a semicircle around me. Each inhaled deeply as a schoolboy might with a cigarette, leading to fits of coughing. Each took a few puffs, then passed the cigars among themselves, showing no concern for how many mouths had already been on it.

Gunnar was the exception among the friendly bunch. According to Mae, it was he and his son Hans who had pulled me out of the icy water, saving my life. Gunnar grabbed his cigar without a smile or a nod of acknowledgment. He broke it in two as he walked away and gave half to his son Hans before returning to his chores. Gunnar didn't need a light. He chewed the unraveling cigar as it wagged up and down from the corner of his mouth. A brown ooze of juice dripped down his chin when he bit off small cigar chunks, slowly packing the moistened and masticated tobacco into his cheek with his tongue. Once fully packed, he spat a stream of juice that landed a good six feet from his boots. He scowled disapprovingly at the rest of the men lazily smoking and chatting, before stowing the rest of his gear and preparing to launch his boat.

Hans was the opposite of his dad. He shook my hand vigorously with a smile as warm as a July heatwave. Tall and handsome, he had jet-black hair, deep dark eyes, and plenty to say.

"We thought you'd lost your marbles the way you floundered in the water," Hans said. "Like you'd gone crazy."

"I couldn't find my way out. I almost died."

"What a ruckus," he said. "At first, you fought like a drunken devil. You went down and didn't come back up, so I reached underwater, caught a fistful of your hair, and pulled you back up. You passed out before we made it to shore. Dragging your limp body out of the water was tougher than hauling a deer carcass through the woods."

He inhaled deeply, followed by a chain of coughs before handing the cigar off.

"Who hit you anyways?"

"One of the lodge guests. Clobbered me with a whisky bottle. Must not have liked my looks."

"Hans! Get to work!" Gunnar yelled.

The men all snapped back to their chores. Each heartily shook my hand before returning to their boats, still passing the cigars back and forth between them. Once out of the harbor, they set their sails and headed south, disappearing behind Tollefson Island.

Back at the lighthouse, I headed straight for the watch room, hoping Cephas hadn't discovered my chores had been left unfinished. I closed the petcock to extinguish the flame, then filled and pressurized the kerosene tank. I wound and locked the clockwork that rotated the lens and swept the floor. In the lantern room, I trimmed the wick, polished the lenses, lowered the lens cover, and drew the blinds. Once finished, I went back to my cottage for lunch, surprised to find Polly sitting at my table, helping himself to my food. His hand cradled a still-groggy head. A drippy can of beans sat on the counter, and a dirty pot had spilled over on the stove. None of it bothered Polly as he scraped the last beans out of the bowl with his spoon.

"No fish?"

"What are you doing here?" I asked.

"Elsie threw me out. Won't let me in our cottage."

He watched me toss the can in the garbage. I wiped the spilled beans from the stove, put a pot of water on for dishes, and rummaged through the cupboards for something to eat.

"New eye patch, eh? Trying to hide that Frankenstein look?"

With all that had happened, my patience for Polly was as brittle as granny bones, ready to snap at the slightest provocation.

"Think you're a big man?" he asked. "A real lover boy?"

I grabbed a can of carrots and pitched it hard at his head. Polly leaned away just in time to avoid being hit, the can whizzing past his face, making a decent sized dent in the bedroom door. I should've throttled him days ago. The can rolled across the floor, coming to rest underneath the couch.

"Aim's not so good," he said. "Maybe it's those messed up eyes of yours."

He held the spoonful of beans in his pudgy hand just under his chin, the beans dripping back to the bowl. His mood was foul as he nursed his hangover, giving no indication of backing down. I cut a slice of bread from the loaf in the breadbox, slathered it with butter and jam, and sat at the table across from Polly.

"Your new girlfriend make that eye patch for ya?"

I ignored him, which made him more pugnacious.

"I saw you two out there on the shore. You're chasing after that fish lady, ain't ya? Must be a real hotsy-totsy."

He grinned confidently, shaking a little as he laughed, the spoonful of beans still hanging underneath his chin.

"A lodge full of classy women, and you go chasin' harbor rats! I guess it fits with that facial deformity of yours." Polly emphasized facial deformity as if choking on the words. I tried to ignore him, but he knew he was getting to me.

"You like them harbor rats? Dirty, nasty, and disgusting harbor rats? Breed like rats, don't they?"

I kept eating. He leaned in closer, the spoon still dangling in front of him.

"Everybody calls 'em harbor rats. Even Gates. Especially Gates. 'The plague of the lake' he calls 'em. Water maggots."

Polly laughed, then swiped his messy spoon up against my cheek, leaving a patch of cold beans sticking to the stubble of my beard. I knocked the spoon out of his hand, sending it spinning across the floor.

"I'll reach down that pudgy throat of yours and rip your liver out," I said. "Maybe cook it up for lunch."

Polly's face lit up with a big smile, thrilled that I'd lost my temper.

"Jonah and the maggots." He laughed. "What an ugly, disgusting bunch of kids you two would have."

His scratchy high-voiced laughter lit the fuse. I tipped the table over on top of him. He crashed backward in his chair, the table slicing hard across his gut before rolling onto his face, bloodying his nose. He flopped like a netted fish trying to free himself.

"Stay where you are, Polly, or I'll knock you right back down."

Polly grunted and got up on his hands and knees before lifting himself from the floor. He charged suddenly, fists swinging wildly, as if he believed he could actually fight. I pushed him away. He came right back swinging. I punched him in the jaw, dropping him instantly.

I didn't want to fight him. He was too pathetic. It wasn't fair. I just wanted him out of my cottage. He crawled to the kitchen counter and pulled himself to his feet.

"Get out of here, Polly. Otherwise, I'll knock you all the way back to Duluth."

He stood at the counter with his back to me, his head bobbing up and down as he worked to catch his breath.

"Get lost, Polly. I swear I'll . . ."

When he turned, his silly smirk was gone, replaced by a look of hatred. His eyes were fixed, his movements slow and intentional. He wiped the blood from his face with his sleeve. He now held a fillet knife in his right hand.

Everything sped up. Every little movement. Each stab, slash, or jab happened too quickly, drew too close. Two stabs, one toward my chest, the other toward my face. A series of short jabs aimed at nothing in particular. I backed away. He followed me around the overturned table, slashing the blade to his right, then to his left. I jumped over the table to get away. He tried to follow but tripped, ending up on his face.

I ran through the door, hurdling the front porch stairs and landing on the walkway. I backtracked to the side of the cottage, ducking out of sight just as Polly flew through the door and lumbered down the stairs. As he hit the walkway, I blindsided him, driving him hard into the railing along the cliff, nearly pushing him over the edge. The knife slipped from his hands, glittering as it fell down the cliff before lodging in the massive boulders below.

Polly hung precariously over the top bar, only his spindly legs hanging on the lighthouse side of the railing. The rest of his weight dangled over a one-hundred-foot drop on the other side. His legs, wedged up in my crotch, kept him from falling. Unfortunately, his weight was about to pull us both over. I wrapped a leg around a rail post, getting just enough leverage to keep us both from falling.

Elsie screamed as she ran her nine-months-pregnant body from the cottage. She beat me with her fists and kicked me with her pointy-toed shoes, trying to break me loose from her Polly, not realizing that I was the only hope for saving his life. With her kicking and his wriggling, Polly slipped even further over the rail. Losing my grip around his gut, I reached around his neck with my left arm, pulling his head back to keep our collective center of gravity closer to the safe side of the rail. He let out the raspy, high-pitched squeal of a man being choked to death, while grabbing at his shirt collar to relieve the strain against his throat.

Elsie grabbed my collar, trying to pull me off Polly. Her extra weight helped. I pushed against the rail with one hand, pulled Polly's neck back with the other, still keeping my leg wrapped around the railing post. Slowly, his belly inched up over the railing. Once the ridge of fat above his belt cleared the bar, we both collapsed backward onto the pathway.

3 GOOD & EVIL

I'd been a real cream puff since the war. Never so much as a heated argument in my six years on the farm. Nothing but complacency and restraint, even while losing Jenny. Now, since arriving at Stony Point, there'd been three brawls in only a few days. Each had been in self-defense. But this latest fight with Polly concerned me. True, he'd had a knife, but I'd never considered him much of a threat. His lumbering stride made him easy to run down. I knew I could catch him and stop him. Then, in a split-second, I crossed the line, thinking I might really kill him. There was no consideration of good or evil, right or wrong. If I'd lifted his body an inch higher, he would have gone over the edge and died. Never before had I been so nonchalant about killing someone. Even during the war, there was never the desire to kill. Only the will to survive.

Elsie went off to her cottage, sobbing. Polly stomped off to the lodge, screaming about assaults, attempted murder, and sending someone to jail. I was suddenly alone, sitting on the gravel pathway, trying to catch my breath. I considered following him to plead my case but couldn't stomach the thought of it.

Instead, I headed into the woods, taking the narrow footpath that started west of the lighthouse, toward the Highway One construction site just north of the lodge. There, the workers drove mule teams that hauled the wagons, scrapers, and graders used to level and compact the nearly completed roadbed. After zigzagging between the piles of gravel, sand, and fill, I caught the trail on the other side, turning southwest along a high ridge running parallel with the road. From there, one could see all of Stony Point harbor—the lighthouse to the left, fishing village to the right, and the lodge occupying everything in between. Straight below, between the strip of highway under construction and the bottom of the ridge, the warehouse and dormitory buildings were nestled in among the towering white pines, their dark-green shingles barely visible among the trees.

As the sights and sounds of Stony Point Lodge fell away behind me, I slowed my pace. The smooth path and coolness of the woods calmed me. I followed the trail down off the ridgetop to a creek that meandered through a ravine of rock outcroppings, running clean and clear through a series of pools, separated by stretches of rapids.

Mae had told me about Barberry Creek, where she and Rose would go to get away from the lewdness of the lodge. She spoke fondly of swimming in the pools, playing along the shoreline, climbing the boulders, and resting in the warm sand. "No rich or poor there," Mae said. "No haves and have nots. Just life the way God intended it to be."

I stood quiet, wondering if I'd been followed. The only sound was the water cascading from the pool off to my right with a steady, timeless ripple—a sound of peace. Two squirrels climbed through the maples, jumping from branch to branch, eating the flowering remnants from the developing seed pods. Dragonflies flickered back and forth, gliding above the water's surface. Trout rose at the point where the rapids became still, feeding on the hatching nymphs. I took off my boots and lay down on a strip of sand, the pool on one side, the small patch of maple and pines on the other. My coat rolled up under my head, I watched as the light filtered through the leaves. My mind began processing the day's events, wondering how close I'd come to killing Polly, knowing that Cephas would consider it another of Jonah's curses, once again corrupting his holy place.

Pastor Koors from my old church in Aitkin used to preach the story of Jonah. "A powerful verse proclaiming God's compassion and never-ending love," he would say. "About a loving and merciful God that forgave the wicked people of Nineveh, sparing these idolatrous and ruthless people from destruction."

The hell, I thought. Unending love and compassion for everyone but Jonah, a man who never asked to be a prophet and never volunteered for the job. Nonetheless, God kept riding him, spooking up a terrible storm to halt his escape, causing him to be thrown overboard, and sending a giant fish to swallow him up. After three days in the belly of the whale, Jonah relented. He risked his life to save his mortal enemies. But in the end, it was the Ninevites who got the fullness of God's love and mercy, for nothing more than a few days of fasting and wearing sackcloth. And for the rest of eternity, Jonah is remembered for his disobedience and resentment. What a topsy-turvy world, where good deeds are punished and wickedness forgiven.

I could only assume I'd be fired. My mind sorted through a short list of options. The most repulsive was returning to Aitkin. I couldn't bear the inevitable comparison of my destitution and Jenny's success. Me with no job and no prospects, while she held court from the fanciest house in town with her rich husband. The measure of how far I'd fallen would be too painful, too obvious, and too inevitable. Besides, I didn't even have the money for the train ride home.

Eventually, the clear water, trees, and warm sand pulled me in, letting loose the bundles of anxiety and giving me peace. I dozed off, listening to the wind rustling through the leaves mixed with the sounds of rushing water from the rapids above the pool.

#

A half-hour past sunset, I emerged from the woods with barely enough light to navigate. Each of the cottages was dark.

Polly would be halfway through his shift at the lighthouse, and Cephas was likely sleeping with a few hours to go before starting his time in the cleaning room. I slipped into my cottage to gather my belongings, leaving the kerosene lamp unlit to hide my presence. The sweeping of the lighthouse beam offered enough illumination for me to find my belongings and pack them in my trunk. The packing started as an impulse, under the assumption that I'd be fired, but the more I packed, the better it felt. I thought of all the Stony Point problems I'd never miss, such as Polly's abrasiveness, Cephas's religiosity, Gates's pomposity, the gluttony of the guests, and the daily reminders that I didn't, and could never, belong among the wealth and privilege of Stony Point. For the moment, any thoughts of where I'd go or what I'd do only confused things.

I wiped the table and swept the floor. The stove and the pot of dishwater had cooled hours ago, so I threw the dirty dishes into the sink and wiped the counter. As I finished packing and cleaning, Cephas made his way to the lighthouse to start his shift. Minutes later, Polly walked past the cottages on his way to the lodge, singing, "Yes, We Have No Bananas" in his scratchy tenor voice.

I laid down, intending only to rest but soon slept soundly with intense dreams, the likes of which I hadn't had since my childhood days. I dreamed of working the waterfront in Duluth, wearing dirty old dungarees, ratty shoes, and a broad-brimmed hat to keep the dirt out of my hair and the sun off my face. I was one of dozens, like bees in a hive, all shoveling spilled grain into the cavernous holds of a ship, the large chutes from the elevator looming overhead. The smoke and grain dust in the air choked the lungs. The roar of the conveyor belts and the avalanche of wheat spilling from the chutes was deafening, occasionally pierced by the yelling of the stevedores, ordering us to work faster and shovel harder.

By now, the anxiety that normally would have made me panic faded away. All sights, sounds, and smells faded into the background, as I listened to the hypnotic rhythms of the shovel sliding back and forth along the steel deck, scooping up spilled grain and dumping it back into the hold. There were no feelings of happiness or sadness. No nervous attacks or flashbacks from the war. Just the rhythm of the shovel sliding back and forth.

I awoke with a clear recollection of the dream, troubled by how it both appealed and appalled at the same time. Maybe I'd find my solitude on the docks of Duluth. A peace not derived from isolation but from a disenchanted indifference. An existence with no lords or lepers, no winners or losers. Just the hypnotic rhythms of the shovels sliding back and forth. Where strength and endurance mattered more than one's appearance or social skills. Where a guy could get lost among a sea of immigrants, all speaking their native languages, each of them too alienated, ignoble, and tired to fuss over anyone else's disfigurement.

In the sweeping light of the lighthouse, I walked to the bathroom to pee. Strange that my dreams weren't of the farm, as if returning to Aitkin was already checked off my list. If I had to fail, I hoped to do so in obscurity, far away from Jenny, my family, and the rest of Aitkin County.

I dressed, washed my face, brushed my hair, adjusted my eye patch, and climbed the outside stairs to the cleaning room, arriving fifteen minutes early for my shift. Cephas heard me coming and stood behind his chair, his hands trembling, holding the fireplace poker from his cottage high above his head, ready to take a swing. I stopped in my tracks at the door, surprised by the fear on his face. I didn't think he wanted a fight, but I had no reason to test him.

"You plan to hit me with that thing?" I asked.

"Just you try me."

We stood staring at each other. Sweat dripped down his face, and the swinging of the poker got more erratic as his arms tired. I felt dead calm, trying not to laugh.

"Brought that thing all the way from your cottage?" I asked. "Expecting some trouble tonight?"

Cephas didn't answer but kept waving that poker in a slow, lazy circle. I walked to my chair and sat down as I would have any other night. I pulled my knife and a chunk of basswood out of my pocket and started carving, thinking I'd make a little horse for Rose. Mae and Rose were the only ones that I really cared about anymore. Cephas slowly lowered the poker. He moved his chair as far away from me as he could, then sat down, the metal bar still firmly in his grasp.

"Polly must have told quite a story. Wish I could have been there to hear it."

"Said you almost killed him. Tried to throw him over the cliff."

Cephas watched my eyes, looking for any signs of remorse or agitation that would imply guilt. For him, the lighthouse was his "eye of the Lord, running to and fro," and blah, blah, blah. I grew tired of his religious obsessions, but after forty years of fog, storms, and blizzards, and with only one year left until his retirement, he didn't want some one-eyed malefactor darkening his holy place.

"Still thinking I'm cursed?" I asked.

"Trying to kill Polly doesn't help."

"Did he tell you about the knife?"

As I turned to face him, he fixed his gaze on my carving knife and tightened his grip on the poker.

"You threatened him with a knife?"

"He threatened me with a knife." I tried my best to control the wobble in my voice as my indignation welled from within. "Chased me around the kitchen, stabbing and slashing like a pirate. Would have served him right if I'd tossed him over the cliff."

Cephas pulled his cap off and wiped the sweat from his forehead with the back of his hand, glaring at me as if I'd lost my senses.

"Elsie didn't say anything about a knife."

"The fillet knife from the kitchen. It went over the edge when I tackled him. Onto the rocks along the shore."

"Ha! He said . . . You . . . He . . ."

He watched my eyes for even the slightest glimmer of guilt. I sat unflinching, looking back with firm confidence and no regret. He still struggled to catch his breath, his collar wet with sweat.

"So, I'm fired?"

"Rip-fizzin' right you're fired. Of course, you're fired. Can't just go dangling men over cliffs and not get yourself fired."

Cephas talked tough but looked uneasy. He laid the poker across his legs, then fingered the brim of his cap nervously, rotating it in his hands. For all his bravado, he didn't appear that comfortable with his decision.

"You and Polly going to run the lighthouse? Get her all ready for inspection? Just the two of you?"

"We'll get by. Don't you worry about us."

"Maybe Polly will spend less time at the lodge," I said. "Less time drinking, more time painting, cleaning, and fixing."

I set my carving down to sweep up the wood shavings and dumped them in the trash bucket.

"You want me to leave now? Or should I finish my shift?"

None of this was said with an attitude or ill-temper. He set the poker down on the floor next to his chair, wiped the sweat from his face again, and put his cap back on his head.

"The steamer doesn't come till Wednesday," he said.

"I guess finishing another shift or two wouldn't be so bad. Maybe even finish painting the barn. She's a fine lighthouse. It's been an honor caring for her."

Cephas took the pipe and tobacco pouch out of his coat. His hands trembled more than usual as he scooped his pipe into the pouch, then packed the shag into the bowl with his thumb. I could tell he had his doubts about letting me go.

"I've been a lighthouse keeper for most of my life now. One year left and not sure if I can make it. Never been so much trouble."

Cephas grabbed a match from his pocket and struck it across the floor. The sulfur hissed and sputtered bright yellow before calming into a gentle orange flame. He rotated the match above the bowl, sucking down the fire as he puffed.

"I guess you won't have me to worry about anymore."

Cephas watched the beam gliding across the lake. The wind picked up, blowing the crest of the waves into a fine mist that sparkled like phantoms and fairies dancing across the water.

"It's not just you," he said. "Been bad times since Gates arrived. Polly doesn't even listen to me. He does whatever he wants as long as Gates is happy. There's nothing I can do about it. I look the other way and let them run the show."

"You honestly think I tried to kill him?"

"Wouldn't blame you if you did."

Cephas forced a little smile, then reached down and thumbed the leather binding on his tobacco pouch. An ore boat sailed to the northeast from the direction of Two Harbors, likely making its way to the ports of Toledo or Cleveland. Cephas must have seen it. It wasn't like him to just let it go. I picked up the logbook to record the sighting.

"You have to go meet with Gates tomorrow."

"Gates? He can burn in hell."

"Do it for me. He wants you to go see him."

"Tell him you fired me. Tell him I don't work here anymore."

"He says he has a job for you. Maybe you can work up at the lodge."

"The thought of it makes my eye itch," I said.

Cephas took a long draw from his pipe, then puffed out a plume of white smoke up toward the ceiling.

"Help me out for a couple of days. Go visit with Gates. Then we'll see what happens. Just don't kill anybody."

He watched as I roughed out the legs of the horse, cutting large chips of wood from under the horse's belly. By now, a new pile of shavings littered the floor between my feet.

"One more year. Then I'll go live in Two Harbors with the rest of my family. Maybe we'll do some traveling, go out east to the coast of Maine. Could even visit New York. Gates says if I help him, he'll help me."

Cephas pulled his chair closer to me, leaning in to tell me something important. "He's a powerful man, Jonah. His uncle is the Lighthouse Service District Superintendent, for goodness sake. That's my supervisor's boss. He can revoke my pension even after forty years of faithful service. Forty years of cleaning, polishing, fixing, painting, and bookkeeping. I must've had a dozen lighthouse assistants. I've lived through storms that you'd swear came straight from the bowels of hell. And after all that, my pension rests in the hands of Gates."

#

There was an uncomfortable knot in my stomach as I walked across the back lawn of the lodge. I felt out of place, and the yard crawled with half-drunk dandies. Gates's Dainty Dollies buzzed from person to person, keeping all the drinks sufficiently spiked. Men wandered through sporting stations in small groups, participating in the shooting, archery, golf, lawn tennis, and lawn bowling games, competing as if their family fortunes depended on their success. Attendants at each location barked the names of the winners with great fanfare, followed by wild cheering from the champions and raspberries from the losers. Then again, there were no losers. Every guest had plenty to drink, surrounded by a bevy of beautiful women attending to their needs.

I headed straight for the buffet and got in line behind a young man already sporting a booze-soaked grin.

"You! Frankenstein!"

He put his arm around my shoulders, spilling the whisky from his glass on my coat. "You don't scare me," he said. "Grawwwwr!"

The men around him laughed, reminding me of why I hated the lodge and its guests. He growled a few more times, each a bit louder, each with a diminished response from the crowd. I filled my plate with salad, pot roast, and roasted potatoes. My newfound monster buddy tried holding both his drink and dish in one hand, still keeping the other hand around my shoulder.

"Have you visited the lighthouse?" I asked.

"Nope. Too busy winnin' up here."

"Ever been down to the fishing village?"

He spat at the ground, hitting my shoe.

"Harbor rats! Water maggots. Surprised Gates hasn't got rid of them yet."

I struggled to smile, pretended to agree, and slid a slice of pie onto my plate. Wiggling out of his grip, I wished him the best.

The Dollies were again all dressed similarly, this time in a nautical theme. They wore royal-blue sleeveless dresses with plunging necklines and hems high above the knee. Each dress had a white stripe across the hip and a puffy white bow on the side. They wore white gloves to match the white bucket-shaped hats. As I watched them work the crowd of guests, it struck me how similar they all looked—each of them with startling beauty, but not one of them stood out from the others. It was as if they had been selected and outfitted for the purpose of all looking identical. Perhaps to keep the men captivated while at the same time keeping them from growing too attached to any one particular girl. By design, Gates had made his Dainty Dollies beautifully interchangeable.

"How about a little bit of zip for that drink of yours?"

One of the Dollies slipped her arm in mine. Her sparkling eyes and welcoming smile left me warmly complaisant. She waited until she had my full attention before pulling the flask from her garter.

"No thanks, I . . ."

"I won't take no for an answer," she replied.

She topped off my glass, then slipped the flask back into her garter with her left hand, her right still wrapped around my arm.

"You must be real important," she said. "Gates wants to meet with you. He's in the back where it's less crowded."

She led me through the crowd past the archery range, toward a small group of men that Gates was chatting with. Upon seeing me, he excused himself, then waved me over.

"Hey, fella! Glad you could make it!" He put his arm around my free shoulder, giving me a shake that felt more commanding than cordial. To him, I was always "fella," as if he couldn't bother to learn my real name.

"Sit down and have a drink."

Gates led me over to an empty table at the edge of the lawn. He sat facing the crowd. I set my plate and glass down and sat across from him. The woman stood by my side.

"Daisy, this fella works at the lighthouse. I didn't know if you two had had a chance to formally meet."

"Pleased to meet ya," she said. With one quick move, she spun around and sat on my lap. Startled and without thinking, I stood, dumping her onto the ground like a rag doll in front of me.

"You dirty pig!" she cried.

I tried to help her up, but she pushed my hands away. After getting to her feet, she brushed herself off, slapped my face, and then stomped off toward the buffet tables. Gates laughed, looking both surprised and disgusted by my inelegance.

"Unbelievable," he said. "Any red-blooded male would be thrilled to have her sitting on his lap, but you dump her like a sack of potatoes. Don't you like girls?"

"I don't like people. Certainly not any of the people up here."

I sat down, using my fork to separate the pot roast, potatoes, salad, and pie on my plate to keep them from touching.

"Cephas said you wanted to see me."

Gates stared at me as he sipped from his glass, his surprise and disgust melting into a look of wonder and disbelief.

"So, you didn't like Daisy?" he asked.

I didn't answer as I cut up my pot roast.

"And they say you tried to kill Polly. Is that right?" He seemed amused by my quirkiness, showing no signs of concern, disgust, shock, or disbelief.

"Did you call me up here to talk about Polly?" I asked.

"They say you tried to throw him off a cliff," Gates persisted.

I took a sip of my drink and changed the subject. "Where'd all these women come from?"

Gates scanned the grounds, obviously pleased with the collection of young ladies. "Beauties, eh? You won't find these girls on the streets of Duluth, that's for sure."

"Why don't the men just bring their wives or girlfriends? Wouldn't that make things easier?"

Gates leaned back in his chair, scratched his nose, noticed a little dirt under a fingernail, and cleaned it out with his thumbnail.

"This is a hunting lodge," he said. "No place for wives or girlfriends at a hunting and fishing lodge."

I glanced around at the men in pressed slacks and sweaters wandering across the manicured lawn in their two-tone shoes, like fraternity brothers at an Ivy League college reunion.

"You kidding me? These men look like hunters and fishermen to you?" I asked. "And why does every single one of those Dainty Dollies look exactly the same? Same clothes, same makeup. You can't even tell them apart."

"If the men want a family vacation, they can go up to the resorts on Isle Royale. This is a hunting lodge."

From a distance, Gates appeared sophisticated and refined. Talking to him face-to-face revealed a crudeness, impatience, and hostility. Like someone who had recently come into money and lacked the polish that comes with being rich all your life.

"Let's get to the point," Gates said. "You're gonna help me with the fishermen."

I didn't bother to look up. Instead, I ate some potatoes, then washed them down with my drink.

"The fishermen like you. They trust you. So, you're gonna help them find a new place to live."

"They have a place," I said.

"No, they don't," Gates said firmly.

He took a sip but never dropped his gaze, daring me to argue. I trimmed the fat off my pot roast before cutting the meat into small squares. Gates softened, then took another sip of his drink.

"They like you. Take a box of cigars from the lodge, bring it down with you, and pass 'em around. I hear they like those cigars. And bring some chocolates for the women. Talk to Gunnar. He's the one in charge. Tell them we can build a comfortable place on the other side of the lighthouse where they'll have more room and privacy."

"Why don't they just stay where they are?" I asked. "And why are you asking me?"

"They're squatters."

Gates spit the words out like they were bitter on his tongue.

I didn't mean to be offensive. I didn't care what happened at Stony Point. I intended to be on the next steamer headed back to Duluth. I sensed his growing displeasure with my lack of cooperation, but he maintained his composure.

"Look, if you want to help your friends, then talk 'em into leaving. We'll build homes on the other side of the lighthouse for them. Get 'em out of those tar-paper shacks and into something new."

Gates took another sip, leaned over, and put his hand on mine. It made my skin crawl. "Cephas says you might be losing your job. Get this done, and you can work at the lodge."

"Doing what?" I asked, not that interested. I pulled my hand out from under his and wiped it off with a napkin. I couldn't imagine what kind of job I'd want to do for Gates.

"I don't know. Cooking, cleaning, fixing . . . I really don't care. Take your pick," he said. "So, when you gonna tell 'em?"

"They've been here forever. They own their place in the harbor, don't they? Why would they leave?"

"They're squatters! If you won't make them leave, I will. I guarantee it. I'll slap 'em with torts, petitions, and injunctions till they're drowning in paper. They'll be spending more time in court than on the lake fishing. I'll sue 'em until they're too poor to go to the poor house."

Gates spoke loudly, forcefully, which quieted the cheers and raspberries from the nearby games. The guests watched from a distance, curious about all the fuss.

"Fella, listen to me. You're doing them a favor by getting them to move."

I went back to finishing my food, eating up the last scraps of meat and potatoes. Gates stared as I ate, waiting for an answer. I got up to leave.

"Well?" he asked.

"None of my concern. Cephas fired me. I'm leaving. Taking the next steamer back to Duluth. Talk to them yourself."

Gates lunged to his feet and grabbed me by the collar. He drew the other fist back as if about to throw a punch. He decided against it as he noticed all the guests listening in.

Dropping his hand on my shoulder, he whispered in my ear. "I hope Cephas keeps you around. We have lots of unfinished business."

#

Gates walked off into the crowd with a happy grin, shaking hands as he went, making everyone feel important and welcome. I looked intently through the mob, trying to pick Daisy out from all of the other Dollies. For the life of me, I couldn't remember a single feature that distinguished her from the rest. I finished my drink, relishing the memories of my morning along the shore with Mae. She had a smile that reached out, pulled me in, made me feel warm. Daisy just made me nervous. Mae had an inner beauty in spite of her simple living. Daisy was simple in spite of her outward beauty. For all the hard work and hardships, Mae never showed self-pity, regret, or a sense of inequity. She rose above it all with grace. Daisy wanted everything, regardless of what she deserved.

I finished my drink and headed off in the opposite direction from Gates, around the outer edge of the lawn. The cheers and jeers from the crowd had become louder, fueled by the spiking of the drinks, which had begun hours ago. Exuberant cheers erupted from the game winners, followed by boos and hisses from the losers—all in good fun, of course.

I glanced in the windows as I walked along the side of the lodge, watching attendants cleaning the rooms. Paintings with hunting and fishing scenes covered the knotty pine walls. Electric wall sconces made from antlers hung on either side of the bed. Fresh flower arrangements sat on the Adirondack-style tables and nightstands. No muddy boots, canvas duck pants, or Pendleton plaid shirts in sight. No rifles leaning in the corners or boxes of shells spilled out on the nightstands. Chances were there was never a deer carcass hung, a waterfowl plucked, or a fish cleaned on the premises. Even Gates and his millionaire buddies couldn't honestly consider this a hunting and fishing lodge. I suspected the real reason for the designation was to keep the wives away.

The front of the lodge facing the road stood every bit as grand as the opposite façade facing the lake. A large stone wall dominated the middle of the building, reminiscent of the lighthouse granite promontory from which Stony Point got its name. Roughhewn wood columns framed entrances to the right and the left of the rock wall, with a patio running across the front and steps cascading down to the circular driveway. The front lawn was artfully planted with decorative shrubs around the edges. The driveway, snaking across the lawn toward the main road, was lined with crabapple trees, now less than a week away from full bloom.

It felt peaceful to be free from the crowds. Other than the workers along the road, I had the whole front of the building to myself. In the distance, the shotguns boomed from those shooting skeet, and the clamorous noise from winners and losers could still be heard—just loud enough to help me remember those things about Stony Point that I'd never miss.

The driveway down to Highway One was smooth, fresh asphalt, with a smell that brought me back to better times. I used to hunt and trap along the train tracks next to the farm. On warm summer days, the air hung thick with the tang of creosote from the coated railroad ties. Now, the oily rich odor from the paved driveway helped me recall those good times when people thought of me as a smart, handsome boy. A kid with hopes, dreams, and a promising future.

Reaching the road, I could barely see the dormitory and warehouse buildings hidden behind a dense thicket of trees. They would have gone unnoticed if I hadn't spotted them from the ridge the day before. Painted green, with brown shingles, they blended perfectly with their surroundings.

The warehouse stood at the end of a winding dirt path from the road, four heavy carriage doors and one service door across its front facade. Along the sides, both walls featured rows of frosted glass panes, providing privacy while still allowing light in. To the right of the building stood a small station for servicing vehicles, with air pumps, jacks, and a gravity-fed gas pump, the kind you'd find in newer filling stations.

Tall masts jutted twenty-five feet above the peak of the roof on both ends of the building. A horizontal wire ran between the two masts while a vertical one ran from the middle of the horizontal wire into the building. From my years in the Army Signal Corp, I recognized it immediately as an antenna, likely attached to a radiotelegraph system inside the building.

Radiotelegraphy wasn't new to these parts. There had been installations in Duluth, Grand Marais, Isle Royale, Calumet, Marquette, and Port Arthur since before the war, providing wireless communications for the safety of mariners across Lake Superior. But private radiotelegraph systems were quite rare because of the cost and experience required to run them. It was intriguing that Gates would have something so important here on the edge of the wilderness to require the immediacy and security of radiotelegraphy communications. By now, my curiosity burned.

The service and carriage doors were locked tighter than the Aitkin National Bank. The carriage doors were bolted from the inside. A thick metal hasp bolted through the passage door, secured by a large brass padlock the size of a farmer's fist. With time to kill, I walked around the building, checking likely hiding places for keys along the way. I looked under the mat at the doorway. I ran my fingers along the molding above all the doors and windows. I reached up into the eaves, checked the nearby trees, and looked under the rocks near the door, but couldn't find the key.

Expanding beyond the building, I checked out the Mae West style gas pump with a ten-gallon tinted glass tank at the top. The narrow body and wide base were painted the same dark green as the building. A black hose connected to the glass tank on one end, while the other end hung from a hook at the top of the pump. A hand crank protruded out of the base like a crooked leg.

The pump looked brand-new, which made sense with the roadway not yet completed. The glass tank looked shiny enough to make me wonder if it had ever been filled with gas. The only thing that looked amiss was an access panel next to the hand crank, hanging slightly off-kilter and missing a screw. When I pulled the access panel open, I found what I was looking for—the hidden service door key.

The warehouse felt secluded. I had to listen real hard to hear the guests up at the lodge. Everyone else must've had more important things to do than worry about somebody snooping around a warehouse, which appeared to be empty. With the hidden key, I opened the service door. Gliding silently inside, I listened for movement or voices, but the only sound came from the light wind rustling through the trees up above.

The place looked like a millionaire's lumberyard. Twelve new Chevrolet Superior one-ton stake trucks lined three-deep, all facing out toward the four carriage doors. Each truck carried enough two-by-four lumber to build half a bungalow, packed solid all the way from the truck bed to the canopy top that covered the cab and cargo area. Back in Aitkin, the farmers owned old Model T Fords, all rusted, worn, and battered by years of hard work. The trucks owned by Aitkin Lumber fared worse than the rest, always hauling heavy loads over miles of unpaved roads. These trucks appeared fresh off the assembly line, every bit as cleaned and polished as the lodge itself. I couldn't imagine why Gates would need twelve truckloads of lumber or where these trucks might have come from with the road not yet completed.

The telegraph station sat in the far back corner of the building in an area the size of a small closet. Hanging on the wall above a tabletop, the loosely assembled contraption of controls, wires, terminals, switchers, and ringers reminded me of the radiotelegraph systems used during the war. A paper tape printer similar to a stock ticker sat on the left end of the table for recording messages as they came in. To the right hung a pair of headphones used to listen to the messages. In the middle of the table stood the telegraph key for transmitting Morse code messages. The equipment wasn't exactly the latest technology but was far more sophisticated than your typical amateur wireless telegraph.

Next to the telegraph key, there was a small pile of books. On the top, an old army manual for radiotelegraph systems caught my eye, being one that I remembered from my time during the war. Below that, a green book titled Codes and Cryptography stood out with its gold type and cream-colored pages. On the bottom of the stack was a ledger similar to the lighthouse logbooks.

I took a seat and leafed through the ledger, finding page after page of apparently random letters arranged in large blocks of text, each block preceded by a date code. The content was meaningless in spite of the clean and precise penmanship. The information contained in the ledger had clearly been encrypted. Having been in the Signal Corps, I knew the considerable effort required to encode and decode messages; only the most sensitive messages could justify such effort.

Most ciphers used on the battlefield were of the "simple substitution" variety, easy to encrypt and decode but not all that secure. I could tell at a glance that the code used in the ledger was far more complicated. Throughout all the blocks of text, only six characters were used—A, D, F, G, V, and X. This sparse subset of letters alone stirred a faint recollection of codes encountered or studied during my days in the war, although these memories were too faint to offer any helpful insights.

I jumped at the sight of a shadow moving across the windows, not the kind that comes from a branch blowing or a cloud floating by. I could see the shape of a head and shoulder moving slowly from one frosted pane to the next in the direction of the service door. I set the ledger back on the pile, grabbed a large wrench from the workbench, and hid behind the truck furthest from the intruder. The passage door slowly creaked open, then softly closed.

An unnerving stillness filled the warehouse. My mind froze. The door was unlocked, giving the person who had entered good reason to suspect my presence. We both hid silently in our respective corners for an uncomfortably long time, until the quiet tension eventually messed with my mind. Branches rubbing against the building sounded like footsteps. I mistook the wind blowing outside for the intruder's breathing. Uncertain of the person's location, I felt trapped.

Needing a better vantage point, I climbed to the roof of a truck with the wrench firmly in hand, using the protruding two-by-fours in the back of the truck as handholds and footholds. It was the third foothold, halfway up the back of the truck that gave way. It appeared to be nothing more than a two-by-four end, yet somehow it let loose with a mechanical thunk as I stepped on it. Inexplicably, this triggered the whole back end of the truck to swing open like an iron gate.

What appeared to be a truckload of construction lumber turned out to be a large, well-disguised secret compartment, occupying the full width and breadth of the truck bed. The sides and top were walls of dimensional lumber running front to back. The back featured a cleverly concealed metal hinged door, covered with a mosaic of mismatched two-by-four ends, and the door latch was concealed as one of these. As the door swung open, I fell to the floor, the wrench clanking like a dinner bell against the concrete.

Once again, I froze, listening intently for any sound that might reveal the intruder's whereabouts. The room was dead silent. Even the branches and the wind stopped their rustling. I knelt on the floor and pried the hidden door open far enough to reveal the contents of the secret compartment. It was filled with cases of Canadian whisky.

If only I'd been more accommodating with Gates. If I hadn't been so nosey, I would never have stumbled upon the trucks, wireless telegraphs, hidden compartments, or the whisky. I could have been visiting the fishing village with a box of cigars in one hand and a box of chocolates in the other. I now feared for my life when I could've been spending the afternoon with Mae. It seemed so convenient to have found the key. Now I wished I'd left the building undiscovered.

The intruder began to move, his steps agonizingly slow. He walked with hesitancy, as if he might turn around at any moment to leave, yet he kept plodding closer, step after tortuous step.

I knelt down to look underneath the trucks. There, among

the tires, axles, and driveshaft, were the wingtip shoes and dark pant legs of the intruder. He stood in the row against the far wall, having moved from the front door to the last car in the row, directly across from me. I watched as his left foot slid back, making way for his knee and two hands as he lowered himself into a crouching position.

Before I could react, his upside-down face came into view, looking straight back at me from underneath the truck, his dark oiled hair hanging down. I jumped and ran, hoping to reach the exit door ahead of the stranger. At the front of the warehouse, my feet flew out from under me as I tried to take the corner, slipping on a pile of sweeping compound. My head slammed against the heavy metal hinge of the carriage door.

#

Looking up from the floor, I saw a friendly face staring back at me. I'd seen so many faces from the lodge that I couldn't place it until he pulled out the silver cigarette case.

"You scared the dung out of me," I said.

I pulled myself up onto the running board of the nearest truck and used a handkerchief to blot the blood out of my hair. Gus offered a smoke and gave us both a light. He looked casually elegant in his two-toned shoes, dark flannel slacks, and a cream-colored cable-stitched sweater.

"Why are you here?"

"Trying to keep you from killing yourself," he answered.

Gus brushed his pants with his hands, then pushed his sweater sleeves up on his forearms, making him appear even more casually elegant.

"How's your brother?"

"I'm not here to talk about Franklin. You've been here less than a week, offending everybody. Half the people think you're a murderer."

"Like I care what all those dandies think. I came up here to mind my own business. To be by myself. I'm not looking for trouble."

"Not looking for trouble?" Gus asked. "You've broken into someone else's warehouse. You're nosing around in other people's business. You call that not looking for trouble?"

He watched as I made a small pile of sweeping compound with my foot, lighting it with the cherry end of my cigarette. It burned slow for less than a minute before I stomped it out.

"What were you and Gates fighting about?"

"He wants me to get the fishing villagers to move."

Gus sat next to me on the running board and flicked the ash of his cigarette on the floor. "Would it hurt so much to help him? Right now, he doesn't like you, and he's a guy you don't want as an enemy."

I took a long drag off my smoke, looking up into the rafters of the warehouse. They looked clean as a whistle, hardly a cobweb between the new oatmeal-hued timbers.

"Isn't he afraid of getting caught?" I asked.

"Gates? Caught doing what?"

"Well, to start with, what about all those gals?"

"No hanky-panky as far as I know."

"What about all those flasks?"

"Gates says he doesn't serve any alcohol. Says he doesn't know where the Dollies get it."

"They say the men's steamer trunks are empty when they arrive and loaded with Canadian whisky before they leave."

"Like I said, Gates says he doesn't serve any alcohol."

"And people believe him?"

I counted the wooden rafters as we spoke, which agitated Gus. He grabbed my arm, pulling my attention away from the roof and toward him.

"You ask too many questions. Quit sticking your nose into places that'll get you into lots of trouble. Stop messing with Gates."

"Why Stony Point?" I asked.

Gus crushed his cigarette butt out on the floor. He stared at the ashes between his feet before kicking them under the truck.

"He's here because he's smart," Gus said. "Smart enough to profit from all those young millionaires in Duluth just begging for ways to spend their money. This little harbor is miles away from prying eyes. There isn't a safer or more profitable place to run his business."

"Bootlegging?" I asked.

"I never said that," Gus said. "And talking that kind of nonsense will get you killed. It'd serve you well to forget all about this lodge."

"And these trucks. You going to tell me he's in the lumber business?"

Gus stood, brushing off the dirt from his trousers. I grabbed him by the elbow, leading him to the back of the truck. Pressing in on the ends of two-by-fours, I found the hidden latch that gave way with a firm mechanical clicking sound. With a light pull, the hidden back door swung open, revealing the hidden compartment filled with cases of whisky. Gus didn't even watch, looking more concerned than surprised by my revelations.

"Lumber trucks coming out of the north woods," I said. "Who'd believe they're hiding compartments full of booze?"

I went to the next truck, pushed in on several two-by-four ends until the latch clicked, and the back swung open, revealing another stash of whisky. Gus grabbed a new cigarette, lit it, and then took a few long puffs.

"I bet Gates can't wait to get these trucks on the road," I said. "Once the highway's completed, they could go to Duluth, Minneapolis, or St. Paul. Heck, Highway One would take them all the way down to St. Louis, Kansas City, or even New Orleans."

As I stubbed out my cigarette, he brought his case and lighter out. I took another cigarette, and he gave me a light. He put his silver case back in his pocket, then pressed the lighter into my palm.

"Here. I stole this from Franklin, so think of it as a gift from him."

A silver Ronson Wonderliter. No doubt the finest thing I'd ever owned. I kept my hand extended out toward Gus, unable to believe he really meant for me to keep it.

"Just take it. Don't be an ass. I'll tell Franklin I lost it. He has a drawer full of them, so he won't even miss it."

He liked to act gruff, but he had an undercurrent of kindness in everything he said or did. I held the lighter in both hands. It would have felt too presumptuous to actually play with it or put it in my pocket. Gus grabbed me by the elbow, hard enough to impart extra meaning to the words he spoke.

"Quit snooping. Forget everything you saw up here. Keep your mouth shut, and keep your distance from Gates. Don't talk with anyone about anything related to Gates. Not friends, not the other lighthouse keepers, and definitely not the police. He's a powerful, scary man."

#

I thought a lot about what Gus had told me about keeping my distance. Great advice. Made perfect sense. But I had a habit of making bad situations worse. My dad used to call it "pulling a Rosco."

Rosco was one of many dogs we had had on the farm. All of them had stayed outside or in the barn. Most had decent temperaments and knew how to behave, but not Rosco. He never listened. We tried bribing him, scolding him, even beating him, but none of it worked. "Just stupid," Dad would say. But I thought he was real smart, not letting anyone push him around. Turned out, Dad finally had had enough. One day, Rosco disappeared. A few days later, I found his carcass in the trash pit behind the barn. It scared me because Rosco and I had lots in common.

I could've been more accommodating with Gates. A smart, sensible person would have been more amenable, at least pretend to make an effort to help. Most people respect authority. I usually resent it, thumb my nose at it. It's not that I cared about prohibition. I had no moral objections to bootlegging or speakeasies. But I couldn't ignore the take-over of the harbor at the expense of the villagers. When faced with such an abuse of power, I forgot about consequences and pull a Rosco. The bigger the abuse, the bigger the Rosco.

After locking the service door and putting the key back, I took a deer path that ran through the woods on the north side of the lodge. From the path, I was close enough to hear the banter from the booze-soaked guests but could avoid being seen. The black flies swarmed, the branches overhanging the trail scratched and scraped as I went, but traveling undetected made these annoyances bearable. I intended to bypass the lodge's lawns altogether, but the path came out near the boxing ring, where the attendants prepared for the fights. The sky had darkened with thunder clouds that had rolled in from the southwest as I walked among the guests. Gates paced across the canvas with his gloves laced up. He grabbed the top rope as he surveyed the crowd, picking me out almost instantly.

"Looks like rain. Only time for one good fight. Fella! How about you?"

I didn't even look up. I kept working my way through the hubbub, heading for the path back to the lighthouse. As I went, the guests squeezed in on me, pushing me toward the ring.

"You! Fella!" Gates called. "Come on up. Just one round. What's your hurry?"

The smiling and laughing men closed in tighter, making it harder to push through. From behind, someone grabbed me in a bear hug, while someone in front lifted my legs, carrying me toward the ring. They threw me on the canvas, and I crawled to the other side to squeeze out, but the crowd closed in around me with their hands in the air, pushing me back. The attendants quickly pulled me to my feet, leading me into the challenger's corner to lace up my gloves.

"Save your fighting for the fight!" Gates said. "I don't want you all tuckered out. Take a couple of deep breaths and quit being such a baby. Boys, let's hear it for this fella."

I made one last attempt to exit the ring, but was repulsed, cheered on by an increasingly frenetic crowd. I'd never been to a fraternity and never witnessed their rites of passage, but this had all the characteristics of a good hazing. Having seen the previous matches, I knew I could hold my own for a few rounds, so I relented.

They laced up my gloves, pulled me up on my feet, and climbed out, leaving only Gates, the referee, and me in the ring. Faces and hands bobbed back and forth, creating a large circle of chaos around the ring, an undulating mass with no definition or detail. When the bell rang, I pulled my gloves up against my jaws and my elbows tight against my ribs.

Somehow, Gates snuck in a left hook to the body, a right hook to the head, and an uppercut before I was set. The first punch did the most damage. It hit just under my elbow, crunching against my ribs and shooting a bolt of pain through my side. The right hook to the side of my head didn't connect, but the uppercut slammed into my jaw, swinging my head around. A gob of spit shook from my jowl and flew past as if in slow motion. I took a few steps back, careful not to get caught on the ropes but hopeful that I could gain a few seconds to get my bearings. Gates didn't hold back. He stalked me across the canvas, trying to pin me up against the ropes. I did my best to keep my distance.

By now, the sights and sounds from outside the ring had faded into the background. Time slowed, measured by jab after jab as he tested and provoked, looking for an opening. Instincts from my boxing at Fort Jackson began to surface. I recognized patterns—a jab-jab-right cross to get me to open up inside, a jab-cross-left hook, to catch me off guard, and body punches to make me lower my defense. I avoided the ropes, protecting my face and body as he followed me. In response, he got more aggressive with his combinations.

He had no interest in split decisions or a couple of knockdowns. Gates wanted that sensational knockout punch that would thrill the crowd, leaving no doubt about who was boss. The kind of KO that spins a guy around, legs going limp, upper torso flying away in the opposite direction, arms drooping straight down to his side, and face falling flat onto the canvas.

He connected on more than his share of punches, causing enough damage to wear me down. I tried not to square up to him, leaning more toward the right to protect my good eye, but this created openings. After a series of left hooks to the body, I dropped my guard just enough for Gates to connect with a damaging uppercut, landing squarely on my chin and dropping me to the canvas.

On my hands and knees, chants for Gates echoed in my head. Blood dripped from my mouth and splattered onto the canvas. Off to my right, the light-blue sleeve of the referee waved past my head. I didn't know the count and didn't really care.

I knew I could beat Gates if only I had both eyes. With only one, there was no depth perception. I had a limited range of visibility and couldn't help but favor my one remaining good eye, leaving the other side vulnerable. A guy with only one eye shouldn't be boxing.

Gates attacked as soon as I stood up. I tripped, trying to avoid a jab, once again ending up on the canvas. This time I took the full count before getting up, letting my head clear. I sprang to my feet with barely enough time to fend off Gates's continued attacks.

He out-boxed me to the point of humiliation, and he didn't let up. He pressed with jabs and combinations, looking for openings. I didn't bother to throw a punch, instead, keeping my guard up and creating separation. He chased me around the ring, trying to pin me up against the ropes. As his frustration and overconfidence grew, his footwork got sloppy, and he started leaving himself open, not protecting himself the way he should. His right hook reached out too far. He wanted to do some real damage to my good eye, focusing on it every chance he could. The more I turned away to protect it, the more he reached, swinging out away from his body and letting the punch hang out there too long, leaving his right side wide open.

Finally, I connected hard with a right cross down the pipe, making him pay for his carelessness. I unleashed a flurry of my own combinations, landing a left uppercut, then another right cross to the jaw, sending him reeling. He pulled back but tripped, opening himself up for another volley. Starting with a few body punches to loosen him up, I followed with another right cross, left uppercut series. I kept swinging and connecting until his legs collapsed, landing him face-first on the canvas.

My heart nearly exploded as the crowd went suddenly silent. The clouds grew dark as night, and the wind howled as the ref pushed me out of the way, clearly unnerved by the turn of events and the damage done to Gates. I didn't know if he could get up or not. I scanned the guests surrounding the ring, their round faces all perplexed by what had happened. This time there were no cheers, no prize bottles of whisky, and no congratulatory words of encouragement.

The rain came suddenly, hard and cold, with drops that stung as they hit. I slid out of the ring, unlacing my gloves as I went. The crowd parted, and I made my way across the lawn toward the lodge, dropping the gloves to the wet grass. I never looked back. I huffed and coughed, more from the growing hatred than the exertion.

Plenty of stares followed me into the building, with my clothes soaked from the rain and my face bloodied from the fight. In the kitchen, I chipped ice from the icebox into a rag for my swollen lip, then leaned over the sink to spit blood. I found a partial box of Gates's carnation boutonnieres with four perfect flowers remaining on the counter. One at a time, I dropped them, grinding them into the floor with my muddy shoes.

Most of the men stood nervously watching as I left the kitchen and entered the great room. Polly and his group of friends were the only ones not to notice my presence, continuing to sing their off-color drinking songs in the far corner. Polly was already late for his shift and appeared wobbly on his feet. It wouldn't be the first time Cephas would have to cover for him. I grabbed a handful of cigars from the humidor and stuffed them into my right coat pocket.

As I looked up at the architectural drawing, I took offense at the new marina occupying the space where the fishing village should have been. I tore it off the wall, crumpled it into a ball, and stuffed it into the humidor. Without a glance back at the crowd, I tracked mud and dripped blood through the great room on my way out.

#

Cephas had told me to smooth things over. Gus had warned me to stay away. Yet somehow, I'd ended up in the ring, fighting Gates. I could have let him win. Instead, I humiliated him in front of his guests. I even crushed his boutonnieres.

I thought it best to hide out until the steamer's arrival, then slink away like a forgotten memory. Once in Duluth, I could find some rock-bottom job along the waterfront where no one would have any reason to bother with a one-eyed outcast.

My plan gave me a chill. For years, seclusion had been my escape from social complications. I'd let myself believe in the purification, reflection, and self-reliance of aloneness, and I imagined an attachment to the hermits, monks, and ascetics who'd gone before me. Through the years, I'd become convinced that isolation would be my cure for the lingering horrors of war and the pain of lost loves.

I scrubbed the blood from my hands, hair, and face in the lake next to the lighthouse dock. The shock of the cold water numbed the pain and washed some of the day's contention away. I opened up the boathouse, removed my wet coat, and found an old towel to dry my face and hands. It didn't feel so claustrophobic with the doors swung wide open, leaving me a great view, the lighthouse to the left, the village to the right, and the crashing waves just a few feet in front of me.

In the bow of the boat, I rested up against the sail bag with a pair of life preservers underneath, making a lounge that felt every bit as comfortable as my bed back at the cottage. The rain stopped, but the winds from the southwest grew stronger, stirring the waters into a rhythmic crash. I rubbed the side of my jaw, now scabbed over from the fight, and noticed that two of my teeth felt loose. I hoped that Gates also had enough damage to regret goading me into battle.

I lit a kerosene lamp, took out my knife, and then pulled out the carving that I had started the night before. The general shape of the horse was roughed out, but that's as far as I had gotten. Settling in against the sail bag, I finished carving the horse's head—its ears pricked, nostrils flaring, as if startled and about to bolt. With little flicks of shavings, I smoothed the horse's shape around the belly and across the back, then shaped the mane and tail, carving wind-swept tufts befitting of a wild stallion in a fierce storm. Working down the sides, I gently sculpted the rounded contours of the fore and hindquarters, staying true to the musculature and bone structure of the animal. From there, I cleaned up the legs and added more shape to the mane, neck, and tail.

At four o'clock in the morning, a small sliver of light appeared along the eastern horizon, leading me to believe I had a few more hours to finish the piece. That was when I heard the sound of engines—first the trucks coming down from the lodge, then the boats as they entered the harbor. I extinguished the kerosene lamp and closed the boathouse doors, leaving an opening large enough to watch the goings-on at the harbor without being seen.

The boats were similar to those from the previous nights, one ten feet longer than the other, both with cabins fore and large cargo holds aft. They turned to face out from the pier, sliding smoothly alongside the pilings as crewmen secured the dock lines. Neither boat shut down its engines, showing no intention of staying any longer than they needed to. Crewmen quickly transferred the cases from the boats onto the trucks. Once loaded, the trucks ascended along the same dirt road from which they came. With the work done, the attendants filed up the stairs to the lodge, and the boat crew disappeared into the cabins of their ships.

The shore quickly went quiet, except for the idling of the boat engines. Winds and waves hushed. The gulls stood silent on the shore, facing out toward the water, waiting for their time to take flight. In the dead silence, two men walked down the stairs from the lodge, breaking the spell.

The larger man was dressed in a cream-colored suit. The shorter man struggled to stay on his feet. The larger man helped the other as they walked along the pier, before climbing into the larger of the two boats. The crewmen wasted no time casting off the lines, leaving the boats to slip away toward the mouth of the harbor.

#

As the boats were leaving, a soft, warm glow rose from behind the fishing village. For a moment, the shacks had a friendly shine uncharacteristic of that dark and shabby corner of the harbor, but that moment didn't last. The softness turned severe, and the glow became godawful as flames engulfed the buildings. The village became an apocalyptic quagmire of yellow-orange bursts. Swirling fingers of fire climbed the birch, aspen, and pine trees, blossoming into windswept fireballs at the tops. Thick black columns of smoke rose like small tornados from the burning buildings and floated out into the harbor. The tar-paper shacks exploded with bursts of fury. Within minutes, the warehouse and icehouse were both ablaze, the fire working its way through the buildings, blowing out windows and doors with yellow-orange blasts.

I grabbed a boathook from the boathouse and ran, driven by a soldier's instincts and reactions. The sounds and sights of the conflagration, the thick choking smoke, and the screams returned me to the trenches. Villagers appeared as apparitions, moving through the flames, running from the shacks to the shoreline like soldiers retreating. The cries came from all corners, rising above the thunderous roar of the fire, frighteningly similar to the sound of wounded and dying doughboys stuck in the no-man's land between the warring armies.

The villagers frantically launched their boats, wading waist-deep into the icy water before climbing over the gunwales to escape the flames. Men rowed from shore, gathering in the middle of the harbor with a barrage of embers showering down upon them. As the confusion subsided, the villagers' cries and screams gave way to mournful wailing—the kind that comes as the chaos ends and the body count begins.

I got my bearings as I approached the village. Ahead of me,

flames and smoke from the buildings obscured everything. The wind blew hard from the southwest, making an approach from the lake impossible, so I headed up the hillside where clearings opened among burned-out areas, and the clouds of thick blackness dissipated. Cephas ran along the walkway by the cottages, still too far away to help, while a handful of lodge guests watched from the lawn above as if the spectacle was all for their early morning entertainment.

Finding an opening where the flames had subsided, I crossed the charred ground to the village, hoping everyone had escaped safely. Nothing but square outlines remained of the tar-paper shacks, having collapsed into glowing piles of rubble. Burned remains of cookstoves, mattresses, chests, or trunks stood out like tombstones among the burning embers.

On my way out of the village, I found a protrusion stretching out from under a burned bed, a sickening sight of human mutilation that one never forgets and never gets used to. Two legs from under the burned mattress bent in unnatural ways. The skin was bubbled and deformed, mottled with blotches of cauterized blood and charred flesh. I hooked the mattress with the boathook and flipped it off the body. With great effort, I lifted the dead weight over my shoulders into a fireman's carry. An oozing line of blood trickled down my shirt as I plodded toward the back of the village with the urgency and intensity of a battlefield rescue. I moved along the edge of the hillside to the waterfront, a safe distance from the fire.

It was a young man. As the villagers' boats returned to the shore, I laid him on his back, straightened his legs, and crossed his arms over his torso. I held my hand above his mouth, not able to feel an exhale, then watched his chest, which showed no movement up and down. Having just arrived, Cephas knelt across from me, trying to catch his breath, his eyes wide from the horror of it all.

"Pray for him," I said.

He muttered what might have passed for a prayer but sounded more like the inconsolable summons to a deity who wouldn't answer.

"My God . . . Oh my God . . . Oh dear, Lord . . . Oh please, God . . ."

Kneeling next to the young man, I sensed none of the life that once occupied his cold gray body. Any essence of humanness was now far removed. Cephas knelt, still muttering supplications, but I could barely hear him above the heavy wind and crashing waves. A swirling energy swept across the smooth stones of the beach as if carrying away all that remained.

Mae stumbled across the shore with one hand clutching her neckline and the other against her mouth, muffling horrific sobs. Anna and Nora, the two other women from the village, each fell down next to Mae, collapsing over the body. It was Hans, the one who had pulled me out of the water to save my life, the son of Anna and Gunnar. Anna threw her arms around him, convulsing as she laid over him.

For me, all the adrenaline and instinct slipped away. The horrors of what had happened caved in on me. I walked toward the still burning tree line, stumbled to my knees, and vomited.

4 DARK TIMES

With no place to come home to and the dead left unburied, the fishermen loaded the boats and headed for their fishing grounds. They couldn't take the time to properly mourn. They couldn't afford the loss of a day's catch or suffer damage to the only nets they had left by leaving them to become overloaded. The body laid out on the shore attracted a growing crowd of lodge guests along the top of the hill, although none of them showed any inclination to assist. As Anna, Nora, and Mae methodically went through preparations of the young man's body, the men watched from afar with the detached interest of anthropologists.

Burial would be late in the afternoon. They washed the body, laying it out on the smooth stones. I brought linens from the lighthouse: washcloths for cleaning the ash and burns away, towels for drying, and bed sheets for wrapping the corpse. Anna, Nora, and Mae stayed with Hans all morning, much of the time just sitting next to the body. Rose, much too innocent to have witnessed all that she had seen, spent her time collecting colorful stones from the shore or lying in Mae's lap.

I'd make his coffin from wood stored in the barns behind the keepers' cottages. The work kept me from thinking too much about the horrors of the night before. Back at the farm, we made almost everything, leaving me plenty handy with tools, but I'd never made a coffin. I wanted to do it right. The fisherman deserved it. It was the least I could do for the young man who had pulled me out of the water and saved my life.

While I worked, the details of the conflagration rolled through my head, a vivid replay of exploding tar-paper shacks, warehouses collapsing into balls of fire, and the villagers screaming as they ran to escape. But before the real horrors, I remembered the two men boarding the motorboats, one tall and one short. Both had left just as the village fire began. I tried not to jump to conclusions over who might be responsible for the blaze. I didn't even know if the fire was intentional or an accident. Still, I couldn't get the thought out of my mind concerning the two men leaving as the fire began.

Elsie's sobs were heard long before she and Cephas entered the barn. She was a nervous sort. Being at the end of a pregnancy and having a husband like Polly would make anyone anxious. The two walked in almost sideways, each with an arm around the other, Elsie, with her face buried among the flaps of Cephas's jacket. He seemed relieved to get her seated in a chair next to the workbench and gave her a handkerchief to wipe her eyes and blow her nose. Cephas tucked in his shirt as he circled my work area. He appeared interested in my coffin-making skills, but from his questions, it became clear he had something else on his mind.

"Where were you last night?" he asked. "And what happened to your face?"

"I stayed in the boathouse," I said. "Didn't think I'd be welcome at the lighthouse."

I assumed he knew of all the trouble I'd caused the day before. He thought I had met with Gates to smooth things over. Instead, I knocked him flat on his back in the boxing ring. Surely someone must have complained, but Cephas had a blank stare that told me he knew nothing of the fight. Gates must have been too busy with other stuff to squeal on me.

"I asked you about your face . . ."

"None of that matters right now," I said. "What matters is the villagers."

Cephas's expression turned sour, either over my avoidance

of his question or my concern for the fishermen. He started to ask me again, then thought better of it. Elsie went on sniffling, wiping her eyes, and blowing her nose.

"And your job is to watch the lighthouse, not to build coffins."

He was in a mood, having worked all three late-night shifts at the lighthouse since neither Polly nor I had reported for duty.

"Plenty of able-bodied men in the village," he said. "They can handle this kind of work. You have your own chores."

"One less able-bodied man in the village, in case you hadn't noticed."

I considered this common sense. He reacted as if it were insubordinate, raising his voice with a quick, sharp reply.

"And in case you hadn't noticed, I worked all three shifts last night because both of my assistants were off doing God knows what. As long as you're on my payroll, you're here to care for the lighthouse, not to fuss over the villagers."

Cephas and I faced each other, the beginnings of a coffin laying between us on a pair of sawhorses. I attached braces to the coffin's bottom boards as we spoke. He watched me work, his arms crossed over his chest. Elsie listened while the two of us argued, her eyes peering over the edge of her handkerchief.

"Is there any room for charity in this holy place of yours?" I asked. "You say our job is the safety and salvation of mariners. Is there any safety and salvation left for our neighbors? Those villagers, who now have nothing?"

It wasn't intentional, but our eyes locked in a stare. Without looking away, I put my tools down and rested my hands on the casket base in front of me.

Cephas finally looked away as he spoke. "You're the last person who should be giving advice on running a lighthouse or being a Christian." After a quick scan of the barn, his glare returned, colder and more resolute than before.

"Aren't you supposed to be gone by now? Sailing back to Duluth?"

"There's a coffin to build, a grave to dig, and a hundred other things that need to be done," I said. "I can't leave."

Only hours ago, I'd made the decision to leave Stony Point, even if it meant taking some rock-bottom dockworker's job. Now it seemed detestable to go.

"Besides, I'm the only assistant you have now."

"Where's Polly?" Cephas asked.

"He's gone."

"You mean he's at the lodge?"

"No, he's gone."

Elsie stopped sniffling and looked up from her handkerchief, her eyes red and swollen. I put the screwdriver down, looking between her and Cephas, surprised that neither of them knew he'd left.

"Polly left with Gates this morning."

Elsie covered her mouth with the now soaked hankie. Cephas made no attempt to hide his surprise.

"I thought the two of you would know," I said.

"Are you sure?" he asked. "I thought Gates was up at the lodge."

"Darned sure. Saw them get on the boat myself. Right after the fire started."

I grabbed a few nails and held them in the corner of my mouth. With a hammer in one hand, I lifted the sideboard up to nail it to the coffin base. Cephas unthinkingly picked up the other end, helping to hold the board in place.

"Where'd he go?" Cephas asked. "What are they doing?"

I nailed the board in place as Elsie blubbered and quaked. Cephas asked all the questions, but I suspected neither of them really wanted to know the answers.

"All I know is you're a bit short of help up here, and the harbor's in some serious trouble. I'd hate for you to be the only one left to put it all back together. Might help to have me around."

Cephas held the other longboard in place, then helped with the shorter sides. With the boards fastened, I sanded the edges, giving it a finished look.

"So, the villagers. Where will they live?" I asked. "They have no food or home. We can't just leave them with nothing."

Cephas didn't answer. His hands trembled, and he suddenly found some reason to leave in a hurry. He put his tobacco pouch in his coat pocket before helping Elsie to her feet.

"Maybe my cottage," I said. "I'll stay with you, Cephas, until they get back on their feet."

Elsie and Cephas were already out the door. If they'd heard a word of what I'd said, they gave no indication. Now alone, I carved a Jesus fish into the top of the coffin, with a cross where the fish's eye would be, and rays projecting out from the fish as if ascending—a fitting emblem for such an honest Christian fisherman. I rounded each of the edges and corners slightly with the plane. Leaving the coffin in the barn, I loaded the wheelbarrow with a shovel, pick mattock, and rake and would spend the next few hours in the meadow south of the village, digging a grave.

#

Mae and Rose joined me out in the meadow. By the time they arrived, I had already picked out the gravesite, cut an eight-foot long rectangular patch through the heavy mat of wildflowers and grass, and made a large dirt pile next to it. I put my shovel down and met them halfway from the hole to the edge of the meadow. Mae and I embraced, a long lingering hug, much more meaningful than the friendly and playful cuddles from before. She looked tired, though still pretty. There were tears, but the sorrow wasn't all-consuming. We watched as Rose ran off to pick bouquets of northern bluebells and wild columbine, weaving through the meadow, from flower patch to flower patch.

"I wanted to thank you," she said. "The whole village wants to thank you."

We held each other, which tempered the trouble and pain if only for a few moments. A soft breeze blew through the grass with a rhythmic ripple, not unlike the waves of Superior. The wind had shifted from the night before, coming off the lake with a comfortable coolness. She brushed her hair back with her hand, then sat on a log next to where I worked. I picked up my shovel while she watched Rose playing twenty feet away, making a large pile of wildflowers.

"That's her papa's grave," Mae said, pointing in the general vicinity of Rose's pile. "My husband, Knute. He died last year."

Mae's eyes and cheeks were still moist from the tears, but she somehow managed a soft, warm smile. She found a way to set her grief aside for the moment.

"Rose and I come here often. In early May, the flowers poke right out of the snow as if they can't wait for spring. That's when I know winter's finally over."

She watched me work as I threw shovels of dirt out of the grave onto the dirt pile. My coat was off, my sleeves rolled up, and I'd worked up a pretty good sweat.

"Knute hated Gates," she said. "The two of them fought all the time. Gates wanted us out of the harbor. We'd find our nets cut up, our boats damaged, or our boxes of fish dumped into the harbor. We knew Gates did it but couldn't prove it. One night Knute went out to check on the boats, but he never returned. The next morning his body washed up onshore. The sheriff declared the whole thing an accident."

Mae clenched her fists as she spoke, her arms swinging back and forth, accentuating her words.

"He had the nerve to suggest it was an accident and all Knute's fault!"

She spat on the ground in disgust, spitting as impressively as any seasoned dockhand. I must have looked surprised because Mae unapologetically blushed. She looked embarrassed about the spitting but firm in her disgust over her husband's suspicious death.

"Didn't they investigate?" I asked. "Did you tell them about the vandalism?"

"Sure. The sheriff knew all about the damage, but he didn't care. He didn't dispute what we said, he just didn't care. Said we should've moved."

Mae smoothed the wrinkles in her dress, then glanced back at Rose. She calmed herself and sat back down. As I dug, she picked long blades of grass, weaving them together into a braid, adding new blades as needed.

"I saw Gates last night," I said. "He left on one of those boats just after the fire started. Think he had something to do with it?"

"Of course," Mae said. "But the sheriff will rule it an accident. He'll say it was our carelessness. Tell us we should move. Treat us like we're worthless and stupid. But we know Gates did it."

Working from the waist-deep grave, the shovels of dirt had to be lifted twice as high to clear the edge of the hole. I wiped my face with my hankie, then brushed my hair back under my cap.

"I'll tell the sheriff what I saw. That'll help, won't it? Tell 'em I saw them leave just after the fire started."

Mae smiled, slowly shaking her head back and forth, politely and kindly dismissive. "I'd die if something happened to you," she said. "Please, don't go stirring up trouble with Gates."

She continued to weave, her nimble fingers manipulating the grass into what now looked like a shallow bowl. I went back to digging.

"My brother Bjørn says you're like Askeladden," she said.

"Who's Askeladden?"

"He's the hero in an old Norse folktale. He's the underdog. The one who doesn't have anything. People don't treat him very nice."

"I don't know if I want to be Askeladden," I said.

"But he's the hero. When the princess is in danger, everybody else tries to save her, but they can't. They fail miserably. They all think they're so strong and smart."

I took my handkerchief from my pocket and wiped the sweat off my face. "So, this Askeladden. Does he save the princess?" I asked.

"Oh, yes!" Mae was quite animated, appearing many years younger than she had just moments before. The story took her back to her youth. "Askeladden is really smart. He sees things that others don't. He can see deep inside people and knows who is honest and who is dishonest. He has a good heart and a good mind. His brothers all fail because they think they're such big shots. Askeladden wins because he's humble, courageous, and good."

"And does he win the princesses' heart? Even if he's all dirty and sweaty?" I asked.

Pleasantly surprised by the implication of the question, Mae blushed. She smoothed her hair back and straightened out the folds in her dress.

"Well, I don't know about that," she said.

Somehow there's always a thick root that crosses through whatever hole one might be digging. This one was two inches in diameter, running diagonally across the plot. I set the shovel down, pulled out the pick mattock, and started chopping the root along the edge of the grave. Mae continued with her stories.

"Askeladden tricked a troll into cutting wood for him, to save his family."

"How'd he do that?" I asked.

"With a ball of cheese! He pretended it was a stone and made the troll believe he could squeeze water from it. He scared the troll so badly that the troll cut all of Askeladden's wood for him."

"Sounds like those trolls are kind of stupid."

"Oh, they're stupid, all right. Askeladden even took all the troll's silver and gold."

I stopped chopping the root and leaned on the pick to listen. She was somewhere else, reliving a better time. Rose continued with large handfuls of wildflowers, placing them against the wooden cross at her father's grave, the cross barely visible among the overgrown grasses. That Askeladden character didn't impress me. All it took to be a Norwegian hero were stupid trolls, inept royal families, and lazy, good-for-nothing brothers.

"Where did the gold and silver come from?"

"Trolls always have a chest full of gold and silver," she said, as if everyone knew about the treasures of trolls.

What a crazy story. I almost told her so, but the stories comforted her and helped pass the time. Rose crawled up on

Mae's lap, tugging on her dress.

"Papa er i Himmelenhimmelen?" Rose asked.

"Ja, Himmelenhimmelen," Mae answered. "Yes, heaven."

"Hans også?"

"Hans also."

Rose squirmed in Mae's lap, unable to get comfortable, making small outbursts to verbalize her discomfort. Mae tried to calm her, tried to stop the squirming, which made Rose all the more unsettled.

"Hjem?" Rose asked. "Kan vi gå hjem?"

Tears pooled again in Mae's eyes as she hugged Rose, stroking her back and rocking her in her lap.

"Kan vi gå hjem?" she asked again.

"Rose wants to go home," Mae said bitterly. "What do I tell her? She has no home."

"Papa? Kan vi gå hjem?" she cried, thrashing about, trying to free herself. She continued to cry for her papa and beg to go home, growing louder and higher pitched until the words were unrecognizable. Mae did her best to calm Rose, getting kicked for her efforts. All the playfulness of the Askeladden story was gone, overtaken by the painful realities of a fatherless, homeless five-year-old girl. Rose pushed away from Mae, returning to her father's grave to rearrange the grouping of flowers. As I climbed from the now shoulder-deep grave, Mae stood, wiped her eyes, and brushed the dirt from her dress.

"You've helped so much. What would we have done without you?"

Mae gently slipped her arms around my neck, drawing me in tight, her face resting against my chest. I wrapped my arms around her waist. What began as a hug turned into a long embrace. Her gesture of gratitude blossomed, lasting much longer than a simple thank-you.

"But we can't let Gates get away," I said.

Mae drew me in, kissing my cheek over and over again until I quit talking. Then her lips met mine.

When it came to love, I was a clumsy apple-knocker. Since my injuries from the war, I'd lost all sense for flings, flirtations, and romance. I'd convinced myself that such wonders no longer suited me. I considered myself too burdened with the troubles of life and scars from the past to waste time with courtship. Now Mae and I had something meaningful. A closeness I hadn't felt for a long time. I might have ignored the spark right from the start, but now I couldn't hide it. I couldn't stop thinking about her, and she seemed to feel the same way about me. We hugged and kissed for longer than I could have hoped for, until Rose finished her arrangements of flowers, returning to reclaim her mother's attention.

#

Late that afternoon, I finished the grave and returned from the meadow. The steamer had come and gone, and my trunk was still hidden in the boathouse. The fishermen worked at the lighthouse dock, their day's catch strewn across the wooden planks. Fillet knives flashed as they cleaned. With two quick swipes, both fillets peeled away from the carcass. A quick flick of the wrist and the rib bones flipped away. Another swipe and the fillet was skinless. They tossed the perfect fillets into a pile in the middle of the pier, waiting to be packed. Up until now, the fishermen had sold their fish fresh, boxed on ice. Now with the icehouse destroyed by the fire, their only option was to salt the fish, packing them in barrels with alternating layers of fillets and salt, then sealing the barrels with tar once filled.

After the cleaning, Bjørn and Gunnar came with me to the lighthouse to get the coffin. Bjørn was pleasant and soft-spoken, grateful for my help. Gunnar had a much harder edge, a permanent scowl and nervous fidget that made me believe he could explode at any moment. No doubt, he suffered greatly from the fire and losing his only son. I should have been troubled by his gruffness, but somehow, I felt a kinship to him. Hell, for what he'd been through, he had the right to act any way he wanted.

Gunnar ran his hands over the smooth top of the coffin, tracing every rounded corner, reflecting on his boy. "A real fisherman," Gunnar said. "Hans could tell a story like no one else. We'd be on our way home from a long day of fishing, then he'd start making fun of Bjørn. He'd bounce around, lively like a Hardanger fiddle, talking all gladsome and gay as if piss were pudding and lice were lingonberries. Just that big, goofy smile on his face, and we all knew he was pretending to be Bjørn."

"Ja, then he starts yelling crazy like Napoleon," Bjørn said. "Stuffs his hand in his shirt and struts around the boat, screaming at everyone. That's when we know he's making fun of Gunnar."

"And God forbid anyone should make a mistake," Gunnar added. "Hans would retell it, making us all appear as dim-witted, hapless trolls. By the time we arrived at the village, we were all happy and laughing as if coming home from the local saloon."

Gunnar grabbed me by the shoulders with his scruffy hands, strong enough to startle me. He still scowled, but his eyes filled with gratitude. "Fine work," he said. "Life's unfair. Hans was more of a man than anyone here. Doesn't even have a decent pair of trousers or a shirt to be buried in. This coffin's the best thing he has."

Gunnar and Bjørn each took an end and carried the coffin out the barn door, past the cottages, and onto the tram. I watched from the walkway as the tram slowly crawled down the hill with the pine box straddling the chair backs. At the bottom, they carried the box across the shoreline toward Hans's body, still lying on the rocks in the shade of a large pine tree between the lighthouse and the burned-out village. Bjørn and Gunnar placed the body into the coffin, and the men carried it across the shore, heading off to the meadow to lay Hans to rest.

By eight o'clock that evening, Cephas was at the lighthouse working Polly's shift, and my old cottage buzzed with activity. Elsie piled blankets and linens on the beds and stocked extra food in the cupboards. I filled the coal bucket and stoked the fire in the stove. With an ash can at my feet, I peeled the vegetables for corned beef stew. Soon, ten potatoes, a dozen carrots, five rutabagas, and six onions were peeled, chopped, and soaking in a pan of cold water. Elsie braised four cans of corned beef in two large pots on the stove, then added all the vegetables with enough water to cover. After seasoning it with a heavy dose of salt and pepper, she left the pots to simmer. We both sat down for coffee. She wore a green dress and looked like a watermelon as she leaned back in her chair. Breathing hard from the work, her skin glowed with sweat. She looked like she might deliver at any moment.

"I know Polly's been mean," she said. "I don't know why he gets that way. Just jealous, I guess. He worries that Cephas likes you more than him."

I took a long sip of my coffee, trying not to show my disgust. I couldn't blame Elsie for defending her husband, but I didn't have to forgive and forget.

"Not that I want him beaten up and thrown over cliffs," she said.

She may have been fishing for an apology, but she wasn't going to get one. After a moment of awkward silence, she changed the topic and grabbed the coffee pot to freshen up our cups.

"Your eye patch looks nice," she said. "My daddy once told me the reason sailors wore eye patches. Not because they'd lost an eye like you. They did it to keep one eye trained for darkness for when they had to go below deck. Below deck, they'd flip up the patch, and they could see real good. Isn't that smart?"

"Sure is," I said. "Maybe Polly needs an eye patch for when he comes back from the lodge at night. Might stop him from falling down."

I regretted it as soon as I said it. She bowed her head, and when she looked back up, her eyes got all watery again.

"Elsie, I didn't mean . . ."

She wiped her eye with the back of her hand.

"It's ok. He spends too much time partying. Says Gates needs him up there, but I don't like it one bit. My daddy never drank. He said it was a sin. And if you ask me, that lodge is no place for a husband and father." She forced a smile. "So, when do you think he'll be back?"

I had nothing but a blank stare for an answer, not that she

expected one. She blew her nose, then changed the subject.

"So, how's that new girlfriend of yours?"

"She's not a girlfriend," I said.

"Oh, I don't know about that. She likes you. I can tell. Us girls know these kinds of things. I'd say she likes you a real lot."

Elsie took a long sip of her coffee, letting the words sink in. I smiled politely, thinking about the afternoon in the meadow and my clumsy attempts at romance. I suspect love could sit right on my lap and give me a big kiss on the lips, and I still wouldn't recognize it. I could barely admit my newfound love to myself, much less to Elsie.

"She's real pretty, don't you think? And her little girl is such a cutie. I could just squeeze her!"

Elsie set her cup down, forced a smile, and rubbed her belly.

"You don't even know them," I said.

"Well, I'd like to get to know them. We need more women and children up at the lighthouse. I need someone to have coffee with, cook with, and raise kids with. You marry that girl and bring her up here. She needs a good husband like you, and you need a good girl like her."

"Maybe she's not interested."

Elsie waved her pudgy little finger and scolded me as a schoolmarm might rebuke a pupil. "Don't say stuff like that. You're a real catch. I can't believe I have to lecture you about courtship."

She checked on the stew while I threw more coal into the stove.

"Now, where do you think Polly went off to?" she asked. "He didn't even pack a bag."

Neither of us really wanted an answer to that question. I could only imagine the worst possible reasons for him leaving on one of those bootlegger boats while the village burned in the background.

I left to retrieve my steamer trunk from the boathouse, carrying it over to Cephas's cottage. By the time I returned, the smells from the kitchen had drawn me in, reminding me of the home cooking back on the farm. Elsie added cornstarch to thicken the broth and tested the potatoes. It would have been best to let the stew simmer, but the villagers had returned from the burial hungry enough to eat tree bark. I lit the kerosene lamps and laid out pitchers of water, plates, bowls, glasses, and forks on the table just as they began to arrive.

Everyone was gracious, famished and tired. I joined them as Elsie ladled out generous helpings, serving the villagers first. Some sat, and some stood; none of them had much to say. Mae sat on the other side of the room, helping Rose with her food. With plenty of stew left, Elsie pushed seconds on anyone with a near-empty plate.

I retired at 9:00 p.m. to get some sleep before my shift. I awoke at 2:00 a.m. to begin what would be a long six-hour lighthouse shift because of Polly's absence. The villagers still had the kerosene lamps ablaze as I walked to work. Bjørn sat with his head in his hands at one end of the table, while Gunnar pounded his fists at the other end. I couldn't hear the conversation, but his explosiveness was unmistakable. Bits and pieces about the fire—how it started, who should be blamed, and what would become of the village filtered through. Words like murder, retaliate, arrest, and hanged peppered Gunnar's tirade, revealing his conclusions and the candor with which he shared them.

Bjørn appeared worn and beaten, as did Mae, Anna, and Nora, who stood right behind him. Mae was the only one still willing to argue with Gunnar, lashing out at every opening, her eyes puffy and red from crying. Besides Mae and Gunnar, everyone else seemed too tired to continue, yet from my perch up in the lighthouse cleaning room, I noticed the kerosene lamps continued to burn well past 4:00 a.m.

#

Mae and Rose stood along the walkway at the base of the lighthouse as I finished my shift. Mae offered a tired smile, obviously exhausted. Rose noticed the carved wooden legs peeking out from my coat pocket and pulled out the horse that

I had carved the night before. She hugged it and stroked the horse's mane without the enthusiasm she'd shown with the previous carvings.

"She's overwhelmed," Mae explained. "Not really herself."

Mae reached out and gave me a hug. A nice long hug. "We lost all her other figurines in the fire. She misses them. She played with them all the time. Even slept with them. She never let them out of her sight."

Rose reached up and took my hand, surprising both Mae and me. She didn't look up or say anything, just wrapped her hand around my pointer and middle finger. It could have been a mistake or a lapse of judgment on her part, but I took it as a display of affection. I stayed still, not wanting to disturb the magic moment. Rose fixed her gaze out across the lake, watching the clouds and seagulls.

"I can carve more animals," I said. "Maybe a pig? A goat? A chicken?"

Rose didn't look up and didn't answer, appearing calm and comfortable.

"Looks like Rose has grown fond of you," Mae said. "All the villagers are fond of you."

Mae hugged my arm opposite of Rose. I stood still, enjoying the attention from both of them.

"You really impressed Gunnar. He almost cried about the coffin. He's devastated. He misses Hans so much."

Mae picked Rose up and kissed her on the cheek. Rose's little hand slipped away from my fingers.

"Gunnar says you must have some Norwegian fishermen blood. He says it's a waste of a good man that you should be a lighthouse keeper. He thinks you should be a fisherman."

Rose focused on my face as Mae spoke, appearing neither happy nor sad, just curious.

"He says we can trust you, and he doesn't trust anyone," she said. "Bjørn thinks you're Askeladden, and Gunnar thinks you're Norwegian. You've become a real favorite."

Mae's humor came across as half-hearted. Her eyes had a twinkle and a sadness at the same time, and her smile was tight and forced.

"Sskal du vekk?" she asked. "Are you going away? Some people say so. Not that I could blame you. Not with the way you've been treated."

I wrapped one arm around Mae, and one around Rose as Mae held her. Mae choked up, trying to fight back her tears.

"What are we to do?" she asked. "What kind of place is this to raise a little girl? No ice, no warehouse, no belongings, and no home."

I handed Mae my hankie. She wiped her tears and blew her nose.

"I already lost a husband. Now they say you'll be leaving soon."

"I'm not leaving," I said.

Mae wiped her eyes and cheeks. She hooked her hair behind her ear and forced a smile through the tears. "They say you lost your job."

"Funny," I said. "I don't even know. Cephas doesn't want me to stay, but he doesn't want me to leave either. I'm the best assistant he has at the moment."

"I know there are plenty of people who have it much worse than us," Mae said. "But it's so hard right now, and I worry so about Rose."

Elsie came out of her cottage and waddled down the path toward us with happy, expectant excitement. "Am I interrupting anything here?" she asked.

I introduced her to May and Rose. She hugged Mae as if they were separated-at-birth sisters, patting her on the back the way a mother might burp a baby.

"You all come with me right now," Elsie said. "I just baked some cookies, and I have coffee on."

"I have work I need to do," I said, wishing I could have spent more time alone with Mae and Rose.

"Well, pooh. We'll just have to go without you then." She held hands with May and Rose, leading them down the path to her cottage. "I won't say anything bad about you, I promise."

#

With a wheelbarrow full of shovels, rakes, tools, and lumber, I went to work along the shore, hoping to make life easier for the villagers. Before the fire, the fishermen cut, boxed, and iced fillets in the warehouse with tables high enough to clean fish comfortably and supplies nearby for efficient processing. Now they had to pickle their fillets in barrels, and all the work had to be done on the lighthouse dock, sitting Indian style, or standing alongside in the freezing water.

Using the wheelbarrow, I moved a number of barrels from the meadow where they'd been stored, stacking them along one side of the boathouse. On the other side, I built a waist-high table, long enough for four men to comfortably fillet fish. All of this was on lighthouse property without Cephas's approval, but at the moment, I didn't really care. Bags of salt left by the steamer the day before had been sitting unprotected along the shore. I stowed these bags in the boathouse up off the ground to keep the salt safe and dry.

After finishing the fish-cleaning stations, I made my way across the shoreline to the village site, now reduced to cinders and rubble. The area felt surprisingly small with the buildings all leveled, filling a space no larger than a football field. I loaded the charred debris from the warehouse and tar-paper shacks into wheelbarrows, dumping the refuse in a small swampy area nearby. I carefully saved any artifacts found, no matter how insignificant. Heavy items such as cookstoves or chests were neatly arranged along the burned-out tree line toward the back of the village. The smaller items went into boxes, including buttons, dinnerware, pots, and pans. I collected a dozen fillet knives with burned handles, boxing them separately, thinking I could carve new handles for them. Interestingly, I found a pair of scorched kerosene cans that must have been thrown into the brush near where the fire started. I piled them up along with the other large items.

With the rubbish gone, I raked through the smooth stones, removing ash and debris until the village area sat indistinguishable from the rest of the shoreline. I left no traces of the tar-paper shacks. The original cinderblock foundation of the warehouse and the slightly charred dock stretching out into the water toward Tollefson Island were the only visible remnants of the old village.

Clearing out the old village was a strange gesture. Initially, I intended to help reclaim the harbor for the fishermen. Mae was definitely on my mind as I worked, thinking my efforts would give her hope for reclaiming their home and harbor. But what kept me going was a desire to obstruct, to thumb my nose at Gates, to let him know he hadn't beaten us yet.

I never used to trouble myself over the welfare of others. Before losing my eye, friendships and opportunities came easy, and I often took them for granted. Only in retrospect could I now recall the less fortunate, those lingering in the shadows, rarely speaking up, hardly visible, and never taken into consideration. The inequities and injustices they suffered were sometimes overt, but more often systemic, happening in the natural course of society. After losing my eye, the delineation between the haves and have nots became readily apparent and abhorrent. And like Rosco, I could no longer blindly defer to privilege and authority. With the shoreline cleared, my next steps in the coming days would be to help rebuild the village, one tar-paper shack at a time.

After a full morning's work, I found Cephas in his cottage serving up some hash and eggs—a much more enjoyable lunch than the can of beans I had planned for. Pulling the biscuits out from the bread drawer, I set them on the table and poured us each a cup of coffee. He covered his food with ketchup, stirred it all together into a hodgepodge, and buttered up both of his biscuits.

"Why didn't you just leave?" he asked, staring at me from across the table, knife in one hand, fork in the other. He was neither harsh nor decisive in his tone. He seemed to genuinely wonder why I would put myself through it all.

"I dunno. I like the lighthouse. I want to help the villagers if I can. And then there's Mae . . ."

"I heard about the fight," Cephas said. They say you sucker-punched Gates. I sent you up to smooth things over, and you knock him out cold."

"Who said I sucker-punched . . . ?"

"I told him."

The words boomed from the bathroom, a deep voice I'd never heard before. A barrel-chested man emerged from the doorway, still tucking in his shirt, buttoning his pants, and pulling up his suspenders. He wore a black bowler hat, pulled low on his forehead, which shadowed his eyes and gave him a sinister look.

"J.T. Bailey," he said. "Lake County Sheriff. I watched the whole fight. Gates had you good and beat until you sucker-punched him."

As J.T. sat at the table, Cephas picked up his plate and coffee cup, moving to the sofa on the other side of the room.

"Didn't come here to talk boxing though. I'm here to talk about the fire. Have a seat."

I looked to Cephas for assurance, but his eyes stayed glued to his plate as he scooped hash and eggs onto a biscuit. I sat at the table across from J.T.

"Jonah Franken? That's your name?"

I nodded yes and set my coffee cup down.

"New lighthouse assistant? Only been here about a week, right?"

I nodded. He was right, although it felt like months since my arrival. He pulled a small notebook and pencil from his shirt pocket, flipped the notebook to an empty page, and began writing.

"So, where were you the night of the fire?"

"In the boathouse," I answered. "Right down along the shoreline."

J.T. stopped writing and looked up, staring at me from across the table. His lampshade mustache hid his top lip, and his squinty eyes almost hurt to look back into.

"I slept in the boathouse. Thought Cephas would be pretty sore at me for fighting with Gates."

J.T. continued to stare, his hand frozen in place since I'd begun talking.

"Not like I was hiding or anything. I planned to leave on the steamer the next day. Thought I'd just sneak away."

J.T. sat motionlessly. With my nervousness increasing, I couldn't stop myself from blabbering. "Y'see, me and Polly got into a fight a few days ago, and Cephas wanted to fire me. Then I had the fight with Gates 'cause he wanted me to make the villagers move. So, after all that, I planned to leave. That's why I was in the boathouse."

"Sounds like you've been fighting with everybody," J.T. said.

The sheriff looked down at his pad of paper and went back to taking notes. I felt panicked, having said everything all wrong.

"Tell me what happened that night," J.T. said. "After you got in the boathouse."

"Two boats came. Just before sunrise."

From the corner of my eye, I watched Cephas jerk his head up, looking alarmed.

"Two big boats. They unloaded the cargo, then the trucks took the boxes up toward the lodge."

J.T. set his pencil down, leaned back, and crossed his arms over his chest. "What cargo? And who makes deliveries in the middle of the night?"

I glanced over to Cephas, who stared back with an intense, nonverbal censure.

"Can't say," I said. "I mean, I don't know. T'was none of my business."

J.T. picked up his pencil and began to write again.

"Then there were these two guys," I said. "They boarded the boat just as the fire started. Maybe they did it. It was Gates and Polly, I'm pretty sure."

Once again, Cephas looked up, alarmed.

"Gates and Polly climbed aboard just as the fire started to spread, then the boats took off. So maybe they had something to do with it."

"Left on the boat, you say? Both Gates and Polly?"

"Yes. Right after the fire started."

"You sure?" J.T. asked.

"Positive," I said. "Saw 'em leave right from the boathouse."

J.T. took his hat off, wiped his oiled hair back with his hand, then set the hat on the table next to him.

"Nothing you've said makes any sense. There're a dozen people up at the lodge willing to testify that Gates left hours earlier, long before the fire started."

"But I saw him leave," I said. "Both of them left."

The sheriff scratched the top of his head, then took a minute to catch up on his notetaking.

"So, the boats left. Then what happened?"

"I ran to the fire, found my way into the village, found Hans, and pulled him out. He was already dead."

"Anybody else around?"

"No," I answered. "The villagers were all in their boats. Cephas arrived just as I pulled the body up along the shore."

J.T. gave a quick glance to Cephas, then resumed the painful interrogation.

"Any kerosene cans missing from the lighthouse?"

"Not that I know of."

"We found charred kerosene cans near where the fire started. They don't use kerosene at the village or at the lodge. The only place the cans could have come from was the lighthouse."

I stared at my coffee cup, not knowing what to say.

"Did you start the fire?" J.T. asked.

"No! Why would you say that? I tried to help the fishermen. It's Gates who wanted them gone. I'd never do something like that. Especially not to Mae or Rose."

I choked up at the mention of Mae and Rose. J.T. leaned across the table, his face uncomfortably close to mine. "You and Mae have a lover's spat? Maybe that's why you planned to leave."

"We're just friends," I answered.

"You wanted to be more than friends?"

"No. I mean, sure. But what's that got to do with it?"

J.T. closed his notebook and pushed away from the table. He stared silently at the harbor from the window.

"Hans saved my life," I said. "He pulled me out of the water when I was drowning."

"Another thing," J.T. asked. "Why were you down at the village today? You must have known there'd be an arson investigation. Looks like you destroyed every lick of evidence we might find down there."

"You think I'm a suspect?"

"More like a prime suspect," J.T. said. "Can't think of anyone more likely. We'll have you up to the lodge for more questioning once things settle down." He put the notebook and pencil back in his shirt pocket, picked up his hat, and stood. "Don't go leaving Stony Point. We'll be talking again soon."

#

My knees buckled as I reached the table. I sat with my cold cup of coffee in front of me. Cephas stayed on the sofa in the far corner of the room.

"You believe me, don't you?" I asked. "I spent all day yesterday burying Hans and all morning cleaning up the harbor for them. I'm the only friend the villagers have up here. You know it wasn't me, right?"

Cephas slowly walked back to the kitchen, putting his cup and plate in the sink before leaning against the countertop.

"Like I said before, it's not that you're bad. You're just cursed. Every sailor knows a Jonah brings bad luck, and the Bible says, 'If your eye is bad, your whole body is filled with darkness.' Here I am trying to get through one more season and retire, but I'm stuck with a cursed one-eyed Jonah, who gives me nothing but trouble."

"But you know it wasn't me, right? And the sheriff must know I'd never do something like that."

"The way you blabbed your mouth off, he must have thought you'd lost your mind. Why did you bring up the boats? And why in blasted blazes did you have to drag Polly and Gates into it?"

"That's the way it happened, I swear," I said, pounding my

fist on the table.

"What were you doing down at the harbor today?"

"I cleaned it up. Made a station at the boathouse for cleaning the fish. Removed the garbage from the old village. Made it so the villagers can get their harbor back."

"Mae ask you to do it?"

"No, I just did it."

"Nothing but trouble," Cephas said.

I went to the bathroom to pee. I washed my hands and splashed my face with water. The face looking back at me in the mirror looked suddenly ten years older. A few weeks ago, I was full of hope and promise, traveling into the wilderness on a new adventure. Since then, it had been nothing but pain and complications.

Cephas stood at the window, looking out on the harbor as I came back into the main room. "What else are you planning to build down on the shore?"

"Nothing," I said.

"Looks like you'll be building a whole city down there."

He pointed out toward the harbor where a large boat approached the shore.

"That your barge?" he asked.

A boat and a crew of ten pulled into the harbor. As Cephas suggested, it carried enough lumber and supplies to replace the village three times over.

"How are you going to pay for all that?" he asked.

"I didn't order it. I don't have that kind of money. I barely have enough money to get back to Duluth."

We watched as a small army from the lodge made its way down the stairs and lined up along shore to meet the barge as it pulled up. The workers on the barge built a ramp to shore with some of the larger boards, then directed the attendants on how they wanted the lumber stacked. While the crew watched, the attendants unloaded, stacking dimensional lumber in a pile to the right of the lodge stairs. Bags of cement, boxes of nails, spikes and hardware, timbers, and narrow-gauge rails similar to those used for the lighthouse tram filled in the area where the icehouse once stood.

By the time they finished, the once-white uniforms of the attendants were covered with stains and blotches of pine sap from the lumber, leaving them more like grimy deckhands than the pristine lodge employees from only a few minutes ago. With the barge empty and floating higher, they tied it off against the charred posts of the old pier.

"They're already building something north of the lighthouse," Cephas said. "They've been working on it all morning. Looks like little shacks."

On the small strip of shoreline northeast of the lighthouse, the walls and roofs of four little huts neared completion, spreading out along the shore with no particular order or symmetry, scattered like dice shaken from a dice cup. Holes had been cut for doors and small windows, but neither the doors nor the windows were yet installed.

"The villagers call that area Stygg Havn," Cephas said. "Means ugly harbor in Norwegian. It's really not a harbor at all. The bay's shallow and rocky, has no protection from the wind. It would be dangerous for fishing boats, even in the best conditions. In a nor'easter, the boats would crash up against the rocks a half-mile out from shore. Certainly no place for a fishing village."

"It's the new village that Gates told me about," I said. "He made it sound like Valhalla. Those shacks look smaller than my old tent at boot camp."

The workers, both at Stygg Havn and at the old village, had an efficiency in how they went about their work, similar to how the attendants conducted themselves up at the lodge. They knew exactly what they had to do, needing no direction from anyone as they went about their business.

"Seems like Gates is the only one with enough money to buy all that," I said. Cephas mumbled and sat at the table.

"It must have taken weeks to arrange for a barge-load of lumber, supplies, and laborers," I said. "How would anyone know that the village would burn? The fire was all part of some bigger plan, if you ask me."

"Well, I didn't ask, so shut up and do the dishes," Cephas said.

"But you believe me, don't you?"

"Shut up."

"So, am I fired or not?"

"Just do the dishes."

#

More visitors arrived at the harbor that afternoon, tying up at the lighthouse dock shortly after Cephas went to the cottage to rest. I almost woke him, worried it might be inspectors from the Lighthouse Service, yet the boat was too small for official business. The men didn't wear uniforms. It was a pleasure boat, a double cockpit mahogany speedster, maybe twenty-five feet long. I decided to check it out before disturbing Cephas.

The captain disembarked as I reached the bottom of the steps along the shoreline. He jumped out of the boat as soon as the engine shut down, tying both bow and stern to the lighthouse dock, then stuffing a seat cushion between the dock and the boat to keep it from rubbing. It was Gus.

"Are you going to help me or just stand there and supervise?" he asked.

We wrestled a wicker wheelchair from the back cockpit, pulling it to the dock and wheeling it next to where the passenger sat.

"I finally talked Franklin into coming up with me."

Gus's brother Franklin glanced back at us, a handsome young man with facial features similar to Gus, only not as muscular. He had a small blanket around his waist that covered his lap, but from the dock, I could tell he'd lost his right leg.

The boat drew a crowd of guests down from the lodge. After Gus introduced me to Franklin, he helped his brother onto the engine compartment behind the front cockpit. From there, Franklin scooted himself to the dock and lifted himself into the wheelchair.

"Getting too busy down here," Gus said. "Ok if we go up to

the cottages?"

Franklin didn't talk much. We loaded his wheelchair onto the tram next to where he sat. At the top of the hill, he pulled himself up into his wheelchair, and I rolled him to the walkway overlooking the lake. Franklin grew increasingly annoyed and insulted with every attempt we made to help him get around. I nervously repositioned his chair for the most advantageous view, while Gus fretted about the crowd of guests gathering around his boat.

"You two get to know each other," he said, heading back to the tram.

Gus was gone before I could protest. I looked desperately for anyone who might help me with Franklin. If only Mae were near. She would've had the social graces to keep him entertained. She'd have him all settled in, conversing like lifelong friends.

"Want some coffee?" I asked.

"No."

"Something to eat?"

"No."

I fidgeted alongside him, wondering what to say. Neither of us was any good at carrying on a conversation.

"Quite a lighthouse," I said. "Has a third-order bivalve Fresnel lens made in France. The lamp is a Heap air-pressure pneumatic. Some great technology."

As soon as the words escaped, I realized my mutterings were the same pretentious puffery spewed out by Polly when I first arrived. Franklin glanced at me like I was a boor, then looked up at the light.

"Let's go take a look," he said.

I fidgeted.

"Look at what?" I asked.

"At the lighthouse. Let's go inside."

I rolled him in and closed the door behind us. As I rolled him toward the main room, he grabbed the railing to the spiral staircase, stopping my progress.

"What's up there?" he asked.

"Oh. That's the watch room. Where the clockwork

mechanism is."

I started pushing him again toward the main room, but he held tight to the rail and lifted himself out of his chair.

"We're going up," he said.

I grabbed his arm quickly to keep him from falling as the chair rolled back against the wall.

"We can't. Gus wouldn't approve."

"You going to baby me like everyone else? Tell me all the things I can't do?"

The railing was on Franklin's right side, the same side as his missing leg. He hopped up the stairs with his left foot while steadying himself with his right arm on the rail. It had to be tiring, but he kept going, taking only two rests along the whole spiral stairway. Once up in the watch room, he fell to the floor, out of breath but laughing uncontrollably.

"Get me a chair," he said.

I grabbed him under the armpit as he hopped to the chair to sit. He adjusted himself and leaned forward, taking in as much of the view as he could, laughing wildly as if he'd just cheated death.

"What's so funny?" I asked.

"Gus. He'll skin you alive when he finds out you hauled me up here."

"Can't blame me," I said. "This was all your idea."

Franklin's wet, sticky wheeze interrupted his bouts of laughter. I wondered if he might be sick. He pulled a hankie out of his pocket and covered his mouth as he coughed. Eventually, the hacking subsided, and he went back to enjoying the view.

"People ever baby you?" he asked. "Treat you like you're a little kid?"

"Hasn't been a problem here. They treat me like a punching bag."

I pushed the chair closer to the window, giving Franklin a better view.

"I guess Mom used to baby me," I said. "Dad did too. There really wasn't anyone else back on the farm."

"It's like you're not a human anymore," he said. "Like you're a plant that needs to be watered, rotated, pruned, and repotted. They're more worried about keeping you from dying than letting you live."

While I tried to think of some meaningful reply, Franklin lifted himself out of the chair, lurching toward the ladder up to the lantern room, hopping over to stand at its base.

"What's up there?" he asked, having already pulled his one leg up to the second rung of the ladder.

"Nothing. Get down."

His leg swung up on the fourth rung, and I could tell he was tired.

"Better not let me fall," he said.

I grabbed the ladder behind him, not knowing what else to do. As he struggled up, he jammed the stump of his bad leg right into my shoulder, which hurt like hell, but I kept climbing up behind him, not wanting him to fall. Two more rungs and his head rose up into the lantern room.

"This must be that 'salved smelly lens' you told me about," he said.

"Bivalve Fresnel lens," I corrected.

As I pushed, he laid his torso on the lantern room floor and rolled over, bringing his leg up from the ladder. Soon, he stood next to the lens, both hands on the railing.

"Don't touch anything," I said.

Franklin shifted his weight and moved his leg toward the door to the lantern gallery catwalk. I stuck my shoulder under his armpit, put my arm around his waist, opened the door, and guided him out. Having come this far, it would be a shame not to let him experience the best part of the lighthouse. He stood holding the railing, the wind blowing his hair into a tangled mess. I helped him sit on the catwalk with his leg hanging over the edge, and that small crazy laugh of his returned, interspersed with bronchial coughing. I sat next to him as we watched the lake. Gus stood on the dock below, surrounded by lodge guests who were admiring his boat.

"Does this go any higher?" Franklin visually searched the walkway for another ladder or set of stairs.

"Trying to get us both killed?" I asked.

Franklin grabbed my leg with a much stronger grip than I would have expected. "Did more today than in the whole six years since the war. Six wasted years. Makes me sick to think about it. How did you get so lucky?"

I'd never felt lucky. Cephas thought me cursed, and the sheriff considered me his prime suspect for the village fire. Some luck.

"It all depends on how far you fall," I said. "I'm from a small farm with nobody around. I guess I had only my parents and my wife, Jenny, to disappoint. Sounds like you were the big cheese, and the whole city of Duluth mourned your new handicap. You were the crème de la crème, while I was a drop in the bucket. You had lots farther to fall, that's all."

Franklin shifted his weight to get more comfortable, pulling himself closer to the railing.

"Speaking of falls, they say you beat the crap out of the champ in the boxing ring," he said. "A one-eyed Dempsey knocks out the 'Great Gates.' Must've made him real mad. Do you think it made him mad enough to burn the village?"

"You think so?" I asked. "Because the sheriff thinks I did it. I told him it was Gates, but he says there're people at the lodge willing to confirm his innocence."

"A pack of lying thieves if you ask me," Franklin said. "Are you man enough to fight them?"

"Why should I care?" I asked.

"I suppose you'll just pretend it never happened," he said. "Kiss up to Gates like everyone else does."

Franklin rocked back and forth, watching the workmen along the shore.

"Looks like Gates has plans to take over the harbor."

"Not my concern," I said, not being totally honest.

Franklin squeezed my leg again, pulling himself around to face me, his eyes showing an exhilaration and intensity uncommon for a man who had just spent the last six years of his life watching ships from the sun porch of his family's home.

"I knew Gates before the war," he said. "I finished law

school with him, and we both planned to specialize in real estate law. When the Great War started, I enlisted. Gates found some way to avoid the service, but before I shipped out, he talked me into my first big investment. It turned out to be a big scam. If I'd been home, I would've recognized it and put an end to it, but I was overseas. I couldn't do a thing. While I served my time in the trenches, he milked every last red cent out of the property. By the time I returned, the property was in bankruptcy."

Franklin spit a big gob over the edge and watched it fall before splattering on the rocks below. Something a teenager might do.

"Gus told me to mind my own business," I said.

"Tell Gus to go to hell." Franklin again spat over the edge, this time not bothering to watch it fall.

"Guys like you and me don't get chances to be heroes. We're too busy being coddled. People think we can't handle it. Here's your chance to be a man, beat Gates, and save the village."

"And how do you expect me to do that?" I asked.

"It's like boxing. Gotta find his weakness."

"What weakness?" I asked.

"Gates must have a few. Just keep your eyes open, and I bet you'll find something."

He wiggled his torso, shifting his weight from one side to the other, trying to get comfortable. "Find a way to expose his operation, put his business at risk, or embarrass his guests. Those are the things that will do him the most harm."

Franklin scratched the end of his bad leg hard enough to appear painful.

"Gates is worthless without his rich young Turks. Those millionaires are fickle and self-centered. They'll drop Gates the minute there's any sign of trouble. Find something that scares the guests. His speakeasy is all fun and games until someone gets caught, and family reputations are tarnished."

He pulled a twenty-dollar bill from his wallet and a fountain pen from his pocket, then wrote his name and address on the back of the note in a flowing cursive script. "Here's my home address," he said, handing me the bill. "Should take only a few days to receive your letters. Let me know as soon as you have some dirt on Gates, and we'll nail the bastard."

I couldn't remember the last time I'd had a twenty-note in my hands. I inspected it front and back, finding it hard to believe it was real.

"More than my weekly pay," I said. "You always use twenty-dollar bills for stationary?"

"It's not like I carry a pad of paper with me," he said. "Would you prefer a smaller denomination?"

I slowly shook my head no as he put his wallet and pen back in his pocket.

"Franklin? Franklin! Where are you?"

Gus's nervous cries interrupted us, rising up from the base of the lighthouse. I jumped to my feet. Franklin laughed.

"I can't believe you dragged me all the way up here," Franklin said. "Gus will skin you alive."

#

It took a half-hour to get Franklin from the lighthouse, Gus cursing us both the whole way down. After they left, I spent my afternoon and evening in the lighthouse with a scrub brush, brooms, a bucket and mop, and polishing cloths. Cephas knew there'd be an inspection soon and asked me to stay on to help prepare for it. I began cleaning in the lantern room, washing the large windows inside and out.

The lantern room was a perfect vantage point for watching the construction crews. They'd arrived earlier by barge and were now spread across the shore on both sides of the lighthouse. To the northeast, three men finished building the Stygg Havn shacks. The shabby small huts looked to be nothing but oversized outhouses. Their size, lack of quality, and undesirable location made them temporary at best. They'd be buried by the December ice off the lake, known to pile six feet high along that unprotected part of the shore.

Back at the old village, workers transformed the harbor in ways that were of no practical use to the fishermen. A crew of eight prepared footings for a brand-new trolley that would carry guests up the hill, from the shore to the lodge and back. After clearing the vegetation from the hillside, they drilled holes into the rock using star drills and sledgehammers. Then the men cemented metal rods into the holes, creating anchors for footings that would be poured later. They temporarily laid the track sections in two parallel lines next to the footings, ascending the hill to create a visual statement as to the purpose of the project, leaving little doubt that it was now Gates who controlled everything.

The rest of the workers set about making a showcase of the old pier. Laborers removed the charred decking and stringers and burned them in a pile on the beach. Two builders worked from dinghies, using draw knives to strip the charred wood off the still-usable posts. A second team bolted new stringers from post to post, while a third group nailed new decking to the stringers. After dinner, two men wrapped the upper half of the posts with rope, creating an upscale appearance. The new lumber had the coloring of dried clay. The dark-brown posts complemented the lighter colored decking. Combined with the pale yellow of the late day sun and the slate-blue water, the harbor that once looked like a trash heap now had a warmth and appeal worthy of a picture postcard—a wharf now too classy for something as vulgar as commercial fishing.

By now, I'd washed the windows, cleaned the walls, swept the stairs, and mopped the floors from the tip of the lighthouse down to its base, leaving the inside with the clean, chemical smell of bleach and Borax. The rambunctious chatter of the lodge guests was now muted, as the young millionaires finished their dinners and moved inside for an evening of cards. The villagers slept. Cephas finished his dinner in the cottage, then prepared for the start of his shift.

For the first time since my arrival, it felt as if the whole harbor was my own. I meandered across the shore, then up to the lodge and across the deserted back lawn, still lit by the electric lights from the porch. Normally, an army of attendants worked the lawns well into the evening, preparing for the next day's fun and frolic. But with Gates gone, the discipline and protocol that regularly ruled the lodge had gone soft. None of the game stations had been torn down, leaving golf clubs, shotguns, bows, arrows, and baseball equipment scattered like little jewels across the back yard.

Closer to the lodge, the buffet tables were stacked with more food than you'd find at any church potluck. I filled a plate with a fried chicken leg, slices of roast beef, roasted potatoes, and chocolate-chip cookies, all foods that I could eat with my fingers as I wandered. Inside, the men sat at tables of four, smoking cigars and concentrating on the cards in their hands. Dollies, each wearing identical short-hemmed red evening dresses and a long string of pearls, circulated from table to table to freshen drinks and impart their "good luck" for the men as they played. Their dresses each had four inches of beaded tassel along the hem, which swished and swayed with every move they made, adding a backdrop of elegance and sensuality to the games.

An unlit kerosene lantern hung from a hook in the corner of the lodge, likely used by attendants and the Dollies to find their way back to staff dormitories along the unlit paths. Having finished my food, I set the plate down and picked up the lantern, thinking there could be no better time for a return trip to the warehouse to get a closer look at the radiotelegraph system.

My earlier conversation with Franklin, about finding a way to beat Gates, rolled over and over in my mind. The two of us shared a mutual disdain for Gates. Both of us had witnessed his cheating and abusive ways. Gus warned me to stay away from Gates, but Franklin egged me on, challenging me to "be a man" and "act like a hero." Gus argued for me to be rational, while Franklin reignited my anger, disgust, and sense of justice. I needed a closer look at the ledger, the one I'd found earlier as I poked through the warehouse. There had to be something important, dangerous, and incriminating locked within those blocks of encoded text. No one goes through all the effort to encrypt, then decode a book full of messages without good reason.

An uncovering of his bootleg operation? The implication of

all those young millionaires putting family reputations at risk? The revelation that Gates set the fishing village ablaze? One way or another, I suspected that the secrets would destroy his operation and tarnish the reputations of half of Duluth's leading families. This was just the bombshell that Franklin and I hoped to find.

I walked from the lodge to the warehouse with an unlit lantern, not wanting to draw any attention. The moon was bright, making it easy to find the key hidden where I'd left it in the gas pump. I opened the door, slipped inside, lit the lantern, and turned down the flame to a soft golden glow. At the radiotelegraph station, I found the small stack of books, along with new tape that had come off the ticker, marked with the dots and dashes of Morse code. Without bothering to sit, I wound the ticker tape into a tight spool and slid it into my pocket. As I grabbed the books, the door in the far corner opened, then slammed shut.

"Who's in here?"

The deep voice bellowed out at the front of the warehouse, kitty-corner from my spot in the back of the building. I knew better than to hope it was Gus. The voice was too deep and stern.

"Who's there?"

The man had a lantern much brighter than mine, casting a sharp white light that bounced off the ceiling and across the room.

"Not supposed to be here," he said. "Come on out."

I watched the glow from his lamp as he slowly moved along the far side wall, past the line of frosted windows, heading from the front to the back. Occasionally he held the lamp high above the trucks, filling the whole building with light. I set my lamp down next to the radiotelegraph station, leaving it as a decoy. I hoped he would follow my light, expecting to find me.

"Can't stay here forever. I'll find ya sooner or later."

I stayed in a low crouch to hide behind the trucks, carrying the ledger and the books in my left hand. Working my way from truck to truck, I slowly crept in the direction of the front door.

He moved toward the corner where I'd left my lamp. As he crossed the back of the building, I ran for the exit, slamming the door on my way out.

"Stop! Stop right there," he shouted. Thudding footsteps approached as I clumsily fumbled with the door lock from the outside, the books awkwardly held underneath my arm. I closed the hasp over the eyelet just as the man's full weight slammed against the door. His fists pounded, and his feet kicked at the door as I snaked the large brass padlock into the eyelet, finally snapping the lock shut.

"Smack bastard! Open the door! If I have to tear it down, you'll be good as dead. Open the door!"

I was already in the woods, bursting through the underbrush, doing my best to stay on my feet and keep moving. Behind me, he cursed and continued to pound on the door. By the time the door crashed open, I was fifty yards into the woods, lying frozen behind a felled tree, the books held tight in my arms.

He waved his lamp high above his head as he scanned the expanse of woods that surrounded the warehouse.

"You're dead," he shouted. "You had your chance. I'll find you. You're as good as dead."

Lying on my side, I lifted my head ever so slightly to catch a glimpse of his location. I watched the glow of his lantern as he made a complete circle around the warehouse. By now, my breathing had settled into a soft, inaudible rhythm.

"Beat you to death with my own hands when I find you."

I heard the swishing of a stick as he poked and slashed into the underbrush. Rolling onto my back, I looked at the canopy of leaves above me, listening to the sounds of his cursing and thrashing about. I listened for what must have been an hour and a half until he went silent. Fifteen minutes later, the lantern glow retreated up the driveway to the lodge. My knees stiffened as I stretched into an upright position, watching the light move across the front lawn and up to the main door. Walking timidly in the shadows, I moved slowly along the edge of the lawn toward the lighthouse. The sight of anyone outside of the lodge drove me back into the woods. I wasn't in any hurry because I still had hours to go before the start of my shift.

#

I knew the cottage would be empty because Cephas was working his shift. I needed a hiding place for the books, a place where neither Cephas nor Gates would find them. The bookshelves in the main room came immediately to mind.

Through the years, Cephas had amassed quite a collection of books, manuals, and pamphlets related to his profession. Some he could have read many years ago, some might never have been read. Still, they filled his bookshelves next to the fireplace, giving off an aura of expertise. The bottom shelf held various rules and regulation booklets from the lighthouse service, including Instructions to Lighthouse Keepers, Organizational Duties of the Lighthouse Board, Light List of the Great Lakes, and Price List of Standard Articles. Cephas even had a book specifically covering lighthouse keeper uniform regulations.

The middle shelf held a complete series of monthly Light House Service Bulletin pamphlets, dating back to 1912. Inside them, a reader might find information on lighthouse technology, reprimands for keepers, disasters faced at other lighthouses, and stories of lives saved by heroic keepers.

The top shelf included books on navigation and communication, as well as a handful of instruments used by lighthouse keepers, such as binoculars, a bearing compass, and a crystal radio. I decided to stick my newfound books behind the largely unread books in the bookshelf, making them both readily available and safely hidden.

With my hiding place found, I began reading the ledger. There was something oddly familiar about the large blocks of apparently random letters. It triggered some distant awareness just beyond my recollection. The date and time of each message prefaced the blocks of characters. The dates began the previous summer, taking a break from October through April. As for the blocks, they had no spaces, numbers, or punctuation, and most of the alphabet was missing. The blocks appeared as random repeats of the letters A, D, F, G, V, and X. After setting the ledger under my chair, I opened the green book, Codes & Cryptography. Its subtitle described it as "A Guide to the Current State of Ship-to-Ship and Ship-to-Shore Communications." The cover art included depictions of a variety of numeric and alphabetic codes.

I found exactly what I needed in chapter 3, titled "German Army Field Codes— The ADFGVX Cipher." The title couldn't have been clearer. A-D-F-G-V-X were the same six letters used over and over in the string of characters from the logbooks. As the chapter explained, the code's popularity came from its reliability for wireless communications because the dot and dash patterns for the six chosen letters were least likely to be misinterpreted when sent using Morse code.

At the heart of the cipher's encoding and decoding was a six-by-six matrix similar to the one below; both the horizontal and vertical axes were labeled ADFGVX. Inside the matrix were thirty-six randomized characters—all of the twenty-six letters of the alphabet plus the numerals zero through nine.

	A	D	F	G	V	X
A	6	9	q	0	h	p
D	y	1	a	e	m	4
F	d	f	o	n	2	1
G	v	c	3	r	k	x
V	b	7	w	z	5	s
X	8	i	t	u	9	j

Using such a matrix key, characters (such as g) are easy to

encode or decode, representing it by the combination of the side header (A), followed by the top header (D), leading to g=AD. With the matrix above, "whisky" would be encoded as VF AV XD VX GV DA (or VFAVXDVXGVDA with the spaces removed). The code would also include what they called a columnar transposition, making it nearly impossible to crack, as long as the randomized six-by-six matrix and transposition keyword were kept secret. Once encoded, messages could be sent by signal flags, flashing lights, or telegraph.

None of this helped me decode the strings of characters in the logbooks, but I now had some valuable information. I'd learned how the messages were encoded and that I would need the transposition keyword and the easily recognizable six-by-six matrix to decipher the messages. The fact that the messages were sent via wireless telegraphy opened a whole new realm of possibilities for what secrets the logbooks might contain. These entries could have been communications sent to or from ships, nearby cities, or locations as far away as Duluth, Port Arthur, or Detroit. They likely coordinated shipments of booze, the booking of guests, the payment of invoices, and the collection of receivables. Cracking the code could very well expose all of Gates's operation, and uncover accomplices, no matter where they were located.

I dog-eared the ADFGVX Cipher chapter before placing all three books on the shelf behind the Light House Service Bulletins. Taking a notepad from my desk, I went outside and sat on the stoop to write to Franklin.

Franklin,
Found a book full of messages. Must be real important, sure to be lots of incriminating stuff. Can't wait to look into it closer.
Jonah

The stars shone brightly in the sky, bright enough to reflect little pinpoints of light off of the smooth-as-glass lake. The air was fresh, still, cool, and comfortable. I stuffed my letter in the envelope and addressed it to Franklin. I placed the note in the lighthouse outgoing mail to be picked up by the steamer in the morning. I felt more hopeful than I had in days. Maybe the lighthouse was a holy place after all, a place where justice bloomed and corruption withered.

#

I arrived for my 2:00 a.m. to 8:00 a.m. shift feeling refreshed despite my lack of sleep, looking forward to a night of whittling. I carved just as Cephas smoked. His was a complex ritual of scraping the ash from the bowl, cleaning the bore with a pipe cleaner, filling the pipe from the tobacco pouch, tamping the shag, then circling the lit match over the bowl to create an even burn. Every fifteen minutes, he would repeat the whole process over again, keeping his hands busy and his mind sharp. My carving went beyond just keeping busy. My creations flooded my mind with thoughts of Mae and Rose, helping me to relive our time spent along the shore as I worked.

I might've carved another doll or animal for Rose but decided to make something for myself. I considered carving a little model of the lighthouse, a paperweight with waves crashing over a large boulder, or a miniature version of my cottage. But none of these lit a spark. They had shape and texture, but no feeling and emotion. Instead, I decided to carve Mae.

There are some basic rules for carving a face. The most basic is the "rule of thirds," marking three equal areas from the bottom to the top of the face. The first area is from the chin to the base of the nose. The second from the bottom of the nose to the eyebrow, and the third from the brow to the hairline. These basic rules help make any carving look natural, guiding a novice carver toward achieving respectable results. What they don't provide is the individuality, personality, and emotion that comes with good carving. This takes an acute eye and a precise hand. The carver sees and interprets things that novices don't notice.

Mae's hair, for example. I remembered it as if she was sitting right in front of me. She parted it slightly to the left, her auburn waves combed and pinned over her right temple before cascading across her shoulders. It made her feminine and lovely. Much more attractive than the harsh, boyish bob-cut styles worn by the Dainty Dollies up at the lodge.

I remembered Mae's eyes angling slightly upward as if recalling happy thoughts. Her nose narrowed to a soft roundness at the tip. Her high cheekbones and accentuated jaw emphasized her athleticism, and a dimple above her chin did a perfect job of framing her lips. With images of her flowing through my head, the wood carved itself. Quickly, the face took shape, the knife flitting from one detail to the next—the sweeping lines of her hair, the fine detail of her tender eyes, and the fullness of her pleasant, subtle smile. Time flew. I forgot about pressurizing the tank, I didn't wind the clock mechanism that rotated the lens, and I hadn't bothered to make a single note of any ships passing by. Not until the clomping sound of feet outside on the lighthouse stairs. Only then did I remember my normal chores. If it were Cephas, there would be hell to pay.

"Prob'ly not supposed to be here," Bjørn said. "I hope you don't mind."

He was a pleasant surprise. Leaving him below, I climbed the circular stairs to the watch room to catch up on my chores, pressurizing the kerosene tank, and cranking the clock mechanism. In my absence, Bjørn picked up my carving from the floor, as if drawn instinctively to the face taking shape. He rubbed his thumbs along the cascading hair and brushed the small shavings from the facial features. I watched from above as he rotated the head back and forth to catch its expressions in differing lights and shadows.

"Just a little hobby of mine," I said, walking down the spiral staircase. I offered him the chair that Cephas normally sat in.

"It's Mae," he said. "The likeness is incredible."

I hadn't finished the carving, but it did look like Mae. The secret was to capture the unique and prominent characteristics of the subject. If that was done well, the individuality shined through, even unfinished.

"Well, it could be almost anybody," I said, slightly

embarrassed to be worshiping her so.

Bjørn handed the carving back. I set it on the floor, nudging it on top of the wood shavings under my chair.

"Jeg ville takke deg . . . I wanted to thank you," he said. "How nice it is to have the fish-cleaning station. Filleting on the dock kills the knees."

I nodded and put my knife away. He pulled a bag of tobacco and some papers out of his shirt pocket.

"Times are hard," he said. "I mean, fishing is always a hard life, but now we just don't know what to do."

He shook a clean line of tobacco across the rolling paper, grabbed the drawstring of the pouch in his teeth to close it, and then rolled the paper and tobacco between his thumbs and forefingers, making a serviceable cigarette with a dexterity that I couldn't have matched after years of practice. He put the smoke in the corner of his mouth and fumbled for a match.

"Tomorrow we're bringing in most of our nets. Only leaving a couple out. We lost all the ice when the icehouse burned. Our only option is to salt the fish and pack it in barrels. Twice the work and half the pay. It's not worth it."

Bjørn found his matches. The cigarette lit up with an extra burst of flame as the twisted paper end ignited.

"Some of the men are setting traps, hoping to catch foxes, beavers, martens, or minks to sell the pelts. So far, they've only caught skunks. It's as if nothing's going our way."

Bjørn reached down to pull the carving out from under my chair, once again giving it a thorough inspection.

"You know, Mae adores you."

"I've hardly seen her since the burial," I said. "I guess things have been too busy."

Bjørn crossed his legs and took a drag off the cigarette, already half gone.

"Her husband Knute was a hothead, kinda like Gunnar. A strong guy who could scare the piss out of people he didn't like, and he hated Gates. It drove him crazy to see the lodge being built, and when the guests started arriving, he couldn't accept it. One night he broke into the shed where they keep the electric power plant for the lights. He cut both the gas line on the engine and the belt to the generator. The whole building went dark for a full weekend. The guests went haywire, and Gates popped his rivets."

I chuckled, thinking this guy must have been pretty resourceful. I would have liked him if I'd met him.

"The next night, Knute disappeared, along with his boat," he said. "Made no sense. He would never go out late at night alone. The next day, his boat washed up on shore past Castle Danger. The tiller and the oars were sawn nearly all the way through, so they broke as soon as someone used them. Somebody set him off with the wind blowing away from land with no way to steer or row back. They probably expected he'd blow out to the middle of Superior never to be seen again."

He dropped his cigarette, crushed it out with his foot, then pulled the tobacco bag and papers back out to roll another.

"Everyone knew Gates did it. Just like we all know he started the fire," Bjørn said. "Heck, as soon as I smelled the kerosene, I knew it was Gates. The way the flames tore through the village—it had to be him."

"Did ya tell that to the sheriff?"

"He never asked," Bjørn said. "You'd think a sheriff would ask the villagers what happened. I mean, we're the ones who lost our homes . . . and Hans, our boy."

Bjørn choked on his words and wiped his eyes, barely able to speak Hans's name.

"A courtesy, if nothing else. He could just pretend. Act like he had actually investigated the fire. Give us reason to believe that we might even matter. But no, he never spoke to any of us."

"He thinks I started the fire," I said. Hans stared back in disbelief.

"I was the first one in and the last one out during the fire, and he saw me cleaning out the harbor the day after. Said I destroyed evidence so I wouldn't get caught."

"Everybody knows Gates did it," Bjørn said.

"That's what I told him. Said I saw both Gates and Polly leave right after the fire started. Left by boat. Haven't been back since. Sheriff said a dozen guests are willing to testify for Gates, saying he was nowhere near the village."

Having finished rolling his cigarette, Bjørn put his tobacco pouch back in his pocket.

"Poor Mae and Rose," Bjørn said. "First, her husband, then her home. Already suffered more than any young woman her age should have to bear. She's tired of losing the people and the things she loves."

Bjørn didn't bother to light his cigarette, just hung it from the corner of his mouth. He took one last look at the carving of Mae and brushed the face clean.

"They said you fixed up the harbor," Bjørn said. "Cleaned up where the village used to be." He stared down at the carving, continuing to brush long after the dust and shavings were gone. "Did you do that for us?"

"Doesn't really matter much," I said. "That was two days ago. Yesterday Gates had a team of men fixing things to his liking, as if he owned the place. He undid all of my work from the day before. Makes me sick."

Bjørn carried the carving of Mae over to the window. He looked out across the harbor, the water still smooth as glass, the stars still reflecting like pinpoints of light.

"Where do we live then?" he asked. "Can't stay at the lighthouse forever. Do they think we'll stay in the shacks? At Stygg Havn? We can't live there. No one could live there. With the harbor gone, there's nowhere for us to go."

"I have a plan," I said. "A way to get the harbor back from Gates. It needs more work, but I'm making progress. And Gates is gone. Maybe he'll stay gone for a long, long time."

Bjørn put the carving of Mae under my chair. As I stood, he grabbed my hand.

"I don't want you fighting Gates. We've already lost too much." His hand shook, and his voice quivered. "Maybe it's time for us fishermen to become miners."

Shortly after Bjørn left, I was surprised by the familiar rumble of boat motors. The bootleg boats always arrived before sunrise on Tuesday and Friday mornings, but this was Monday, and Cephas had said nothing of late-night visitors. A boat came into the harbor, throttled down to an idle, and slid quietly up to the lighthouse dock. There was no unloading of crates and no attendants filing down from the lodge.

A short and pudgy man stepped out onto the dock. He stood on the pier like a statue until a taller man stepped out. The boat departed. The two talked for fifteen minutes, the tall man's arm around the other person's shoulders. They took the stairs from shore together. At the top, Gates walked to the lodge. Polly stood by himself for a half-hour before disappearing into his cottage.

#

Halfway through my morning chores, I sat to enjoy the cool breeze off the lake. From the lantern gallery, my feet dangled over the edge, my arms looped over the railing. I nearly jumped out of my skin as Elsie started yelling from the base of the circular stairs, holding Rose by the hand. A dozen thoughts ran through my mind— Elsie was having her baby, Polly had drunk himself to death, Mae had decided she loved me, Mae had decided she hated me. I raced to the base of the lighthouse, arriving all wild-eyed and coughing uncontrollably.

"Go catch some fish," she said.

I leaned over to catch my breath, feeling another nervous attack coming on. My chores still needed to be finished. It angered me that all her yelling was for want of a few trout. I didn't bother to reply, just started back up toward the lighthouse.

"Go catch some fish! There are too many mouths to feed around here, and we're not having beans again. Go. We're having fish, potatoes, and canned peaches for dinner."

She stood at the bottom of the stairs, her feet spread wide, her hands on her hips, and her belly hanging so far out it looked like a round bobber stuck between two plug lures. Choosing not to quarrel, I sulked my way down to the shore and slipped into the boathouse to organize the fishing rods and tackle box. Mae appeared as I loaded them into the boat.

"Elsie says you'll need some help. I brought minnows from the traps down by the creek."

She stowed the bucket next to the middle seat, then helped push the boat out of the boathouse.

"Elsie said I needed help?" I asked.

"Said you wouldn't know which end of the hook to bait."

I kept pushing while Mae stopped to climb aboard, causing her to lose her balance and fall to her knees.

"Trying to kill me?" she asked. "Is this any way to treat a girlfriend?"

A simple 'sorry' was all I could muster. I didn't mean for it to happen. Maybe I was nervous. I slowed, helped her in, guided the boat into the water, and pulled myself over the gunwale. Mae sat in the bow as I rowed out along the north side of Tollefson Island, planning to anchor at the drop-off where I had caught fish before.

"Can't catch fish here," she said. "It's too shallow. Go out past the island."

I would've argued, but she said it with decisiveness, as if she had the whole lake memorized and mapped in her head. She kept pointing in the direction she wanted me to row until we reached a spot a quarter of a mile beyond the island.

"Here. Drop the anchor here."

The rope slid quickly through my hands, well past the thirty-foot mark from my previous day of fishing. I watched as the pile of rope at my feet grew smaller until the anchor landed with only a short distance of rope left.

"Aren't we too deep?" I asked. I reached over to bait her hook, but she whipped her rod away, nearly hooking my thumb in the process.

"It's just the right depth, and I bait my own hooks, if you don't mind."

She grabbed a fat sucker minnow out of the bucket.

"Gunnar might think you're Norwegian, but I have my doubts."

"I could out-fish you any day," I said. She thumbed her nose at me in response.

"If I catch the first fish, I get a kiss."

"What do I get when I catch one first?" she asked, letting her weighted line sink to the bottom.

"Two kisses."

She laughed, trying her best to show a face of indignation.

"I have a better idea," she said. "When I hook the first fish, you eat two sucker minnows."

I looked into the bucket to find a bubbly slime on the surface. Not that it mattered, but I couldn't tell if the discharge was from the minnows or a fungal growth from a soggy pail that had never been cleaned. Either way, I thought it best to hang the bait pail over the edge to freshen up the water.

"Ok. I get two kisses if I catch the first fish, and I'll eat two suckers if I lose."

We shook on it just as the tip of her rod started to twitch. She stood up and played the line in slowly, responding to each little tug with a slight jerk until she could feel the weight of the fish. Mae set the hook in dramatic fashion, arching back and raising her hands high above her head as she reeled in, the rod bent into a semicircle, the tip pointing straight down into the water.

"Looks like you'll be eating minnows!"

"Gotta land it first," I said.

I lost hope as I watched her finesse the fish. Twice it ran, with the line spinning off the reel, the drag set just enough to tire the beast without breaking loose. The lunker had to be at least forty inches. Mae showed patience, letting it run and reeling it in between the runs. I had the net ready, but when it came time to land it, she pushed me away, grabbing the large trout under the gills, and lifting it out of the water. With a pair of pliers and a hard jerk, she pulled the hook out of the fish's mouth. She ran the stringer through the fish's bottom lip. I tied the other end of the stringer to the boat while she gently slipped the tired fish back into the water. It splashed a few times against the hull as it tried to escape, then settled. By the time I had the unused net stowed, she already had her hook baited with the weighted line sinking to the bottom. She reached back in the bait pail, pulling out two suckers and handed them to me.

"Are you man enough for this?" she asked.

Good thing I had rinsed the bucket out. I grabbed the first by the tail and dropped it into my mouth, letting it wiggle down my throat. The second was harder to swallow, causing a minor gag reflex. Minnows aren't that bad if you just let them swim down your gullet. A bit of a wormy, earthy aftertaste, but nothing that a sip of water won't rinse away. I rinsed my hands and scooped up some lake water to wash it all down. Mae smiled and leaned over to give me a pat on the back and a kiss on the cheek while the trout flopped up against the side of the boat, tethered on the stringer. She sat back down, then pulled my head to hers, giving me a real kiss. A long, meaningful wonderful kiss.

Grabbing her rod from the front, she moved to sit across from me on the middle bench, holding my hand, patting my cheek, and looking deep into my eyes with love and tenderness I hadn't felt in many years.

"Why can't you just leave?" she asked. "I don't want you to get hurt. A good old coward would make my life so much easier."

She leaned over, kissed me again, and then hugged me tightly. I put my arms around her, wishing never to let go.

"Stay away from Gates," she scolded. "No boxing, fighting, or smashing his carnations."

I held her, thinking how disappointed she'd be if she knew about my break-in at the warehouse for the ledger and cryptology books. But physical violence against Gates was now the furthest from my mind. My plan was to outsmart him.

Mae had another tug on her line. A hard hit that left no doubt she had it hooked. Luckily, she didn't make me eat any more minnows. We kissed after each fish, no matter who landed them. After a few hours, we headed back with a total of seven trout, five of them caught by Mae.

#

"You're in trouble," Elsie said.

Mae was already up at the lighthouse checking on Rose. I had just finished filleting the fish.

"Cephas wants you up at the cottage. Says you shouldn't be wasting time fishing."

"You told me to go," I said.

"He doesn't know that. I told him it was all your idea." She smiled. "And I hear that Mae caught all the fish."

"Polly tell you where he went?" I asked.

"Said he went to Port Arthur. Up in Canada. Met some of Gates's business associates. Says he has the opportunity of a lifetime, and we'll be richer than railroad tycoons."

We walked up to the cottages as we talked, Elsie holding tight to the railing and pulling herself along as she went. I grabbed under her arm to make sure she didn't fall.

"Says he'll be reporting to Gates from now on."

"So, he's top brass?" I asked, knowing she wouldn't like him working at the lodge.

"I don't like it up there," she said. "Too much drinking and partying."

Elsie stopped for a minute to catch her breath. "It's hard to breathe these days. I think I'm too small for childbirth."

"So, where are you going to live?" I asked.

"He says we'll move to the lodge! In the worker's dormitory. Can you imagine? Me, the baby, dozens of working men, and all those Dainty Dollies livin' up there? I told him I'll go home and stay with Mother."

Elsie's frankness surprised me. Particularly because her husband and I hated each other.

I assumed Cephas wanted to scold me for going off with Mae before the morning chores were finished. I hoped he would be alone, but he had company.

Gates and Polly.

They all stared at me disapprovingly, as if I was late for a planned meeting. Polly was hardly recognizable. He wore a new suit, new shoes, and a starched shirt, looking almost as fancy as Gates. He had a different air about him too. Still short and round but now more aloof. The smirky smile was gone. The jovial expressions that once made him so entertaining now hid behind a mask of boredom. No waving arms, wild facial gestures, or happy feet. Now he played the role of a big shot.

"Sit down," Gates said.

He kept his eyes on me the whole time as I walked over to the bread box to grab a biscuit, then poured a cup of coffee and slowly shuffled back to the table. I wanted to leave, but Cephas went out of his way to pull out a chair for me next to Gates and waited for me to sit before settling himself. Polly sat with his arms crossed, balancing on the back legs of his chair, one foot against the edge of the table.

"Gates told us his plans for Stony Fest," Cephas said flatly. "Last weekend in June. A big celebration at the lodge. The highway will be open, so he says we'll have dozens of automobiles."

Cephas showed no sign of endorsement or condemnation as he plowed through the details.

"Cars like Packards, Pierce Arrows, and Cadillacs. Might even be a Duesenberg or a Rolls Royce. The kind of automobiles baseball players and boxers drive."

As Cephas droned, my mind went elsewhere. The long strings of letters from encrypted logbooks filled my head. Like Egyptian hieroglyphics, they bewildered with their density and detail, and captivated with the secrets they hopefully held. I thought of Franklin, how he had grabbed my leg with a viselike grip, hell-bent on finding a way to destroy Gates.

Cephas coughed as if to recapture my attention, then continued on about Stony Fest. "The marina will be all set by then. Sailing regattas and crewing competitions. There'll be a trolley running up and down the hillside. Maybe even a fancy motorboat or two for trips up and down the shoreline. There'll be food and drinks along the shore all day, band concerts at night. Gates calls it the biggest blow this side of Chicago."

Cephas glanced at Gates, hoping he'd pick up the conversation from there, but Gates didn't even notice him, just kept a close eye on me. Polly continued balancing on the back legs of his chair with his foot up on the table, scratching a rash on the back of his hand.

"Gates arranged for the lighthouse inspection to happen right before the start of Stony Fest."

The mention of an inspection caught my attention.

"Inspection? Aren't they supposed to be a big surprise?" I asked.

"Right. Well, that's the good part. Gates arranged it so we'll know exactly when it will be. We have a little over two weeks. Enough time to clean, polish, trim, tune, and update our records."

"Tell 'em about the villagers," Gates said.

Cephas's left hand trembled against the tabletop as if he was polishing the surface. He cupped his hands together to stop the shaking, then fixed his eyes on the picture of Jesus hanging on the wall.

"Well, they have to move. They can't stay here. Not with the inspection and Stony Fest coming up."

Polly stopped scratching his rash and looked back and forth between Cephas, Gates, and me.

"I mean, the villagers just can't stay in the cottages. They need to move," Cephas said, wrapping his arms around his chest to keep his hands from trembling.

I buttered my biscuit. Polly went back to scratching, and Cephas stared blankly at his coffee mug. It was Gates who finally broke the silence.

"Hey, fella, the villagers need to go. Understand? This is your fault. If you had taken care of it like I asked you to, we wouldn't have this problem. Just move 'em to those shacks, or they can join some other fishing camp farther up the shore."

"You can't expect them to live in those shacks," I said. "That godforsaken strip of shoreline is too shallow, too rocky, and completely unprotected."

"Well, then, why don't you take them all back to that shithole farm of yours in Aitkin?"

I grabbed the back of Polly's chair as I stood, almost knocking him over backward. He twitched his arms and legs straight out from his body, like a cat thrown from a hayloft.

"How 'bout we just move 'em right back to that harbor of theirs?" I asked. "The one you're trying to steal from them?"

Gates sat with an annoyed scowl on his face, scratching a scaly spot on the side of his nose with his middle finger. "You a misanthrope?" he asked.

I looked around, finding all eyes on me. "I don't know what that means."

"Misanthrope," Gates repeated. "Someone who doesn't get along with anybody."

"Maybe so," I said. "Every time I see you, I get this misanthropical burr up my butt. Feels like I'm sittin' on a porcupine."

Gates finished scratching, then wiped whatever had accumulated under his fingernails onto his jacket. I took a bite of my biscuit, feeling everyone's watchful gaze.

"You a socialist?" he asked.

"Are you an arrogant bastard?" I replied.

"Jonah!" Cephas snapped. "Watch that tongue and show some respect. How many times do I . . . ?"

"Shut up, Cephas," Gates said, holding a hand up toward his face. "It's ok. I like small men with oversized attitudes. Arrogance is a complicated concept for an Aitkin farm boy, eh, fella? If you're asking if I feel entitled, the answer is yes. As far as I'm concerned, privilege goes to the powerful. If you and your chicken-hearted friends disagree, then you go ahead and try to stop me."

I threw my half-eaten biscuit at Gates, leaving a smear of butter on his lapel.

"And if socialism means a deep hatred for assholes who burn villages and kill young men, then consider me a socialist," I said. "A misanthropical socialist."

Polly sat up straight in his chair. Gates wiped the butter off his coat with a disgustingly arrogant laugh.

"Burning villages, eh?" Gates said. "I have a dozen people at the lodge who say I had nothing to do with it. All I need to do is ask, and they'll say you were the one throwing the lit torch into that pile of kerosene-soaked fishing nets that set the whole village ablaze."

The specific detail he gave about how the fire started made me shiver. He didn't even try to hide his tracks. His main point was that he had a lodge full of false witnesses who would implicate and convict whomever he wanted for whatever crime he had in mind. Before I could react, Gates stood, cleared his throat, and thumped his hands on the table. Not so hard to be melodramatic, but hard enough to get everybody's attention.

"Look. Polly's working for me now, to help manage the marina. Hopefully, Jonah here can keep himself busy enough to stay out of trouble. Get the villagers out of here, and make sure everything's neat and tidy for the inspection. If everybody does as they're told, and nobody gets arrested or hurt, then Cephas might finally earn his retirement and pension."

5 ATLANTIS

Stony Point's new harbor officially opened for business on Saturday, June 21, 1924. No more than two weeks after the burning of the village and a dozen days after Polly and Gates returned from their trip to Port Arthur, Canada. There was no looking back, no mourning, no condolences, and no pretense of sympathy for the villagers. Just dozens of attendants and laborers busily erasing any remembrances of the old fishing village, replacing it with a new marina for the sole purpose of entertaining lodge guests.

The thirty-foot Hacker-Craft that Gates and Polly arrived in now adorned the end of the pier like a tiger's eye jewel at the end of a stick pin. The sun glistened across the heavily waxed mahogany deck, and the hull, shaped like an artillery shell, screamed of speed. The midship double hatches sheltered an engine with horsepower suitable for vessels twice its size, and three cavernous cockpits were more than adequate for hauling nine guests at a time up and down the coast.

The shoreline teemed with attendants preparing the new waterfront attractions. Spacious tents stood on both sides of the stairs leading up to the lodge, and tables and chairs were set up for the daily lunch buffet. Two trolley stations were under construction, one along the shore and the other at the top of the hill. The tracks running between the stations had already been laid along the steep incline. Beach umbrellas sprouted like multicolored mushrooms in front of cloth cabanas used for changing into beachwear. Potted palms and ferns dotted the area, infusing a tropical counterpoint into the north shore wilderness experience. Only a man like Gates could reasonably explain why a wilderness hunting and fishing lodge might need potted palm trees.

Having finished their lunches, the guests gathered to catch a closer look at the Hacker-Craft. Most wore yachting attire, white or ivory linen trousers, white shoes, and straw boater hats. The frumps in the crowd showed up in knickers, argyle socks, and newsboy caps, more appropriate for the shooting and golf games held up on the lawn.

"Gates wants to use the lighthouse boats," Cephas said, having joined me along the walkway at the lighthouse. "Would you mind cleaning the two and bringing them to the lodge pier?"

Cephas had been noticeably less demanding and more considerate since our meeting with Gates, asking for help only when absolutely necessary and with an almost apologetic tone. I did my best to go about my daily business as usual, hoping to avoid Gates, Polly, and Cephas.

From the shore, I threw a bucket and scrub brush into the first boat and pushed it into the water, then scrubbed the hull from bow to stern, both starboard and portside. From the inside, I mopped up spider webs, water bugs, and fish slime, then sponged the benches and flooring dry. The sheets were coiled and aligned along the benches, sails stowed across the bench seats, and the bailing bucket stashed under the seat up front.

"That better be clean as a whistle or you'll be cleaning it with your toothbrush," Polly barked at me with his hands on his hips, yelling loud enough for any nearby guest to hear. By now, his new suit showed wrinkles and stains as if he'd slept in it. His crooked sunglasses added to his unkempt appearance and masked his normally bloodshot eyes. He held an empty glass, likely not his first drink of the morning.

"And I want both those boats, not just the one. They should've both been cleaned up by now."

Earlier that morning, he'd lorded over the attendants, ordering them to move, fix, clean, and organize whatever he fancied until they grew tired of his arrogance and simply ignored him. Running out of people to subjugate, he turned on me.

I'd never cared for Polly, but now I worried about him, wondering if arson and Hans's death was weighing heavily on his conscience. Polly acted tough, but the disheveled appearance and sullenness suggested his falling apart. The same guests who once flocked to hear his stories now turned away from him, wanting to avoid the commotion he caused.

While he marched off to berate another group of attendants, I added my own little finishing touch to the lighthouse boats by rubbing a heavy coat of motor oil into each of the bench seats. It gave the wood a nice polished shine and would leave a permanent dark spot on any pair of the white and ivory colored trousers that it happened to come in contact with. It was nothing but a juvenile prank to get back at Gates. For the moment, juvenile pranks were all I had.

Gates spent the afternoon in his new toy. Nine guests at a time piled into the Hacker-Craft, and they cruised up and down the shoreline at full throttle. Every fifteen minutes, the speedboat idled down and slid back to the pier to fill up on gas, replenish the liquor supply, and pick up new passengers for another trip. In addition to his standard cream-colored suit and red carnation, Gates now had a skipper's cap, symbolically suggesting one more thing that he excelled at—powerboats.

The Dainty Dollies' swimsuits attracted lots of attention. Their blue and white striped V-neck tops were made of a tight-fitting ribbed jersey, and the matching blue shorts rose high above the knee. Incredibly, all the Dollies still looked identical, even in their tight-fitting swimsuits. Without stockings or garters to hold their flasks, they carried their booze in dangling beaded purses.

Men took turns shooting skeet and playing volleyball along the shore. Others sunned themselves from the beach chairs, dipped their toes into the freezing lake, or explored the shoreline where the old shacks once stood, searching for the occasional button, pipe stem, or thimble. Like magpies, they collected the little curiosities, stuffing the worthless trinkets in their pockets.

By late afternoon, the villagers returned from fishing, finding their old harbor overtaken. The shoreline was now filled with tables, chairs, cabanas, and umbrellas, while a pair of large tents flapped in the wind over what used to be their warehouse. They cleaned the fish next to the boathouse, layered the fillets and salt into the barrels, and stacked them to be shipped out on the next steamer. Dog-tired, they climbed the stairs, in no mood to talk as they walked by.

Come dinnertime, Polly sat alone, draped across a beach chair, having passed out hours before. Cephas and I woke him and carried him across the shore. He puked once while riding the tram up to the lighthouse and once again on the cottage floor as we put him to bed.

#

The next morning, a motorboat rounded Tollefson Island, throttling down as it entered the harbor. This time I recognized the two of them immediately. Seeing Franklin's wheelchair stuffed in behind him made it an easy identification. I ran down the stairs from the lighthouse and met them as they slid up alongside the dock.

"Hop in," Franklin said. Gus pushed the wheelchair to the side, making room for me in the back.

"Where we going?" I asked as we pulled away from the dock. Before anyone could answer, the boat growled up to full throttle, the roar of the engines making any conversation impossible. With my question still lingering, we rounded the lighthouse and headed northeast along the shore. In a matter of minutes, we'd completed the five-mile trip to Beaver Creek, gliding up against the public pier.

"What are we doing here?" I asked, pulling the wheelchair onto the dock.

"Hopefully, I can talk some sense into you two dunderheads," Gus said, guiding Franklin out of the boat. The two of us helped him into his wheelchair, then we made our way to the cafeteria, a block up from the docks.

"This whole thing is stupid," Gus scolded. "Gates is a dangerous man. He'll tear you both apart."

Inside the café, the three of us sat at a table away from the window. Gus and Franklin both pulled their cigarette cases and lighters out and lit up. Neither of them thought to offer me a smoke.

"Jonah, what if you lose your job?"

"Too late, Gus," I said. "I get fired and rehired almost daily now. Cephas can't stand having me around, but he can't bear to have me leave."

"Rotten bastard," Franklin said. "Must be working for Gates."

"Listen to you. Listen to both of you," Gus said. "You sound like hooligans and gangsters."

"Can I have a cigarette?" I asked.

Franklin fished a smoke out of his case and gave me a light. He grabbed Gus by the arm, gently pulling him until their faces were no more than a foot apart.

"Gus, you'll never understand. You walk into a room and everybody takes notice. Women flirt, men get chummy, and the whole crowd follows your lead."

Franklin paused as the waitress dropped off glasses of water and menus before she moved on to the next table.

"When I wheel into a room, there's always a hush. The crowd parts. And the only conversation I get is pity from the women and asinine words of encouragement from the men. Jonah and I don't want pity. We don't need words of encouragement or protective brothers looking after us. We need our dignity. To stand up for what we believe, to act like men. I'm tired of sitting on the back sun porch, watching ships go by. Isn't this what you wanted? For me to live a little?"

I only had enough money for a cup of coffee, but Franklin ordered us each the Lumberjack Special once the waitress returned to take our orders.

"Don't worry, Gus is paying," he said to me with a wink.

Gus leaned back, looking defeated. Franklin pulled a notebook from his pocket and thumbed through it before conducting our little meeting, as one might expect from a very capable real-estate investment lawyer.

"Jonah, I got your note. You say you found a ledger."

"Yeah. Found it back in the warehouse," I said, very proud of myself. "Right next to the radiotelegraph system. It has entries that began last summer. The last entry came in just a few days ago. I also took some tape off the machine that hadn't been decoded yet."

"You stole a ledger from the warehouse?" Gus asked, sounding mortified.

"He borrowed it," Franklin said. "It's not like a famous work of art or expensive jewelry for cripe's sake." He flipped the notebook to a fresh page and licked the tip of his pen, ready to record my every word.

"So, what did the ledger say?" he asked.

"I don't know."

Gus and Franklin stared blankly as if they didn't understand what I'd said.

"Y'see, it's all written in code. Just big blocks of letters that make absolutely no sense until it's decrypted."

Franklin closed his notebook and set it on the table along with his pen. The waitress set a large platter of steak, eggs, potatoes, and pancakes in front of each of us and topped off our coffees.

"Can you crack the code?" he asked.

"Sure," I replied. "I mean, maybe. I know what kind of code they used. Now I need to find the decryption key. A six-by-six matrix of letters and numbers, plus a special code word. If I find the key, I can crack the code."

Gus slapped the table hard enough to cause the whole cafeteria to take notice.

"Nothing!" he yelled. "You got nothing! You go poking your nose in other people's business, putting us all in danger, and you got nothing. You're grasping at straws. We need to just drop the whole thing right now."

Franklin ignored Gus as he loaded his pancakes with syrup. "You crack the code, then send me a note, ok? Do it right away."

Gus barely touched his food. I had already finished two of my cakes and both of my eggs, saving the steak for last.

"I dug around at the courthouse yesterday," Franklin said. "To find out who legally owns the harbor."

"It's the villagers, right?" I asked. "Gotta be the villagers."

"Well, there's no clear title for any of the land around the harbor. The only deed recorded at the county names Karl Berg as the owner of record, and he's deceased. The county clerk told me his only surviving heir was Knute, who died last year. Knute's surviving heir would be Mae."

"So, Mae owns the property?" I asked.

"Not quite. With no recent deeds, wills, and transfer of titles recorded, the ownership is murky. To make matters worse, Gates has taken advantage of the villagers' neglect and inactivity. He filed his own claims on the land, even paid a few years of property tax. The villagers risk losing all their legal rights if they don't get their paperwork in order."

"How could Gates have any rights to the property?" I asked.

"Squatters rights, I guess," Franklin said. "Lawyers call it 'adverse possession.' He claims to have occupied the lodge property for nearly fifteen years. Says he's had a hunting shack on the land since before they built the lighthouse, uses it every hunting season. They even had old pictures in the file to prove it. His claim is strong enough to tie the land claim up in the courts for years to come. We can't even begin to challenge his squatter's rights until the deeds, wills, and transfer of titles are all updated."

"The villagers can't wait that long," I said.

"Nothing," Gus muttered under his breath. "Both of you. Just wasting time."

Franklin used the last bite of steak to mop up the runny eggs on his plate. He thoughtfully chewed before calmly summarizing our limited options.

"I'll work on the deed. You find a way to decipher those ledgers."

"Is that all we have?" I asked.

"I'm a lawyer, not a magician."

Franklin wiped his mouth before putting the napkin on his plate. He pulled out a twenty-dollar bill, leaving it on the table to pay for the meals with a generous tip.

"Let me know when you crack that code," he said. "And one last thing. Gates has lots riding on this Stony Fest event. He's using it to get all the police, councilmen, and judges in his back pocket. See to it that Stony Fest doesn't succeed. If Stony Fest fails, the whole lodge will fail."

Gus turned pale.

"Time to be a hero, Jonah," Franklin said.

#

As they often did, the fishermen returned from tending their nets in foul moods. They cleaned the lake trout on the table next to the boathouse, the skin, guts, and carcasses thrown in boxes left over from the fire. The cleaned fish was all packed into barrels with salt. They stacked the barrels against the boathouse for the next day's pickup and carried the boxes of guts out into the woods before heading back to the cottage. Before dark, Gunnar checked his traps, hoping for a fox, otter, or mink, but there was nothing but skunks. Truthfully, none of the pelts would have been worth much anyway, being trapped too early in the season before the animal's fur had thickened for winter. Financially, physically, and emotionally, the villagers were barely surviving in spite of all their hard work.

At the marina, two weeks of construction, landscaping, and setup turned the new harbor into the main attraction. Canoes, rowing shells, and sailboats lined the shore in front of the beach umbrellas and cabanas. The trolley stations were ready for paint, while the bandshell and picnic areas were nearing completion. Lodge workers finished planting the formal gardens along the slope, providing a clean boundary around the marina and leaving fingers of greenery stretching out from the hillside.

Gates made a habit of visiting Cephas at the end of each day, bringing dinner and desserts. I stayed upstairs, ostensibly resting before my late-night shift but actually just avoiding Gates. I found I could hear their conversations pretty well from the top of the stairs.

"Nearly sunk three sailboats today," Gates said. "Crap, we only had four races. The boys get so competitive, they lose their senses. And two of the rowing shells capsized. We had to fish both crews out of the water."

"Sounds like too much whisky to me," Cephas said.

"Well, it's not nearly as fun without the whisky. I guess I'll have to hire more lifeguards."

They sat at the kitchen table as they talked, laughing and joking about the ineptitude of the guests and the challenges of running the marina while still under construction. Cephas asked about the upcoming inspection, which immediately caused Gates to complain about the villagers.

"It doesn't matter what you clean, fix, and paint," Gates said. "If those villagers are still living here, you won't be passing the inspection, and you might just wait another ten years before you get that pension."

"Maybe I can explain to them what happened," Cephas said. "Tell them about the fire and how their stay is temporary until they find a new place to live."

"You want your pension, or don't you? You'll still be working this godforsaken rock till you're over a hundred. You'll die with your hands on that clockwork crank up there, never having a chance to retire with your family. This is your chance. You got one more year. Don't blow it."

"It's just that they have no place to go," Cephas said.

Gates paused as Cephas tended the stove. After a squeak of the firebox door, I heard the shaking of ash from the firebox, the clunking of added coal, and another squeak of the closing door hinge before Gates continued.

"I know it's not your fault. If Jonah had done what I asked him to, none of this would have happened. I know you like the kid, but he sure makes a mess of trouble."

"Well, we can't just kick the villagers out," Cephas said.

"To hell we can't. I built cottages for them just north of the lighthouse," Gates said. "Right along the shoreline."

"You mean up at Stygg Havn?"

"Stygg what?"

"Stygg Havn. That's what the villagers call it. It means ugly harbor. They say it's too rocky and small. No room for a warehouse or a pier. Too shallow for the steamer. They'd have to row their daily catch out to the big ship each day."

"Fine then," Gates said, raising his voice. "I'll be sure to visit you twenty years from now when you're an old, decrepit lighthouse keeper, still working in this godforsaken wilderness all by yourself."

"Maybe there's someplace else . . ."

"There's piles of fishermen junk everywhere. All the nets, old fish boxes, and rows of barrels. Their boats are littering the shore. And it's absolutely against regulations for them to be living here at the lighthouse. There really is no other option but to make them leave."

"No, I just . . ."

"You just what? You just better think about getting those villagers to move, or you can forget all about that pension of yours."

My knees ached from crouching up at the top of the stairs, but I didn't dare move, worried they might discover me listening in. I held the railing and slowly stood with hardly a creak of the floorboards. After a pause, Gates continued in a softer, more sympathetic voice.

"Cephas, grab that last piece of pie, and I'll tell you what we'll do. I'll have my boys empty out the villagers' cottage. They can do it after the fishermen head out on the lake. Mae will be the only one around, and she won't make a fuss. You and I can be discreetly hiding out up at the lodge. By the time the fishermen get back, all their stuff will be moved to that Stygg place."

"What about Jonah?" Cephas asked.

"I'm sick and tired of that fella. Send him out to catch fish.

If he gets in the way, we'll take him out in the woods, chop him to pieces, and feed him to the raccoons."

"You wouldn't . . ."

"Stop worrying. Just be up at the lodge first thing tomorrow."

After hearing the clinking of plates and silverware being placed in the sink, I could see the shadows of the two men as they moved toward the door.

"Say, I'm missing some books from the lodge. You haven't seen them up here, have you?"

"What do they look like?" Cephas asked.

"One's a ledger. The other two are just books. You'd know if you saw them."

"Doesn't sound familiar. Want me to ask Jonah?"

"Hell no. Forget the whole thing. I have to get back to the lodge. It smells like a sewer up there. The whole back patio is thick with some foul stench. I have to keep the guests drunk and pray for heavy wind, at least until we find out what's stinking the place up."

#

At the lighthouse, the day started out thick, hot, and muggy, even at sunrise. Cephas said things were even worse for the guests in the lodge, where the stench and swarms of flies filled the back porches—all an unpleasant expression of something rotten, yet to be uncovered. The attendants started work early, many of them moving the brunch buffet down to the shore, setting up the tables and chairs near the waterfront. The remaining workers sprayed the patios to kill the flies and dug through the gardens, trying to find the source of the smell.

I left my lighthouse chores unfinished, so I could catch the fishermen before they headed out to tend their nets. I had no intention of letting the eviction happen without a fight. Gates thought of us as too meek or stupid to stand up to him. Each victory made him stronger and more determined. It was time for his victories to end.

Bjørn and Gunnar prepared their boat as I approached. When I told them about the infestation up at the lodge, Gunnar laughed.

"Stinks to high heaven?"

"Gates says it smells like a slaughterhouse," I said. "Says the guests need to be good and drunk; otherwise, they can't sleep because of the odor. That's why they're moving everything to the marina."

"And the place is covered with flies?"

"The whole backside of the lodge," I answered. "Hairy bugs as big as your thumbnail. They're spraying insecticide on everything that moves, but the swarms keep coming."

"Just like a slaughterhouse," Gunnar mused.

The two slowed their pace, delighting in the lodge's misfortunes. Gunnar sat down in the boat, uncharacteristically enjoying the morning, humming a Norwegian folk tune.

"Any idea where the stench and the flies came from?" I asked, already having a strong suspicion.

"I bet Gates blames you," Gunnar said. "He doesn't like you much."

"You, of all people, know it's not me. They think it's an animal carcass. If this turns out to be a prank, some jokester will end up on the bottom of the lake with a boat anchor tied to his leg."

Gunnar snorted his contempt for my warnings and for Gates.

"Which leads me to the real reason I'm here." I had no delicate way of saying it. The words just spilled out. "Gates plans to evict all you villagers today."

In an instant, Gunnar's demeanor turned from dismissive to scornful. "Thinks he'll move us to that pig-hole Stygg Havn, I bet." He jumped back into his work as if he'd heard enough, loading supplies into the boat.

"Steamers can't dock there. Damned ship would need to anchor outside the bay. We'd have to transport the boxes and barrels a good quarter mile. Gates wouldn't care if we had to row the fish all the way to Duluth!"

"They were talking about it last night," I said. "How they plan to kick you out."

Gunnar threw his lunch pail in the boat, the two sandwiches getting soaked as they fell into the slimy water between the ribs behind the forward thwart.

"How about we burn this marina to the ground and take our harbor back?" Gunnar said. "Maybe torch the lodge while we're at it?"

Bjørn fetched the sandwiches, shaking the water off before putting them back in the lunch pail.

"This is our place," Gunnar said. "It's been ours for generations. Gates burned it to the ground, and now he wants us at Stygg Havn so he can run his fancy marina. He'll get more than rotten fish guts from me if he plans to kick us out."

The men from the other four boats gathered close to find out what the fuss was about while Bjørn did his best to calm Gunnar. Gunnar pushed him away.

"Now's the time for us to take back what's ours!"

None of the other villagers seemed stirred to violence.

"You can't beat 'em that way," I said. "He has a dormitory full of men you'll have to fight before you get to Gates. Better if you outsmart him."

Gunnar ignored me as he threw things around in the boat. The other men listened.

"They're all up at the lodge now," I said. "Once you leave, his men plan to bundle your stuff and move everything to Stygg Havn. Knowing Gates, he'll send enough muscle to overcome any opposition you can muster."

"So, we quit?" Bjørn asked.

"No. You'll be taking those rich millionaires out fishing." I paused, watching their dumbfounded reactions.

"Why in damnation would we do that?" Gunnar asked.

"You need those guests on your side. If they like you, and you show them how to catch lake trout, then Gates can't touch you. He won't throw you out while you have a bunch of his customers out in the middle of the lake."

"Dumbest, chicken-livered idea I ever heard," Gunnar said.

I grabbed Bjørn, pulling him away from the fishing boats, toward the marina's morning buffet.

"No time to argue," I said. "We need to move."

On the way to the marina, I coached Bjørn on what to do and say. He had his reservations, but his only other choices were eviction or going to war against Gates. As I instructed, he climbed up on a table to address the crowd as the guests gathered for brunch.

"Mange takk, mange takk. Many thanks to each and every one of you." Bjørn paused for effect.

The men quieted, surprised by the praise about to be directed at them.

"On behalf of the fishing village, we offer our sincere thanks for your prayers, generosity, and help. We've been living up at the cottage since the fire. We know we've been a burden to both the lighthouse and the lodge, yet Cephas and Mr. Gates generously took on those extra hardships, making sure we'd be safe and comfortable, with a nice place to stay."

I looked through the crowd, watching the men as they listened intently. Bjørn's oration rang as sincere and impassioned as any career politician. The customers wanted to believe his portrayal of Gates as a benefactor, and the extra step of thanking the guests stroked their own oversized egos.

"What could we possibly offer in return?" Bjørn asked. "With so little to give? What we can offer is the best fishing experience on all of Lake Superior. We have the boats, the tackle, and the experience. We want to take you fishing as our way of saying takk for alt, or thanks for everything."

Bjørn went on to describe the size and quantity of the fish they'd catch, as the men queued up to the table, not wanting to miss out. The adventure of catching a nice stringer of lake trout would be new for them, and one of the few things they could actually brag to their families about upon their return home.

Standing at the edge of the table, I assigned customers to the villager boats. Before Bjørn finished his heartwarming expression of gratitude, the first group of guests was already in one of the boats, crossing the harbor toward the far side of

Tollefson Island. By the time he finally stepped down from the table, thirty guests had booked their trips throughout the rest of the week. The attendants looked confused about the new event. Their boss had never launched anything new without telling all the workers. But based on the guests' enthusiasm, they couldn't doubt the idea's brilliance—not until they saw Gates barreling down the stairway from the lodge.

My throat clogged with a strange combination of joy and fear as he pulled up next to me. The only other time I'd seen him without his jacket and boutonniere was in the boxing ring. He wore a dress shirt, dress slacks, and suspenders, looking as if he had left in such a hurry, he'd forgotten his coat. He reached his arm across my shoulder, grabbing a fistful of uniform and holding on tight. Guests might have mistaken it as a friendly, manly type gesture, but it felt more like a wrenching headlock, pulling me away from the table in a manner that was anything but affable. We walked with our heads only inches apart.

"I'll pluck that good eye straight out of your head and stick it right up your butt," he cursed in a low whisper.

Gates briskly snatched a glass from an attendant's silver drink tray as we walked by, knocking the rest of the drinks to the ground. He led me to a table at the foot of the hillside leading up to the lodge. We both sat, watching Bjørn continue the task of scheduling trips for the guests.

"What kind of dumbass trick are you trying to pull?" A cold spray of whisky shot across my sleeve as Gates spat his drink along with his words. I wiped my arm with a napkin.

"The boys love it," I said. "You're mad 'cause you didn't think of it yourself."

Gates stared with an expression cold as stone. "Put an end to it. Right here, right now." His eyes stayed glued to mine, his lips drawn thin, hardly moving as he talked.

"Too late," I said. "Prob'ly fifty guests already booked through the rest of the week. There's a half dozen out there right now. Soon they'll be catching fish and having the time of their lives."

Gates scanned the lake, finally spotting the four boats well past the island. He refocused on me as if expecting an explanation.

"You should thank me," I said. "You call this a hunting and fishing lodge. It's about time the boys enjoyed a little outdoor adventure. Hell, they're bored stiff with those carnival country club games of yours. Give 'em something manly for God's sake." I talked loud enough for neighboring tables to hear, not caring if it made Gates uncomfortable.

"I don't need some crippled Cyclops telling me how to run my lodge," he said.

"Not with a buffoon like Polly running the show," I replied with a heavy dose of sarcasm.

He leaned back in his chair, gulped down half of his drink, and then set the glass back on the table. "A misanthrope. Isn't that what we decided? Nothing but a misanthropical socialist?"

"Just as we agreed that you're an arrogant bastard."

His stony stare finally cracked. He surveyed the crowd, his fists clenching with a slight shake that conveyed strength, not weakness.

"Hold on there, big guy," I said. "No need to cause a scene. These guests have a delicate constitution. They don't want to see their leader losing his cool. Just let the men fish. I tell you what—we won't even charge you. The first week is free."

I waved my hand as if to dismiss him. Gates stood, finished the rest of his drink, and began to walk away, getting as far as the stairs before turning back.

"What do you know about the stench and flies up at the lodge?" he asked.

"I hear it stinks enough to make a vulture puke."

"And what about my missing books?"

"What would a farm boy like me do with books?"

Gates nonchalantly knocked his empty glass over as I spoke. It rolled in an arc across the table before falling onto the ground.

"You're a funny man, Jonah. But sometimes little men with big attitudes get hurt. I mean hurt, real bad."

\#

"Jonah! Come quick!"

Mae yelled from the lighthouse walkway as I approached from the shore. I was still reeling from my grilling with Gates, having had enough excitement for one day.

"Where have you been? Get up here!"

As I stomped up the stairs, a half-dozen possible emergencies rolled through my brain, like the eviction of villagers, Gunnar on a rampage, Cephas having a heart attack or Polly dying of alcohol poisoning.

"It's Elsie! Her water broke!"

In spite of Elsie's condition, her impending delivery had escaped my mind. Mae and I entered Polly's cottage and found her in the bedroom, walking slowly in obvious pain.

"Shouldn't she lie down?" I asked.

"What do you know about childbirth?" Mae barked. "Heat some water, then bring me a bunch of clean towels and pillows."

I wanted to help but was relieved to be out of the birthing room. I put the pot on the stove and rummaged through their closet for linens. Once Elsie's cries weakened, I brought the laundry into the bedroom, piling it on the dresser. Elsie tried to catch her breath as she recovered from her last contraction, slowly walking around the room with Mae.

"These things take hours, don't they?" I asked, feeling a wash of anxiety flood over me.

Mae watched the alarm clock next to the bed, timing contractions as she calmed Elsie.

"Strong contractions about four minutes apart. She's pretty far along. You better get Anna and Nora. Get Polly too."

I left as the next contraction started. After checking the pot on the stove, I headed to the lodge.

At the top of the hill, the large back lawn was deserted. Halfway across the expanse of grass, the stench hit me, and I noticed the swarm of flies hanging like a pulsating gray cloud across the back patios. With the back doors locked tight, I went around through the front and found Anna and Nora in the kitchen. Hearing the news, they quickly set their dishes aside, removed their aprons, and left their dinner preparations behind them.

Polly was harder to find. I searched both wings of the building, expecting to find him in one of the unused guest suites sleeping off a hangover. By chance, I found the narrow stairway leading down to the cellar. He sat in a small dark room in the back corner of the basement, past all the storage and utility rooms. Slouched over a small, unadorned secretary desk, he had no books, pens, or pencils that might suggest office work of any kind, other than a roll of papers in his right hand, used for swatting flies. To his left stood boxes filled with empty whisky bottles. To his right, a pile of dirty plates swarming with flies from a week's worth of lunches and dinners.

Polly was a drink or two shy of passing out. As I shook him, he coughed and gagged. He started with a bad case of dry heaves. I took the papers out of his hand and stuffed them in my coat pocket before grabbing the wastebasket and hanging it under his chin. Within moments he erupted, spewing a greenish-yellow slime with hardly any pieces of food, a strong indication he'd been drinking more than eating.

The short trip to the lighthouse took us over half an hour. It started with a forced cup of coffee at the lodge to sober him up. From there, we walked around from the front, into the foul-smelling back lawn, which made him puke again, this time all over his new suit. We left the soiled coat on the grass and made our way toward the lighthouse, me half carrying him to his cottage. Below us, the group from the first fishing excursion proudly posed for pictures with their freshly caught stringer of lake trout. Both of us jumped to attention, hearing Elsie's cries as she began a new wave of contractions.

Cephas had arrived, pacing the floor in the main room like an expectant father. Rose huddled in the corner with her carved horse and pig figurines, quietly calling for her mother. Rallying as best he could, Polly pushed me away and headed into the bedroom. From there, we heard a few clunks, clatters, and bangs, then the screaming—not just from Elsie, but also from Mae, Anna, and Nora. In a flash, they came running out of the room with Polly in hot pursuit.

"Maggots!" he shouted. "Keep your dirty hands off of her! We don't need no water maggots!"

Anna grabbed Rose while Nora picked up the toys. They flew past us out the front door. Polly picked up a chair as if he planned to clobber Mae. He didn't notice Cephas, who had approached from behind, then tackled and pinned him to the ground. Still too drunk to be decent, Polly screamed with the incoherence of a banshee, continuing his threats against Anna, Nora, and Mae, while Elsie cried out from the other room, halfway through childbirth. Cephas pulled Polly from the floor and sat him in a kitchen chair.

Mae grabbed my hand and pulled me into Elsie's bedroom. "I checked her," Mae said. "She's starting to open, to ripen. Won't be long now, but she's really tired, and we need to keep her calm."

"We? Me too? I can't . . ."

"Yes, you can. That drunken bastard just chased away the only other women in the harbor. Get in here and help me roll her over."

We positioned Elsie on the bed up on all fours, pillows stacked under her chest. Elsie was splayed over the bedding like a dressed deer tied across the fender of a Model T. I never imagined childbirth to be so awkward.

"Shouldn't we just lay her down on her back?" I asked.

"You don't tell me how to deliver a baby, and I won't tell you how to pee standing up."

Mae rolled up towels and stuffed them under Elsie's ankles. This little detail left me totally confused, though I wouldn't have dared to contradict Mae again.

"Time the contractions," she ordered. "From the beginning of the first to the beginning of the next. Use the second hand on the clock. She has one starting now."

The sheet covering Elsie was already soaked with sweat. She half screamed, half moaned between gasps for air while we softly encouraged her, promising it would all be over soon. The contraction lasted forty-five seconds. In three minutes, a new one started.

And so it went for over an hour. Wave after wave of contractions, gradually getting stronger and more frequent. We changed her position twice, moving her to her side, then returning to all fours with pillows stacked underneath. I stayed at the head of the bed, away from all the action, measuring contractions and offering words of encouragement. Her pain tolerance amazed me. I wondered if being shot in the face hurt half as much as childbirth.

With each contraction, my eye socket itched, requiring a vigorous rubbing of the void and an adjustment of the eyepatch—some sort of subconscious sympathetic reaction. Finally, two more pushes, and I sensed that she'd made it over the peak. The tension in the room receded, replaced by a feeling of anticipation. Elsie's screams and moans quieted, the air now filled with a strong baby's cry and an exhausted mother's laughter.

"A boy!" Mae exclaimed. "A beautiful, healthy boy!"

We turned her onto her side, then handed her the baby, all bundled in a small blanket. Mae cleaned the bed as best she could, washed her hands and arms, and then melted into the chair next to Elsie.

"Jonah, go tell 'em the news," she said. "Give us fifteen minutes, then bring Polly in."

Polly and Cephas sat across from each other, both nervous with anticipation as I walked into the main room.

"It's a boy," I said. "Mom and baby are healthy and happy."

The men beamed. Polly had sobered some and looked more respectable. With his hair combed, face washed, and shirt tucked in, he looked like an expectant father and less like the town drunk.

"Mae says it's time to go visit your wife and son."

He got up and followed me into the bedroom. Elsie held the baby close in her arms, talking softly and rocking him slowly. Mae led Polly to the chair next to her bed. She pushed him into it, then scolded him.

"Elsie needs my help, and Jeg vil hjelpe . . . I'll help her. Don't you dare raise a finger against me. We're friends now. If you give me trouble, I'll beat the dickens out of you. You understand?"

Polly nodded politely, looking grateful and sincere. He leaned in to give both Mom and the baby a kiss, nearly crying.

Once in the other room, Mae collapsed into the chair from exhaustion, her arms splayed out to the sides and her head leaning off to the right.

"He's a big boy, head full of black hair," she said. "They're naming him John. They figure starting a life up here in the Superior wilderness must have been like it was for John the Baptist, living in the wilderness of Judea."

Mae forced herself up, brushed her hair back with her fingers, and smoothed out the wrinkles in her dress before heading to the door.

"I need to get Rose," she said. "Day's almost over, and I have a full day's worth of work left to finish."

#

Cephas and I headed back to his cottage, giving the new parents some privacy. He stoked the stove while I grabbed a can of meat and day-old biscuits to make sandwiches.

"Been a hell of a day," I said.

"Damned right. What in blazes were you trying to pull?"

"I don't know what you're talking about."

"This morning," Cephas said. "All that foolishness with fishing excursions for the guests."

"About time someone treated those guests like real men," I said. "They loved it. Did ya see them taking pictures? As proud as if they'd caught man-eating sharks with their bare hands."

"You did it to stop Gates."

I ignored the accusation and pulled the little key off the side of the meat can. With a couple dozen turns, the thin strip of metal curled up around the key until the lid popped off. I cut one slice of the whitish-pink pork product for each biscuit.

"He calls this place a hunting and fishing lodge," I said, sitting at the table. "About time those rich boys acted like men.

Gates should be grateful."

Cephas checked the coffee, tamped the coals in the stove, and partially closed the damper to keep the embers burning.

"You knew he planned to evict the villagers."

"He had no right."

"So, you knew about it, and you wanted to be a real smarty-pants. Well, don't you think for a minute it'll work. There'll be hell to pay. Gates won't stand for this."

"I saved his pompous ass," I said. "Imagine the villagers being forcibly evicted right in the middle of Elsie's childbirth. It would've been you delivering that little boy today."

Cephas set the coffee cups on the table, then rubbed his face with both hands as if trying to wipe away years of unholy inequities and injustices. He went back to the cupboard and pulled out a tin of cookies hidden behind the bags of sugar and flour.

"Mae's quite a woman," Cephas said. "We had a real disaster on our hands, and she took control."

"She's a peach," I replied. Maybe I was biased, but her loyalty to Elsie impressed me, as did her courage and determination in standing up to Polly. I wouldn't have blamed her if she'd run like Anna and Nora. Instead, she stuck by Elsie's side.

"Still, there's bound to be hell to pay."

I laughed, thinking of the ledger. With the code cracked, there would be hell to pay, but it'd be Gates's neck in the noose, not mine. He'd end up in jail, and his well-heeled guests would be tangled in a scandal big enough to destroy them all.

Cephas opened the tin of cookies while I grabbed a sandwich from the plate. The day had flown by. We were starving.

"What's with Polly?" I asked.

"Polly's changed. He's always been an idiot, but he used to be such a happy idiot."

The dry biscuits made the sandwiches hard to swallow. A little lard or butter would've made them tastier. I washed each bite down with sips of coffee.

"He's dark," Cephas said. "Never been the same since coming back from Port Arthur with Gates. Doesn't even come around the lighthouse anymore."

Cephas skipped his sandwich and ate three more cookies instead.

"Not my concern. He's Gates's problem now," he said.

With a clean and starched white shirt and a flawless coat, Cephas showed none of the normal stains, wrinkles, or grime that come from a day of chores. His hair and beard were neatly trimmed, all per lighthouse regulations. His solid reputation as a keeper had been built upon his religious adherence to the rules.

"This place is a nuthouse," he said. "One cottage filled with homeless villagers, another filled with the family of a drunk who spends all his time at the lodge."

We had no reason for ending the conversation there, but it ended. Maybe because we were both so tired or maybe because we had nothing more to say. Soon he left to start his shift, and I went to my room to rest.

I didn't expect to sleep. The thick and humid night air made the bedcovers stick like flypaper. As I removed my jacket, the roll of papers I took from Polly fell from the coat pocket onto the bed. Likely trash, I thought, nothing but Polly's homemade flyswatter. I hung my jacket and trousers on the valet rack.

Sitting on the bed in just my underwear, I thumbed through the papers. Most were flyers from the lodge, announcing the upcoming Stony Fest celebration. Other sheets offered lodge employees extra hours and additional pay to help finish the trolley stations. Great tinder for lighting fires, I thought. Having read the fronts of the pages, I quickly rifled through the stack, finding most of the backsides blank. All blank except one.

On the back of one of the pages offering extra hours for employees, I found a handwritten matrix with six columns and six rows. The thirty-six elements of the matrix were the twenty-six letters of the alphabet, plus the numbers zero through nine, organized randomly. Below the matrix, the word STONY had been printed in large block letters. In my hand, I held what was unmistakably the decryption key, the wondrous missing piece of the puzzle, capable of turning a worthless collection of ledger entries into explosive evidence. A flimsy sheet of paper that would tear Gates to pieces, destroy his operation, and return the harbor forever back to the villagers. It made me nervous to hold it. The importance of it weighed on me. Already on edge, I jumped to my feet when the bedroom door opened suddenly behind me, sending the stack of papers flying across the bed.

"Just remember," Cephas said, casually walking in. "Elsie's delivery cost us a full day of hard work. That means we have to work extra hard."

His words trailed off, noticing the papers fluttering across the bed. I gathered and shuffled them into a pile as quickly as I could, trying not to look suspicious.

"What's all this?" he asked, reaching around me and fingering the pages closest to him.

"Nothing. Just some trash. Some tinder for the stove."

I tried to be cool, but my heart pounded like a loose window shutter on a stormy night.

"This sheet's about Stony Fest," Cephas said. "And this one has to do with working extra hours up at the lodge."

"Perfect. I'll take those. Put them all in the tinder box next to the stove. No more collecting birch bark for starting fires, eh?"

I took the papers from Cephas and stacked them neatly, sticking the whole pile in the box next to the stove. I shut the lid and went into my room to put my pants on. Cephas appeared confused but not terribly suspicious.

"So be ready to clean and paint," he said. "Only nine days until inspection."

By the time Cephas walked out, I was dizzy and disoriented. I removed the matrix page from the stack of papers, returned the rest of the papers to the tinder box, and then slipped the matrix page under my pillow. In the distance came the resonant clomps of the metal stairs as Cephas climbed to the watch room. By the time he reached the top, I had my breathing under control.

The matrix felt too real. Back when I only had the ledger, I could dream of destroying Gates. I could imagine G-men flooding into the harbor, busting booze bottles, and locking up all the lodge employees. It was all pretend and make-believe, until now. Now I needed to be more careful.

I put on my shirt and coat, carefully folding the matrix page and slipping it into my coat pocket. Cephas helped me see just how careless I'd been, leaving papers and ledgers laying around, barely hidden. I needed a better hiding place.

Back in my boot camp days at Fort Jackson, thieving recruits regularly pilfered things like cigarettes, pocketknives, and watches. While the others in my barracks suffered through the losses, I created the perfect place for storing my stuff. In just a few spare hours, I built a false bottom inside my footlocker to keep my valuables hidden. It worked like a charm, protecting my stuff from the vultures who preyed on everyone else. If it worked at Fort Jackson, it would certainly work at Stony Point.

I carried the dresser drawer into the barn behind the cottage. In less than an hour, I had a false bottom cut from laminated wood, fitting snug into the dresser. I lined the drawer's inner perimeter with one-inch spacers, giving the false bottom a solid edge to rest on. With no gaps along the edges, it had enough tension to keep the false bottom in place, even when turned upside down. I drilled small access holes in the original base, from which a stiff wire could push the new laminated wood up, giving access to whatever lay hidden.

Back at the cottage, I hid the ledger, codebooks, and my newfound matrix page under the false bottom. I added clothes and slid the drawer into the dresser.

#

With Polly working for Gates at the lodge, Cephas and I had longer late-night shifts at the lighthouse. Cephas worked from 8 p.m to 2 a.m. I worked the golden hours of peace and tranquility from 2 a.m. to 8 a.m. Very rarely did I have visitors, and when I did, the noisy stairs gave plenty of advanced warning. Those hours were a perfect time for deciphering the ledgers from the lodge.

From the green Codes and Cryptography book, I recalled the

decoding to be a three-step process. First, the strings of characters would be organized into tables, filling in the A, D, F, G, V, and X letters from left to right under each letter of the keyword STONY. I then transposed the columns, arranging the header (STONY) characters alphabetically (NOSTY), which changed the order of all the letters below. The remainder of the decryption required nothing more than a simple substitution using the six-by-six matrix key.

I began with the ledger's first block of text dated June 7, 1923, to test my skills. After ten minutes of drawing tables, reordering matrices, and performing "simple" substitutions, I had my result:

POWERPLANTSABOTAGEDCULPRITPUNISHEDEXPE
CTNOMORETROUBLE

It made the hair on the back of my neck stand on end. I was reading an account of what had to be Knute's murder as the first recorded message in the ledger. "Power plant sabotaged. Culprit punished. Expect no more trouble." I didn't know what I'd find from my decoding of the messages. I'd hoped for something incriminating but never considered it would be so damning in the first block of characters. The seriousness of the situation tempered my elation. Now, being fully aware of how damning the information would be to Gates, I feared the brutality of his retaliation.

I cranked the clockwork mechanism and pumped the kerosene tank before returning to the deciphering. Over time, I became more familiar with the matrix key, and the translations progressed at a steady pace. After a few hours, I had the first few pages decrypted. Half of the messages accounted for the whisky shipments to the lodge from Port Arthur (the late-night deliveries by boat every Tuesday and Friday). The other half listed the names of guests visiting the lodge and the bottles purchased by those guests (rumored to be loaded into their steamer trunks for their trip home).

What a bombshell. With only a small percentage of the

messages decrypted, I'd uncovered information on Knute's murder, an accounting of the lodge's bootlegging activities, and a list of Duluth's high society now mixed up in the illegal operations. Federal investigators could soon be rolling through the stately mansions of Duluth like the plague, from East End to Endion. Prestigious families might soon be crushed from the disgrace. Dozens of politicians, judges, policemen, and clergymen would be implicated, all tangled up in the web of Gates's operations. The whole social structure of Duluth might be torn apart—by me. That was a heavy burden for a disfigured assistant lighthouse keeper.

I thought of Franklin and measured my weak constitution against his determination and resolve. He spoke of dignity in fighting for righteousness and justice. I could see that dignity in Franklin. I used to have that dignity during the war.

Now I could regain that manhood and self-respect. Now was not the time to back down. I pulled the twenty-dollar bill out of my pocket and copied Franklin's address onto the envelope, then penned my letter:

Franklin,

Found the decryption key. I've deciphered a small portion of the messages from the ledger, and you won't believe the dirt uncovered. Ruinous for the guests, but particularly damning for Gates. We'll lock him up for good. I await your reply.

Jonah

#

Stony Point might have been an excellent location for a lighthouse, but it was a brutally inhospitable location for a budding romance. The prying eyes, tight quarters, uncertain futures, and competing priorities left little time for relationships. Mae and I crossed paths plenty, always heading off in different directions, rarely having the time or the privacy for romance. We both had much bigger things to worry about, but for me, there could be nothing more important than her. Nothing would make my life happier than to spend the rest of my days with Mae. I needed to let her know.

At the end of my shift, I packed a lunch for the three of us, including Rose, for a little picnic up to Barberry Creek. She protested, saying she had too much work but finally gave in. I could tell she wanted to go. "Bring your bathing suits," I said.

We had been to Barberry Creek before but never together. The smell of pine and wildflowers aroused the senses with a waft of warmth and stimulation. I carried Rose, her arms around my neck, and Mae carried the basket of food. We stopped just beneath the falls next to a clear pool, where the current painted ripples across the sandy bottom. It took only a minute before I was in my shorts, floating around in the cool, clear water under a canopy of pines and birch. Rose and Mae hid behind a clump of trees as they changed into their suits.

"What's taking you so long? My skin's already wrinkly."

"Must be old age," Mae replied, coming out from the trees. Rose jumped in with a big splash, then popped up with a vigorous dog paddle that carried her out to the middle of the pool. Mae walked in gingerly, slowly acclimating to the water. Of course, I splashed her. It was just too much of a temptation not to.

"Nei! ikke Ikke gjør det! Don't do that!" Mae turned and held her arms up in a futile attempt to block the spray. "I hate that!" she said, distressfully dropping down in the water until her shoulders slipped under the surface.

Mae looked great in a bathing suit. It may have been out of date, but her slim, youthful curves filled it in nicely. I regretted splashing her. I would have enjoyed watching her longer, gracefully easing into the water. After a few minutes of swimming, Rose became interested in hunting frogs along the edge of the pool, giving Mae and me time to ourselves.

"Now, is that any way to treat a woman?" she said, rubbing my hair, then adjusting my eye patch. I held her close. She twitched with a light gasp before sinking in toward me, her eyes softening and her smile sparkling.

"You lighthouse keepers are so aggressive," she said.

"You do this with a lot of lighthouse keepers?"

"You'll be the only one, as long as you learn not to splash me."

She put her arms around my shoulders, and we kissed. A deep, meaningful, long-overdue kiss. Not a fishing boat kind of kiss with lake trout flopping at our feet, but a gentle, tender embrace in a lovely pool surrounded by pine trees, her arms around my neck, and her body next to mine. The lighthouse felt a million miles away. We floated, embraced, kissed, and adored each other for a good half an hour until Rose grew tired of chasing frogs.

"Eewww!" Rose laughed. "Du kysser!"

Mae loosened the embrace, her arms still around my shoulders.

"Bet you're a better kisser than all those other lighthouse keepers," she joked.

"Better than Cephas or Polly?"

She wrinkled her nose at the unpleasant thought. We swam to shore and spread a blanket over a large rock between the pool and the trees. I unwrapped the canned meat sandwiches, this time made with butter and slices of cheese. We also had oranges and apples taken from a basket sent from the lodge, congratulating Polly and Elsie on the birth of their son. It wasn't fancy by lodge standards, but Mae and Rose seemed to like it.

After eating, Rose played along the edge of the pool. Mae lay on her back with her eyes closed while I rested on my side, watching her. Her suit didn't fit as tightly as the styles worn by the Dollies at the lodge, but she still looked like a model or a movie star. I kissed her on the forehead, and she smiled, pulling me down for a nice long embrace and a loving kiss.

"My Askeladden," she said, her smile as brilliant as the rays of sunlight filtering through the trees.

"You mean your little troll fighter?" I asked.

Mae feigned disappointment with a pouty frown and a pinch on my cheek, as if scolding a little boy.

"I heard about your little prank. Setting up fishing trips for all those dandies in their cream-colored pants and fancy sweaters. Those millionaires looked like hobos by the time they got back. All untucked shirts with sweaty pits, sunburned and covered with fish slime."

"Hey, now. They were happy hobos," I said. "Might be the first masculine thing those boys have ever done. And it's about time."

Mae combed my bangs back with her fingers and adjusted my eyepatch. "Bjørn says they're good tippers too. Says we're making more as fishing guides than we ever did catching fish. He says you're a genius. Just like Askeladden."

She gave me a peck, then another, then a long deep kiss that blossomed. Passion filtered through thoughts and senses, unconstrained by place and time, with a loving sweetness and openness that I couldn't help but fall into.

Since the war, I'd become an expert at reading people's faces, uncovering the emotions behind them. I've known the curiosity of kids too young to understand disfigurement and the cruelty from kids old enough to figure it out. I'd seen pity from townsfolk, disappointment from Cephas, resignation from my parents, and revulsion from my ex-wife, Jenny. In Mae's eyes, there was none of that. Nothing but acceptance, adoration, and love. She made me human and healthy.

With Rose off catching frogs, we slipped back into the water, weightlessly floating in each other's arms. I felt like a teenager again, my war year memories washed away, my disfigurement almost forgotten. After so many years, I now had that sense of wonderment from my youth, hardly able to believe the caressing, nuzzling, and embracing, each of us melting into each other's touch.

We stayed longer than we should have, both with a full day's work waiting for us back at the harbor. Rose ran ahead of us to the villagers' cottage. I hoped for one last kiss, but any semblance of romance shattered like broken glass with Rose's screams.

Mae reached the door first, and I stopped right behind her, looking into a completely ransacked cottage. Not just the clothes and belongings thrown about, but every bit of furniture had been turned upside down and scattered across the room. Rose jumped into Mae's arms as we slowly walked in, kicking a narrow path through the rummage on the floor. Every drawer had been emptied, no stick of furniture left unturned. From the window, I could see the barns out back, both with clutter spreading out from the open doorways. The villagers' cottage hadn't been the only target.

"How could he do such a thing?" Mae asked. "What could he possibly want from us?"

Without acknowledging or answering, I turned for the door.

I found Cephas in our cottage, sitting on the only stick of furniture still standing upright—one of the kitchen chairs. Around him lay overturned tables, a couch lying on its back, other dining chairs thrown across the room, and shelves emptied. Interspersed among the larger items were all the accoutrements of daily life, ripped from their proper storage and strewn about. Pots, pans, dishes, and glasses spread across not only the kitchen but throughout the great room. Books, lanterns, shaving kits, items of clothing, linens, and seat cushions seemed scattered not from haste, but to violate and offend.

"What's all this?" I asked, already knowing who had done it and what they wanted.

"Never happened before," he answered. "Wrath of God, I suppose. Or another Jonah curse." He sat straight, his arms crossed and his hands tucked up into his armpits. His whole body quivered slightly as if he was chilled. His mouth had a grimace, lips turned downward, suggesting fear, anger, and disappointment.

I went into my room. As expected, I found my bed tossed, my steamer trunk thrown across the room, and the dresser emptied of its drawers and tipped over. The bottom drawer was my main interest, lying upside down on the floor.

"Must be the Jonah curse," Cephas yelled from the other room. "That's what this is."

I felt the heaviness of the drawer as I turned it over. The false bottom stayed in place. The ledger must have remained hidden.

#

When I first met Cephas, he impressed me as a man of confidence and integrity, appearing as formidable a leader as any of the officers I'd met during the Great War. I could appreciate his faith in God and his adherence to the teachings of the Bible. His religion set the firm foundation for his decisions and conduct. He drew his strength from God. The lighthouse was his holy place, his "eye of the Lord."

All that had changed after the village fire. Cephas spoke less of his holy place. He stopped referring to the lighthouse as his eye of the Lord. He acted fragile and unsure, as if no longer celebrating God's glory, but fearing God's wrath. His faith, his moral compass, and his righteousness appeared to be lost. Now the pursuit of his pension and retirement consumed him.

He didn't bother looking up as I reached the top of the spiral staircase to start my shift. He scraped the ash from the bowl of his pipe and dumped it into the tin can under his chair. I started into my evening chores, winding the clockwork for the lens, checking the kerosene, and pressurizing the tank with a few good pumps. By the time I sat down, he had already swiped the pipe through his pouch, using his thumb to tamp the tobacco into the bowl. He held it in his hand, pointing the stem at me as he spoke.

"Emma always hated the lighthouse."

It was a strange occurrence, the realization that I'd never heard his wife's name before.

"Before the lodge, she couldn't stand the solitude. Each spring she would arrive later, every fall would go back earlier, and her visits home to Two Harbors during the summer would grow longer until she eventually stopped coming altogether."

Cephas lit his pipe, rotating the match around the bowl as he puffed until he had a good, steady burn.

"The lodge only made things worse, with all the drinking and carrying on. She wondered if I'd lost my religion, living amid all this sin and corruption. She couldn't understand why I allowed the decadence right next to the lighthouse, as if I had the power and authority to stop such things."

He folded the leather pouch that held the pipe cleaners, scraping tool, and matches. After a few thoughtful puffs, he put the smoking kit in his coat pocket.

"She almost left me. I begged her to wait for a few more months until I could retire. I said I'd have my pension, and we could live out our final years peacefully and respectably at Two Harbors, going to church together and taking care of her parents. I really thought that might happen."

We watched the beam as it played across the waters, sweeping from left to right. The distance it covered made one man's problems seem insignificant.

"I cleaned the cottage and the barns," I said. "You'd never know they were ransacked. And the villagers straightened out their place. Things are getting back to normal."

He puffed on his pipe as he followed the beam, not acknowledging a word I'd said. I suspected that neither of us believed things would get back to normal, or even knew what normal was anymore. After finishing his smoke, he picked up the tin can under his seat and tapped the ashes from the pipe bowl into it. Without another word, he descended the stairs. Making a quick stop along the railing, he scanned the water one more time before retiring for the night.

I waited for a half an hour to make sure he was sleeping before starting my new undertaking—possibly my most important project since my arrival at Stony Point. From the shop, I gathered a toolbox full of tools, including a coping saw, a brace, drill bits, clamps, files, some sandpaper, and a piece of half-inch-thick maple trim. After the regular chores of winding the clockwork mechanism, topping off the fuel, and pressurizing the tank, I secured the piece of maple trim onto the metal stair rail with a clamp. Near the edge of the wood, I drilled a five-eighths-inch hole, then rounded the inside edges with a rat-tail file. I carefully cut a larger circle around the hole with a coping saw, creating a bulky wooden ring. Then, I returned to my chair with my carving knife, files, and sandpaper, to shape the clumsy loop into a simple, elegant polished band of maple.

As I sanded the ring using progressively finer grades of sandpaper, the wavy grain of the wood began to reveal itself. The ring was small, light, and inconsequential as I held it. Still, I hoped it would convey my love for her. She deserved a real engagement ring, and in time, she might have one, but my proposing to her couldn't wait.

Working with my hands eased my mind. It slowed the worried thoughts over the ransacking and the deciphered ledger. I realized how much I could enjoy the life of a lighthouse keeper, particularly with Mae by my side, if not for the constant abuse from Gates.

With the ring perfectly shaped and sanded smooth, I finished it using multiple coats of shellac and a mineral oil mixture, polishing it in with a soft cloth. The finish transformed the buff-colored wood to a glossy finish, the color of naturally tanned leather. The ring never would have sufficed for Jenny, but somehow, I knew it would be just right for Mae.

#

The morning started with Mae off to help Elsie, Gunnar off to tend his animal traps, and the other villagers off with guests on their fishing excursions. Cephas had a long list of chores for me in preparation for the lighthouse inspection, to which I responded with less than my normal enthusiasm.

Meanwhile, a sweet undercurrent of optimism flowed through the marina and lodge. Gates focused everyone's efforts on the preparations for Stony Fest. He doubled wages for the attendants and construction workers, offering a persuasive incentive for finishing all the projects on time. The biggest and most impressive project was the inclined trolley from the shoreline up to the lodge. Working twelve hours a day, the crew had finished the stations located at the bottom and top, and the attendants gave them a final coat of paint. The stations featured the same rustic combination of stone columns, leaded glass, and rough-hewn log walls that made the buildings so distinctive, only on a smaller scale. A large Stony Point Lodge sign stretched all the way across the lakefront side of the station, leaving no doubt about the ownership of the harbor.

The day the custom-built trolley arrived from Duluth, the attendants painted it to match the stations. The trolley included a custom-made inclined platform for the wheels that matched the steep incline of the track to keep the passenger carriage level throughout the trip up the hill. With the trolley operational, the whole conversion of a ramshackle fishing village into a posh marina was complete.

At the end of the day, Gates set aside an hour to celebrate his workers. He opened a buffet and drink stations near the dock where the construction crews and lodge attendants could take a break from the day's work. He recognized the significant accomplishments of the day and presented special gifts to those who'd made major contributions. For the men, these awards were new pocket watches, pocketknives, cufflinks, or shaving kits. It was the highlight of the day for the workers, who appreciated the celebration and enjoyed the recognition.

Polly and Cephas always attended, but not me. Being dead last on Gates's gift list, it came as no surprise that I wasn't invited. With the day's celebration in full swing, I slipped the boat into the water, rowing to the northeast, past the lighthouse, for my first visit to Stygg Havn. From the vantage of a few hundred yards out from shore, the narrow strip of coastline wedged between the water and the rocky ridge reminded me of the old fishing village. The huts built weeks ago by Gates's construction workers stood off to the left, nestled next to the hillside around a small fire pit. I imagined how a warehouse might fit to the right of the sheds, followed by an icehouse and the reels for drying nets.

At a hundred yards out, things appeared less promising. I bumped up against the first of the large boulders lurking dangerously below the surface. The winds were light, hardly a ripple on the water, allowing me to scan the waters port and starboard for a better approach. But left or right, as far as I could see, dangerous shallows and jagged rocks threatened. I slowly rowed to shore, bouncing from one rock to the next, realizing that even a small storm out of the south would create swells large enough to make the trip in or out of Stygg Havn deadly.

Once on the beach, the same strip of shoreline that appeared sizeable from the water turned out to be no wider than a sports field—plenty of room for a pickup game of football but much too narrow for a village. With no island or peninsula breaking the wind and the waves, anything built on the beach would be crushed by ice in the winter or washed away during summer storms. The little huts wouldn't last a season.

The first hut I entered was empty, other than a few apple crates stacked in a corner. I repositioned one to use as a chair as I considered the room's starkness, wondering how the tar-paper shacks could have been any worse. When the door opened suddenly behind me, I jumped to my feet and tried to turn around all in one motion, causing me to trip over the apple crate. I landed with a pair of wing-tipped shoes just inches from my face. I initially feared it to be Gates until the familiar scratchy tenor voice told me otherwise.

"Why, you're as nervous as a bootlegger's bride," Polly said. He grabbed the other apple crate and sat as I got to my feet.

"Where'd you come from?" I asked.

"Took the path through the woods. Much safer than coming by water." Polly scanned the inside of the shed, noticing the bare walls, open rafters, and lack of a floor.

"What a dump. You thinkin' of moving in?"

"Of course not," I said, trying to sound insulted by the implication. In truth, I knew that Stygg Havn could end up being the villagers' and my only option.

"Why are you here?" I asked.

Polly picked up a handful of rocks and started throwing them against the wall one at a time, not speaking until they were half gone.

"I need to tell you something." He kept tossing pebbles and staring at the shed wall, busy formulating his thoughts.

"Sit down, Jonah. You're making me nervous standing over me like that."

I kept standing. He grabbed another handful of stones and

started throwing them again.

"I never thanked you," he said. "You and Mae saved Elsie and Little John. They might have died without your help. I don't know what I would've done."

Noticing a knothole in the wall of the shed, Polly shifted from mindlessly tossing rocks to aiming for the hole. It gave us both a calming distraction from his clumsy conversation.

"And, yes, I know I've been a real ass."

"That's an understatement," I said.

I sat on the other apple crate and picked up my own handful of stones. Soon, we were both throwing pebbles at the knothole in an unspoken competition, seeing who could get the most through.

"Elsie and I are moving to Duluth. It's time for me to buck up and be a better husband and father. She wants a nice place to raise our family. And there's a special steamer coming tomorrow because of Stony Fest."

"You're leaving tomorrow?" I asked.

"Yes. You need to come too. You can't stay here."

In only a few weeks, I'd seen three distinct sides of Polly. First, the buffoon, telling his stories and singing his bawdy songs. After the village fire, he became a pompous, egotistical ass, supposedly managing the marina. Now he acted remorseful, reasonable, and caring. I didn't feel that I could trust him, but I didn't feel the same hatred I used to.

"I can't leave," I said. "Not now. I won't go without Mae and Rose."

Polly grabbed my hand midtoss to get my attention. "You really need to leave. You have no reason to believe me or trust me, but please listen to me. The sooner you leave, the better. Maybe they can go with you."

"Give up my dream job?" I joked.

"No. Not funny. You really need to . . . Polly choked on his words, trying to tell me something but not able to spit it out. He fumbled through a series of partial sentences, each of them ending abruptly as if coming perilously close to revealing whatever he apparently didn't dare say. Frustrated by his inability

181

to make his point, he stood, throwing his handful of rocks against the wall.

"I have to get back and pack up our stuff. You gotta believe me. Please come with us. If you don't believe me, maybe Elsie can talk you into leaving. Bring Mae and Rose with you. Please."

Polly left after an awkward silence. Having seen him play the court jester for so long, I struggled with taking him seriously. Whether working at the lighthouse or the lodge, I'd never trusted him. But as I rowed back to the lighthouse, I somehow found myself believing in his sincerity.

It was dark when I returned to the lighthouse, and I was grateful to be back at the cottage. I slathered peanut butter and honey on a biscuit and took two of Cephas's gingersnap cookies, hidden behind the bags of flour and sugar. I suspected I'd be fired before he found them missing.

On the corner of my bed, I found the letter, a white envelope addressed to me with Franklin's return address. I set the plate of food on my nightstand next to the alarm clock and turned the letter over and over in my hand, anxious to read his reply. After a bite of the biscuit, I ran the blade of my pocket knife up through the top crease, slipped the letter out, and then carefully unfolded it. It was dated June 23, written two days prior:

Dear Jonah,

I read your letter with great joy, thrilled to hear of your success in decrypting the ledger. Surely this will mean terrible troubles for Mr. Gates.

I have so many questions. How did you acquire the ledger? How did you crack the code? Where is it hidden? Who else knows about it? Please write immediately to let me know!

I will arrive by steamer on Friday, June 27, the first day of Stony Fest. Please have the ledger with you, and meet me on the dock. I have great plans for the ledger and assure you we will soon be celebrating the downfall of Gates and the undoing of his horrid Stony Point Lodge.

Sincerely,

Franklin B. Smythe

After reading it three times, I laid back, having a hard time believing the progress made. The cracking of the code was significant, but then to have the help of someone as capable and connected as Franklin was a real bonus. In our meeting at Beaver Creek, he spoke of delivering the books to his publisher friend at the Superior Telegraph in Superior, Wisconsin. It's a good old-fashioned workingman's newspaper, leaning heavily toward the socialist side of things. A paper that wanted nothing more than to start a union uprising and class warfare, bringing the rich ruling class of Duluth down to their collective knees.

#

Late-night visitors always surprised me up at the lighthouse, and less than an hour into my shift, I heard footsteps climbing the circular stairs. Not the heavy steps of Cephas, nor the foot dragging of Polly. These steps were rhythmic, slow, soft, and steady, like an angel on velvet. Mae. It would be the first time she'd come to visit me at work.

Standing at the top of the stairs, her eyes bounced from the lantern above to the kerosene tank hanging on the wall, to the clockwork mechanism. I swept the wood shavings from my carving under my chair with my foot.

"I couldn't sleep," she said. "Too much happening. Too much to think about."

As she spoke, I stood to pressurize the kerosene tank and wind the clockwork mechanism. Mae watched intently, continuing to share what was on her mind.

"I've been a wreck ever since the ransacking. Every day we lose another piece of our harbor. Now they're building a new bandshell right next to our graveyard. Right next to where Knute and Hans are buried. He might not give a hoot about us, but at least he could show some respect for the dead."

I sat back down in my chair, picked up my knife, and continued with the night's carving project.

"I know we can't stay here forever. But where can a whole village go?" she asked. "Other fishing villages have their own problems, and Stygg Havn's a dump. The men say they might have to give up fishing, and it's the only thing they know."

"Where's Askeladden when you need him?" I asked.

"I'm serious," Mae said. "Askeladden's make-believe." She wove her arm inside mine and laid her head on my shoulder.

"Yeah, I know. But if he were real, I suppose he'd find a way to trick Gates. Maybe get him and all his guests into big trouble. He'd find some accounting book from the lodge to use as evidence against Gates and put him in jail for years, returning the harbor back to the village."

Mae looked stunned. My little tale had way too much detail to be fictitious.

"What book are you talking about?" she asked. "What are you saying?"

"Then, Askeladden could marry the princess. They'd live happily ever after in a little harbor on the edge of the wilderness. They'd raise a family, catch fish, and run a lighthouse."

Mae stuttered, unable to find the words for a suitable response. I stood, helped her to her feet, and led her to the lantern room ladder.

"Where are we going?" she asked, climbing ahead of me.

"The best part of the lighthouse. Through the door to the right when you reach the top."

As we walked out onto the lantern gallery, Mae gasped in amazement. The stars seemed close enough to touch, and our view out onto the lake was endless. I knew she'd be impressed. We sat on the dark side, leaning against the black metal backside of the lantern room. I helped her to sit and draped my coat over her shoulders to protect her from the wind. Her legs swung back and forth, dangling over the edge of the metal grate floor.

"You comfortable?" I asked.

"That depends. You're scaring me. Are you leaving me? If so, you should have told me down in the watch room," she said. "We could've shaken hands and said our good-byes."

"I'd never leave you."

"But Elsie told me they're moving to Duluth, and you are going with them."

"I told Polly I'd never leave without you," I said.

"You mean it?" she asked, looking pleasantly surprised.

She pulled a ribbon out of her pocket, combed her auburn hair with her fingers, and tied it up in a ponytail, leaving little strands falling down around her face. Mae wiped her eyes with the back of her hand, blew her nose lightly into her hankie. We kissed through her tears. There was an energy, a newness, pulling us together and pushing away the troubles and fears. Tonight, just the two of us on our perch high above the rest of the world. I retrieved a small tin box from my pocket, then held it out to her.

"Before meeting you, I had nothing," I said. "How could I have known what a blessing you'd be? You've given me a new life, one with more love and joy than I could ever have thought possible."

Mae looked stunned. I felt a sudden panic, holding the small tin box out toward her. She deserved diamonds and gold. All I had to offer was a wooden ring in an old snuff box. Hardly romantic. Jenny would have taken it as an insult, a crude joke, and an unforgivable sin.

Mae didn't wait. She grabbed the box and opened it herself. With a little squeak of glee, she threw both arms around my neck, pinning me against the railing with her kisses and hugs. I pulled loose, then placed the ring on her finger.

"There's no one in this world I could ever love as much as you," I said. "We'll spend the rest of our lives together, you, Rose, and me."

Mae's left hand trembled in mine as I spoke. Her right hand alternated between covering her mouth and wiping away tears. I choked up just watching her, hardly able to get my final words out.

"Mae, will you marry me?"

Through the sobs and the tears, her answer was barely audible, but unquestionably yes.

Mae wiped her eyes with her hankie and combed her hair back with her fingers. She patted her legs as if to get control of her emotions, then circled the ring around her finger, admiring it.

"It's perfect," she said. "You're perfect. And whatever happens, we'll be together."

The water below sparkled like a million diamonds, illuminated by the beam as it swept across the lake. We kissed, caressed, held each other, then kissed some more. We listened as the party sounds from the lodge eventually calmed, giving way to a deep silence. We watched for shooting stars, smelled the scent of pine, and listened to the waves lapping up along the shore. The night was ours—all the sights, sounds, feelings, and emotions.

Too soon, the first sliver of light appeared on the horizon, and our night of love ended. I walked her back to the villagers' cottage.

"Did you make all that stuff up?" she asked. "Those accounting books, the evidence, and Gates going to jail? Was that all just a story?"

"Are you sure you want to know?" I asked.

"Maybe not. Do you think it'll work?"

"Sure. All I need is a few more days. No blow-ups, altercations, or evictions. Just a few more days and Gates will be running a cellblock instead of a lodge."

6 STONY FEST

"It's back," Cephas said. "Damned smell and flies, back at the lodge."

With only one day to go until the start of Stony Fest and the lighthouse inspection, Cephas had something new and horrible to focus on. He held a pitchfork in one hand and a shovel in the other, having fetched both from the barn behind the cottage. Wearing his work gloves, cotton shirt, and dungarees, he looked more like a farmer than a lighthouse keeper. Below us, the villagers had all four of their boats along the lighthouse pier, waiting for the lodge guests they'd booked for the morning's lake trout fishing excursion. Mae held Rose and waved from the window of the villagers' cottage, looking more concerned than cordial.

"Stinkin' to high heaven at both the marina and the lodge," Cephas said. "Gates is poppin' his rivets."

He rolled up his sleeves, raised the pitchfork high, and held the shovel out for me to take. "Let's go. We don't have all day."

Flies swarmed across the trolley station. Buffets and tables sat unadorned along the shore, abandoned because of the smell. The sailboats and rowboats were still perched high up on the beach. Teams of attendants packed in along the hillside with rakes, shovels, and pitchforks, poking and scratching their way through the tangles of underbrush, looking to find whatever might be causing the smell. Another group wielded pump sprayers and shot clouds of insecticide to knock down the swarms of flies. As the attendants sprayed, the cloud of flies would briefly shift, only to fill back in once the insecticide cleared. Dead bugs piled up, getting smashed into the decking by the men as they worked.

"They say the smell just came out of nowhere," Cephas said, stabbing into the gardens with his pitchfork. "They moved all the food, drink, and events inside."

"It makes no sense," I said. "I've been around animals all my life. A carcass never smells like this. They get eaten by scavengers, they dry out, and shrivel up. They don't just stink up a whole harbor overnight."

While I normally favored any disruption of the lodge or annoyance of the guests, I had a bad feeling about this one. It would have been a well-deserved reversal of fortune if the smell turned out to be some natural event, like swamp gas or a dead moose. Unfortunately, that kind of good luck rarely came my way. Rightly or wrongly, I just knew the accusations and consequences would come crashing down on the villagers and me once they discovered the source of the smell.

Cephas worked like a man fighting to save his life, the same way farmers back in Aitkin responded to fields destroyed by hailstorms or animals dying off from some virulent disease. With his retirement and pension in jeopardy, his exertions were disproportionate to the task at hand. He worked like a maniac, as if the extra flailing about might tip the scale in his favor. I worked alongside him for only one reason—to deflect suspicions that the villagers or I might be to blame.

By early afternoon, the steamship arrived, loaded with guests and supplies for the Stony Fest celebration. As always, a cadre of attendants met them at the boat, along with trucks and busses to take the cargo and young millionaires up to the lodge. Gates stood in the middle of it all, wearing his cream-colored suit and red carnation, greeting most of the guests personally as if they were long-time friends or business partners.

We continued poking and prodding along the hillside as the steamer crew unloaded luggage and supplies onto the dock, keeping everything separated and organized. Piles of steamer trunks, perishables, and dry goods filled in along the length of the pier, creating a narrow pathway from the ship to the shore. Attendants loaded the supplies onto the trucks, moving like an army of ants.

The unloading took significantly longer than usual with all of the Stony Fest passengers and freight, but the quick and unexceptional loading for departure took only minutes. Polly, Elsie, and little John were the only passengers boarding, the only freight being the family's two large steamer trunks.

"A new beginning for those two," I said. "Off to live with her family."

"Don't think so," Cephas replied. "Elsie says they're staying in some big ol' mansion. She blabbed about some new rich friends that Polly met. Says they'll be livin' with some real important people in one of the biggest homes in all of Duluth."

"Like who?" I asked, having a hard time grasping the idea of Polly and Elsie hobnobbing among Duluth's high society. "Maybe one of Polly's buddies from the lodge?"

"Hardly. He burned through any old friends he might've had. They treat him like the plague now."

If the stories of big mansions and important friends came from Polly, one might chalk it up to the big talk of a guy who'd never been constrained by truth. But this was Elsie talking of rich friends, not Polly. Leaning up against the ship's railing, she held John in one hand and heartily waved her good-byes with the other. Polly stood behind her, looking bored.

As the afternoon came to a close, the workers and attendants gathered along the shore for the daily celebration, knowing all too well that there would be no commendations, no buffet, and no drink bar. Everyone circled around a very solemn and somber Gates.

"Today, I have only a few words for all of you. I'll give one hundred dollars tonight to the man who finds where this godforsaken smell is coming from. If it's not found, I'll dock all of you a week's pay. Nobody sleeps until that stink is gone."

He turned and headed to the lodge, where the young guests gathered for dinner. The crowd of attendants and construction workers dispersed slowly, taking their sprayers, rakes, and shovels back for one more assault against the unrelenting smells and flies.

I'd had enough. I left Cephas along the hillside and returned to the lighthouse cottage to see Mae. Only hours ago, we were a pair of young sweethearts—thrilled over our engagement and optimistic about our new lives together. Now we could only worry over the day's developments.

"Gunnar did this, didn't he?" I asked, pointing in the direction of the workers digging and spraying. "Is he the one that caused all the smell?"

"Jeg vil ikke tenke på det," she said. "I don't want to think about it." Mae's reply bit as sharply as my accusation. She stood with her arms crossed, watching the digging and spraying from the window.

"This ruins everything," I said. "Gates will explode, and I'll never get that ledger to Franklin."

"What ledger?"

"An accounting book from the lodge. Jam-packed with enough damning evidence to destroy Gates." I didn't dare mention the part in the ledger about the power plant sabotage and the culprit, Knute, being punished. I decided to wait for a time less stressful.

"And who's Franklin?"

"A friend. I'm meeting him on the steamer tomorrow, assuming we're not all evicted by then."

I pulled Franklin's note from my coat pocket and handed it to Mae. "Here's the letter he sent. The ledger is hidden in my dresser."

As Mae opened the letter, I pulled the bottom drawer from the dresser, relieved to feel the heavy weight.

"What's this twenty-dollar bill for?" she asked.

"Franklin wrote his address on it. Can you imagine? Used it like a worthless scrap of notepaper. I wish I had that kind of money."

Turning the drawer upside down, I banged it hard against the floor until I heard the thump of the hidden cache dislodging, hitting the carpet.

"He sent that other note just the other day," I said. "Setting up our meeting tomorrow on the steamer."

"This doesn't make sense," she said. "It doesn't match."

Mae held the twenty-dollar bill in one hand, the note in the other, looking back and forth between the two.

"The address?" I asked.

"No. The handwriting. It's not the same. These weren't written by the same person."

"That's impossible!" I pulled both papers from her hand. With only a quick glance, the difference in handwriting was evident. The writing on the twenty-dollar bill featured a flowing cursive script, its letters sloping forward with large rounded loops. The note to set up the meeting looked completely different, with large, blocky letters in more of a print style.

"But I watched him write his address on that twenty."

"Someone else must've written the letter," Mae said. "Not Franklin."

My hands suddenly sweating, I reached for the drawer lying upside down on the floor. My perfect plan had crumbled. I had been so confident to have found and decoded the ledger. It felt like such good fortune, as if the downfall of Gates was preordained. I only needed Franklin to do his part by delivering the evidence to the Superior Telegraph Newspaper. What I thought would be a triumph now smelled like a trap, and the prospect of losing it all to Gates gave me a burning pain that felt like fire crawling up my throat.

As I lifted the drawer from the floor, a pile of paper flopped out from underneath. Not the dark leather-bound ledger I'd expected, but magazines printed on cheap stock. The decryptions and damaging evidence that I'd worked so hard for were gone. In their place, a stack of Polly's trashy Black Mask and True Detective magazines, with sinister-looking men and victimized buxom women splashed across the covers. My meeting planned with Franklin must have been a setup, arranged by whoever sent the forged note. The ledgers were gone, possibly already in the hands of Gates. I threw the drawer against the wall, then collapsed onto the bed.

"It doesn't match this handwriting either," Mae said, paging through the lighthouse logbooks. "Got entries here from both Cephas and Polly, and the handwriting on the note doesn't match. So, it's not Franklin, Polly, or Cephas. That really narrows the field for suspects from the harbor."

"We have to go," I said. "It's not safe."

"Go where?" Mae asked. "We're not even packed."

"Better start," I said. "We don't have much time."

I was tired of losing. Franklin had talked big about how we needed to act like real men, but things didn't feel so dignified or heroic, having been tricked, bamboozled, and outmaneuvered.

#

An hour before dusk, hooting and hollering arose from the marina. The workers stopped their spraying and digging, and congregated around the trolley station. Gates stood in the middle of it all with his jacket off, a good six inches taller than anyone around him. Two of the crew had pulled up the decking between the building and the tracks, and removed several boxes from underneath, each surrounded by their own black cloud of flies. A cheer arose from the men as they carried the crates away from the station and onto the shore. The men slapped backs and hugged one another, thrilled with their newfound treasure.

Gates picked up one of the boxes. Three other attendants followed him, each carrying a similar crate toward the lighthouse. Cephas and I watched nervously from the walkway as the men climbed the stairs, quietly and deliberately. The acrid, fetid smell grew stronger with every step as they approached us. Cephas turned away and covered his nose with a hankie.

"You wouldn't listen," Gates said. "Fought me every step of the way. You cried about the poor villagers while they busily hatched plans for stinking up my lodge."

He slammed the box down onto the lighthouse walkway, the thick brown goo splashing from it, along with fish skins, fish heads, animal carcasses, bones, and entrails. He made sure that it sloshed up on our pant legs, onto the immaculate cream-colored brick lighthouse walls. I could feel the coolness of the slime soaking through my clothes and knew that any attempt to rub it off would only work the mess deeper into the fabric.

"Fish and varmints," Gates hollered. "Guts, skins, entrails, bones, maggots, slime, and flies."

He picked up a slime-covered carcass, holding it high for everyone to see. "A skunk! A disgorged skunk! Look at that tail. What sick asshole would use skunks?"

Gates threw the remains at me, then grabbed the second box and flung it across the path, spilling a slimy string of heads, spines, and intestines across what earlier was a freshly raked gravel walkway. Flies coated our legs and arms and swarmed across our faces. Gates kept kicking at the crate, the juice from the fish and skunk parts spraying all over our pants and the lighthouse walls.

"A dozen crates of the worst shit you could ever imagine stacked under the decking at the trolley station. I'm sure they're finding the same crap up at the lodge. Someone must have worked every night for weeks to prepare for this little prank."

While Gates tormented us and methodically befouled the lighthouse, a mob of his attendants struck like a swarm of hornets below us at the lighthouse dock. With screams and hollers, they ran back and forth across the dock, throwing anything owned by the villagers into the lake. The eviction had begun. Before the fish guts, it might have been an orderly and humane expulsion. Now there was an unmistakable bitterness— barrels, fish boxes, fishing nets, fishing tackle, gaff hooks, and anchors were tossed. Even the large reels used for drying fishing nets were heaved into the lake. Everything heavy sank to the bottom. The lighter items floated like the flotsam and jetsam of a shipwreck.

By the time the fishermen reached the dock, all of the villagers' belongings from shore had already been tossed in the water. The fishermen launched their boats to recover whatever they could, many of their possessions already floating off to the middle of the harbor. The mob ignored the men, instead running up the lighthouse stairs to the villagers' cottage where the eviction would soon get even nastier.

I easily pushed through Gates, planning to head off the eviction mob as they approached the locked cottage where Mae, Rose, Anna, and Nora hid. I could have cut them off, if not for losing my footing in the slop and slime and landing hard against the rail. Within seconds, two of the box-carrying goons lifted me from the walkway and hauled me back to Gates. I struggled to get free and craned my neck backward, watching helplessly as the mob broke through the door of the villagers' cottage. They rushed in as Mae, Rose, Anna, and Nora ran out. The women headed down the stairs to the shore as the pillaging continued, the villagers' belongings from the cabin being tossed over the cliff.

Gates grabbed a fistful of my hair, jerking my head around to face him. "You ugly one-eyed bastard." He pulled me in, our noses just inches apart, flies flitting back and forth between us. He smeared a handful of slop across my coat and spit on my lapel.

"Thought you were so smart? You and your buddies thought you had me over a barrel? A bunch of water maggots and a worthless piece of disfigured crap like you?"

I tried pulling away, craning my head to watch the ravaging of the villagers' cottage. Gates droned on, emphasizing his disgust in the villagers and me with staccato expletive-filled outbursts. My muscles ached from grappling with the men behind me, one twisting an arm, the other holding me in a headlock with his arm tight across my throat. Gates still had a handful of my hair and jerked violently every time he needed more attention from me.

Reality, reason, and logic slipped away into a dark, dreamlike state. Fish gut smells, jabbering from Gates, jerky scuffling from the goons behind me, and stabbing pains, all faded to the background. Sensory overload melted into a tunnel vision similar to what I had experienced fighting in the foxholes, where smoke, explosions, screaming, and gunfire melted away in a singular focus on whatever shape lay in my sights. Now I singularly focused on the mob blackheartedly tossing whatever the villagers owned over the cliff. Heavy items dropped like stones, bouncing off the rocks below. Lighter stuff fluttered off with the wind, landing far out into the harbor. Back and forth, they ran, from cottage to rail, with clothes, rain gear, tools, housewares, fishing tackle, and linens. It didn't last long—the villagers didn't own much. Soon, all of the villagers were out in their boats, weaving from one floating item to the next, rescuing what they could. The mob regathered on the shore, pelting the villagers' boats with rocks.

Gates paid no attention to the siege against the villagers and continued his assault on the lighthouse. With a sick laugh, he tossed handfuls of offal up against the cream-colored bricks, leaving patchworks of puke-brown streaks and splotches that reached a good twelve feet above the pathway. After catching his breath, he turned almost sympathetically to Cephas.

"How will you ever pass inspection?" Gates asked, talking as if he actually cared. "Inspection is tomorrow. If you're to have any chance in hell of retiring, you'll be working all night cleaning this mess up." Gates grabbed handfuls of guts, throwing them well out of reach, high up onto the lighthouse walls. "Even those spots way up there."

Cephas stood resolute, his hands folded across his chest.

"Must have been the villagers, eh?" Gates asked. "They must've spent days to make all this happen. Likely took the whole village. Jonah, is this what your little pack of harbor rats has been up to?"

After recovering anything recoverable, the villagers' boats came together in the middle of the harbor, out of reach of the stone-throwing mob. They paused, as if collectively searching for any alternative other than surrendering their harbor. Then, as if on cue, they raised the sails, and the boats headed out of the harbor to the northeast.

I struggled loose, grabbing Gates around the neck, pulling

him down to the ground. His goons quickly pulled me off of him and pinned me flat on my back. Gates struggled to his feet, the slop on his pants and coat weighing him down. I turned away to avoid the guts kicked in my face. Almost blinded, I caught a glimpse of Cephas holding a pitchfork in the background, just as Gates picked up the last crate and dumped it over my face. I shook my head wildly from side to side, unable to breathe, choking on the offal.

#

Feeling the grips loosen from my arms, I struggled to breathe. Cephas drove the attendants away with his pitchfork. I turned over on my hands and knees and watched Gates and his men back off slowly and deliberately, then follow the stairs back to the marina. I sputtered, coughed, then pulled myself to my feet, my heart beating its way through my ribcage. The villagers' boats slid past the large granite base of the lighthouse, heading northeast toward Stygg Havn.

"You ok? Can you breathe?" Cephas dropped the pitchfork and grabbed me under my armpit to help. I pulled away and ran, rushing across the lighthouse property, thinking only of catching up with the villagers.

The path from the lighthouse to Stygg Havn was nothing but a narrow deer trail with plenty of roots for tripping and branches for scraping. Through the trees, I caught an occasional glimpse of the waters out past Stygg Havn but never a clear enough view to spot the villagers' boats.

I emerged from the woods into shadows, the sun having set behind the steep hillside that ran along the length of the bay. By now, the boats had sailed well beyond the shallows, just four small dots out in a huge expanse of water. Traveling at a decent pace with the wind behind them, they moved to the northeast. I ran to the water's edge, yelling and waving my arms, watching for any perceptible response. I just knew Mae wouldn't leave me behind. I knew she'd look out for me, just as I would for her. Still, there was no indication of the boats slowing or turning in toward shore.

It never occurred to me that the villagers' eviction would come so suddenly or with such violence. I knew they couldn't stay forever, yet I expected it to be more orderly, with me leaving as one of them. Mae and I were now engaged. That made me part of the clan, although it didn't feel that way. Not with me onshore and the rest of them sailing away.

The boats were already halfway across Stygg Havn, having sailed even farther from shore. I ran through waves up to my knees, trying to follow their progression, kicking, screaming, and flapping my arms. With legs numb from the cold, I lost my footing twice and fell into the icy water. The boats were nearly impossible to see by now, nothing but specks that disappeared and came back into view with the rolling crests. My whole body ached from the cold. I slowed as they reached the high cliffs of Gull Point, too far away for them to spot me. With no more reason to yell or wave, I stopped and watched as they rounded the cliffs, drifting out of sight.

Collapsing on the shore, I laid on my back to catch my breath. The muffled cheers and laughter from the lodge taunted me. The stench, sight, and feel of my clothes soaked in fish guts offended my senses, in a way much worse than the sickly sweet smell of manure ever did back home. I brushed the slime, chunks of fish, and carcass parts from my pants and coat, watching as the first stars of the night appeared with the darkness.

I felt terribly alone and cast aside. Different from the "by myself" times on the farm. This was more painful—a deep, dark disassociation. Disconnected from everyone. Not belonging at the lodge or lighthouse and now separated from the villagers. A lifetime of aloneness weighed me down, shutting me off from the joy of being engaged to Mae.

Before Stony Point, I had already given up on love. I'd come to the lighthouse looking for solitude. I quickly became an outcast, but I didn't mind. I'd been one before and knew how to get by. I would have worked the late-night shifts at the lighthouse with a comfortable indifference, carving figurines and enjoying the majesty of the lake. Cephas and Gates would have granted me that much. Gates hadn't stolen my solitude. It was the villagers and my affection for Mae that wrested me from isolation and rekindled the flames of love. A love so improbable. Not born from Saturday night dances or church potlucks, but from necessity and coincidence—the bandaging of wounds, little figurine gifts for Rose, and Mae's sewing of my new eye patch. Not your typical courtship. We tangled together before we even began to love. Now the safe, unfeeling state of aloneness was irretrievable. The doors to loneliness and broken hearts were now opened wide.

As the sky darkened, the constellations came into view. I picked out the Big Dipper, Little Dipper, Cassiopeia, and Orion. Constellations for the loners and losers. Constellations that don't judge or criticize. They just listen in silence. I could only hope that Mae too lay on a beach somewhere, staring at the same constellations, missing me just as much as I missed her.

Five hundred yards away on the part of Stygg Havn that approached the shacks, two boats maneuvered through the rocks before landing on shore. I laid low to stay out of sight while men with kerosene lanterns and tools marched from the shoreline to the small shacks. With sledges, pry bars, and hammers, they demolished the huts built only days before, heaping all the nail-infested boards into a large pile. After a good soaking of kerosene, they lit the pile.

Stygg Havn. A place that nobody wanted, built by people who never planned to live there, for reasons that had nothing to do with shelter or community. The builder knew all along that it was completely unsuitable for its intended inhabitants. The villagers rejected it as worse than being homeless. And now it was all mine. My belly of the whale, both hostile and bleak.

The Jonah of the Bible would have prayed. I could only curse those who had left me alone in such a horrible place.

As the men rowed back to Stony Point, I stripped naked and washed in the lake. The ice-cold water triggered spasms throughout every limb and muscle, but ridding myself of the slime and the stench made it worth the pain. In knee-deep water,

I washed the fish parts and stench from the clothes, scrubbing and rinsing as my legs grew too numb to stand. After wringing out the laundry, I hung it by the fire to dry.

The flames reached a good twenty feet in the air, a large plume of black smoke stretching out across the lake. Like a long dark finger, it smudged across the lighthouse's white beam — Cephas's "Eye of the Lord." His place for safety and salvation for all.

#

The wee hours were always magical as a lighthouse keeper. A restful time with the lodge guests finally retired, giving the keep a sense of dominion over everything below—from the lodge, throughout the harbor, and out across the water. A time for smoking pipes, carving figurines, and thinking big thoughts about the nature of the world. A time to reflect on good things—remembering the happy times from the past and planning for those good times yet to come.

The wee hours at Stygg Havn were different. Primordial, naked, and abandoned. I circled the roaring fire like a man consumed. Stygg Havn had no fond memories nor wholesome aspirations. This was a place haunted by dark desires, sabotage, and revenge. A place for settling scores and setting traps.

Gunnar's fish gut and carcass attack both encouraged and disappointed. It had been an extensive endeavor of nights spent filling boxes, Gunnar steeping his sordid stew, then cleverly hiding dozens of the boxes across the lodge and the harbor. How creative and clever. What a thrill to have created such a disruption with the wretched stench and the disgusting flies. Yet, in the end, it had hardly made an impact, just revealed the resilience and invincibility of the lodge. After a day of panic, the mess would be cleaned, the disaster averted. Stony Fest was saved, and the villagers' eviction was complete.

With a long stick, I flicked the burning boards and coals back into the middle of the fire. I needed the heat for drying clothes and the smoke for repelling mosquitos. And the crackling sounds and shooting embers helped me concentrate.

I needed something more impactful, something that would cause more damage than swarms, smells, inconvenience, and annoyance. The ledgers would have been the perfect death blow, exposing the whole bootleg operation, incriminating everyone from the suppliers all the way through the guests. The ledgers would have made Stony Point front-page news in papers across the country, exposing spoiled young millionaires for their excess, hypocrisy, and indecency. Duluth's social elite would have crumbled, becoming the cause célèbre for every Woman's Christian Temperance Union chapter across the country. Unfortunately, the ledgers had disappeared, and there was nothing I could do about it. Not in the wee hours anyway. I needed another way to destroy Gates.

The fire died down into a pile of burning embers and blackened nails. My clothes were mostly dry, and the mosquitos began to bite. The crescent moon hung over the lighthouse, occasionally obscured by clouds. I dressed and went back up to the cottages to get supplies for whatever defilement I might concoct. Hopefully, inspiration would come to me in the wee hours.

#

The cottages and the barns had been ransacked again, even after the eviction. Drawers pulled, cushions tossed, housewares strewn, and personal items destroyed. I took it as a positive sign, an indication that Gates was still searching for something he considered important and threatening, like the ledgers. In the barns, anything once stored up in the rafters or on the shelves now created a hazardous tangle of clutter across the floor.

I muscled a wheelbarrow through the mess to the outside, then loaded it with anything sharp, heavy, or otherwise destructive—any implement of subversion I might find useful. I packed knives, saws, hammers, rakes, and shovels around the sides, surrounding four heavy kegs of nails and screws in the middle.

After navigating the wheelbarrow through the woods to the recently completed Highway One, I had the choice of going right or left. Right would take me to Beaver Creek, the friendly little community where Franklin had paid for my Lumberjack Special breakfast. It would have been the safe choice, leaving behind both Stony Point and my failed attempt as a lighthouse keeper. It must have been the Rosco in me that pulled me toward unsettled scores and injustices, not letting me turn away. Strange that righteousness would be my guiding principle on a night of such crudeness and vulgarity. Rosco won out, and I chose left—to retaliate rather than escape.

I headed southwest. Only days ago, the road had remained unfinished, packed with mule teams, wagons, scrapers, and graders. Now, the finished Highway One stretched from Duluth to the lighthouse, its gravel roadbed nicely crowned and sloped to shed water from rains or the spring melt. It stood a good two feet higher than the ditch running on either side, to keep it from flooding. The surface was as smooth as water on a windless night—no ruts, potholes, or washouts. Cities from Duluth to Grand Marais had claimed that Highway One would be the most scenic roadway in all of the United States, with breathtaking views of the lake interspersed by waterfalls, cascading creeks, and large rock outcroppings. Gates had planned Stony Fest to coincide with its opening, knowing his clientele would clamor for the opportunity to drive the new highway in their incredible automobiles. Rather than relying only on steamer traffic, the lodge would now have the majority of its guests arriving by car.

The stars glittered in the sky, a small sliver of moon doing nothing to chase away the darkness. I noticed the glow of kerosene lanterns around the truck warehouse as I passed, the garage doors swung wide open, men bustling about as if in the middle of their workday. One of the trucks stood running next to the pump, being filled up with gas. Three other trucks waited their turn. Two had their hoods up, men leaning over the fenders, their heads buried deep in the engine compartment. And men with two-wheel carts ran among the trucks, hauling cases back and forth. I walked on the far side of the road to avoid detection.

The lodge came into view a bit farther down the road, glowing bright beyond fields full of automobiles that covered every patch of lawn and garden from the roadway all the way up to the front patio. Not your ordinary Maxwells or Model Ts; these were the Packards, Duesenbergs, Cadillacs, and Pierce Arrows, befitting of Duluth's finest. Across the road from the lodge, a large area had been leveled, creating additional parking for the flood of cars expected throughout the weekend—an area twice as large as the lodge's front lawn, already filled with roadsters and limousines.

A short distance from the lodge, the road descended and narrowed, falling into the sharp hairpin turn carved into the side of a granite cliff. Along the left edge of the road, a row of posts strung with cable created an insubstantial barrier, protecting cars from a fifty-foot drop to the rocky shoreline below. On the right side, a wall of granite rose thirty feet above the roadbed. In the middle of the turn, the road narrowed dangerously, making it a gamble if any two cars should meet on the curve.

As I descended the hill, thinking too much about cliffs, granite walls, and hairpin curves, the barrow's wheel caught the edge of the roadway, jerking the heavy load off to the right. I overcorrected, trying to stabilize the weight, which caused the whole load to dump into the smooth gravel surface. The tools fell off to the side. The kegs of nails and screws lost their tops upon impact. The kegs rolled down the hill, leaving a wide swath of nails and screws stretching across the roadway.

My first instinct was to clean it up. In the dim light from the moon, I loaded the tools and now-empty kegs back into the wheelbarrow, rolling it behind a patch of small pines on the side of the road. With a dirt rake, I attempted to remove the spilled nails and screws. It only made things worse, embedding the little spikes deeper into the gravel, making the roadway even more dangerous.

Stepping back to better assess the situation, the wondrousness of my mess became apparent. Ahead of me lay a glorious road hazard that stranded each of the treasured vehicles already at the lodge and cut off access to all those who would be arriving in the coming days. Gates suddenly had a huge logistical nightmare that would lay a big rotten egg all over his Stony Fest booze party.

I didn't want to kill anybody. The last thing I wanted was some Packard full of men blowing its tires, losing control, and careening full speed over a cliff. I hoped to avoid broken bones or bloody messes. But this nail patch promised to be the major disruption, a calamity big enough to cause real heartburn for everyone involved. Something to attract reporters and photographers, who would uncover and report on all the lawlessness of the lodge. Notoriety that could destroy Gates.

I needed front-page news. Reporters knocking at the doorstep of the Stony Point Lodge, peeking inside, seeing the drunks, and smelling the whisky. If fish guts couldn't destroy Gates, then a bunch of enterprising reporters with a nose for scandal just might. At any rate, I now had a hundred-yard patch of roadway shimmering edge-to-edge with nails. Rather inconvenient for the lodge, whose busiest day had begun.

7 EXODUS

I woke to crushing sounds. Sharp as thunder, rumbling like steam shovels, as deafening as coal dumped into nearby railcars. Cold and stiff from sleeping on the ground, I didn't know where I was or where the horrible noise was coming from. The sun had only minutes earlier risen above the eastern horizon, painting a splash of orange across the morning wisp of clouds.

A glow from headlights came from below, along with enough peppery sweet whisky vapors to leave a man thirsty for a drink. As the crashing noise subsided, it gave way to the sounds of running engines and hurried hushed voices. That's when I remembered the nails. A roadbed full of them, spreading from a rock face on one side, across to a sheer cliff on the other.

I recalled retreating to higher ground after a late-night raking of the roadbed. Now sitting on the hillside as the morning sky lightened, I had a clear view of the roadway, south from the Barberry Creek Bridge, all the way north past the lighthouse. Below were four vehicles, their headlights shining off in all directions. Four spanking new dark-green Chevrolet Superior stake trucks, the same as the ones passed only hours ago, in front of the warehouse. Each suffered from a full set of punctured tires, leaving them scattered across the roadway as a child might leave toy trucks strewn in a sandbox.

The first truck laid on top of two sheared-off guardrail posts, its bumper tangled in the cable barrier that likely saved it from a fifty-foot drop to the shoreline below. The second truck had flipped in an attempt to avoid the first. The last two trucks each slammed into the one overturned, creating a pileup that littered the roadway with fenders, bumpers, running boards, and shiny chrome trim. Steam blasted from the broken radiators, and shards from the windshield shone like glistening jewels across the roadbed. The truck's hidden compartments—disguised to look like full loads of lumber—were torn off, dumping the concealed cases of whisky across the road, where splintered wood and broken bottles mixed in with the broken truck parts. Pools of whisky formed around each of the twisted truck bodies before running off into the gullies on either side of the road.

This was the satisfying retaliation I'd hoped for. Certainly justifiable, considering the brutality of the villagers' evacuation and my own near-suffocation in fish-gut slime. Now a horrendous mess lay before me that would have made Gunnar proud and would surely spoil the Stony Fest celebration. A catastrophe more complex than just a handful of crushed cars. This roadbed of nails and screws sliced straight through the artery of Gates's operations, cutting off both guests and booze shipments—at least until someone figured out a way to make the road safe and passable again. Gates would soon have an army of his men trying to move the trucks from a roadbed too dangerous to walk on. Even if they managed the removal of the twisted truck frames and broken booze bottles, there would still be the challenge of extracting thousands of nails and screws embedded in the gravel. Digging up the highway and resurfacing it seemed the only option, one that would leave the lodge in isolation for weeks.

The road closing had happened at the worst possible time for Gates. Dozens of Duluth's finest automobiles were already at the lodge, now stranded until the roadway cleared. Dozens more were on their way up from Duluth and would need to turn back, with no parking available south of the road closure. And who would have guessed that Gates's bootleg shipments, heading to who knows where, would be the first victims of the befouled roadway?

Even more damaging, news of the accidents causing Highway One's closure would attract hordes of nosey reporters snooping around and potentially uncovering juicier stories of misbehaving millionaires and brazen bootlegging. Only a short walking distance from the wreckage, they would find the decadence that newspapers crave, scandals brazen enough to make the newsworthiness of the accident pale in comparison to the goings-on at Stony Point.

Never before had I caused so much trouble. This went well beyond tipping outhouses or spiking punch. Then again, Gates deserved as much pain and suffering as I could possibly cause. If it resulted in the closing of Gates's bootleg operation and the return of the harbor to the rightful owners, then the closing of the road had a worthy purpose.

For a moment, everything was calm, but I knew the stillness wouldn't last. Leaving the trucks and debris scattered across the roadway, the drivers had already hiked back to the warehouse, walking as a group. Gates was likely still sleeping, calmed by the knowledge that the fish guts, the villagers' eviction, and the Stygg Havn buildings had all been dealt with. Yet some unlucky attendant would soon wake him, inform him of the crash, and set off a firestorm of panic across the lodge and throughout the harbor. I intended to be a safe distance away by then.

Barberry Creek was at the end of the cool and quiet path leading from the ridge into the gully. My footsteps crunched on the leaves and twigs underfoot. The sun poked through the branches with little pinpoints of light, casting colors among the shadows surrounding me. The waterfall rumbled as I approached, an endless cascade of the world's natural order. A woodpecker hammered away at a dead pine tree with rapid bursts that sounded like machine-gun fire, followed by silence, before another woodpecker deep in the woods pounded off its reply.

Dragonflies skimmed across the surface of the pond while swallows darted back and forth above them, catching just-hatched black stoneflies. I walked up one side of the creek, some distance above the waterfall, then walked back down past the pool, retracing the steps Mae, Rose, and I had taken in our earlier visits. I sat on the same rock where we'd eaten our lunch and waded into the pool, where Mae and I had shared long, loving embraces. Today, the magic wasn't there, and even the memories had died.

Finding an aspen branch from along the edge of the woods, I began to carve. Something modest. A simple elongated heart the size of an oak leaf. It took me less than ten minutes to rough out the general shape. As the larger shavings peeled away and scattered across the rock, my mind wandered, thinking about the second ransacking at the lighthouse. It had happened after the villagers' eviction, hours after I'd discovered the ledger already missing from the false drawer bottom. I had assumed that Gates had already found the books, but if he had, there wouldn't have been a second ransacking. This meant someone else must've removed the incriminating ledger from the hiding place, or it was still in the cottage.

With the general shape completed, I smoothed the wood, scraping it with my knife blade at a ninety-degree angle to the wood surface, which planed away any roughness. I scraped as if by instinct, my mind still fully occupied with the ledger, wondering if I might still find it. I had to check the cottage one more time to make sure before I made my escape.

It took me five more minutes to carve the initials J+M across the front of the heart. It wasn't my best work, relatively flat and unadorned. It had none of the usual detail or emotion. It reminded me of a piece that some school kid might make for his sweetheart with his Boy Scout knife. Slightly classier than cutting initials into a tree. I considered something more intricate, but I knew my time would be better spent searching for the ledger.

I swept the shavings into a pile and perched the heart upright in the middle. If Mae passed by, it would let her know how much I missed her. I put my shoes on, rolled my pant legs down, and said my good-byes to Barberry Creek—the waterfall to the right, the pool, and the creek flowing off to Superior from the left. A place that felt so far away yet was nothing but a short walk through the woods from the site of the accident.

#

At the hairpin turn on Highway One, my little nail patch was now quite the attraction. I returned to my perch above the roadway to watch a dozen attendants slowly cleaning things up, collecting unbroken bottles and placing them into cases, or gathering loose truck parts, piling them along the roadway's edge. Gates presided from the middle of it all, wearing dungarees and a Henley collared worker's shirt. He barked at attendants, directing them to rake this, shovel that, lift here, and push there. These were the same men already demoralized by the whole fish gut fiasco, having spent the previous day killing flies and chasing smells. The weeks of incredible optimism in preparing the harbor had now given way to a collective discontent in dealing with the recurrent acts of vandalism. With brunch buffets to organize, games to set up, boats to launch, and drinks to serve, they didn't have the time for such interruptions.

One man among those surveying the crash site wore a lighthouse keeper's uniform with badges and sashes that suggested a much higher rank. He was a short, distinguished man with gray hair and spectacles; I assumed him to be the Lighthouse Service Superintendent, who must have arrived before dawn. The inspection had been planned for the morning and might have already started if not for the accident. The superintendent stood to the side with his arms crossed, shaking his head back and forth disapprovingly in response to the mess in front of him.

A steady stream of guests wandered down from the lodge to gawk, reminiscent of the way crowds watch burning buildings. Some appeared concerned, understanding the gravity of the situation. Most enjoyed the excitement of the big crash. The more adventurous jumped right into the nail-infested roadway to collect unbroken whisky bottles for themselves. Along the roadside, they argued over where the nails and screws might have come from, where the whisky was going, and how best to clean up the mess. Whenever attempts were made to lift an overturned vehicle or untangle the truck from the guardrail, a flurry of yelling and waving exploded through the crowd as guests placed bets among themselves on whether the attendants would succeed or fail. Gates couldn't have orchestrated a more entertaining morning. The sailing, rowing, and games would have to wait. The crash had become the day's main event.

From my vantage point on the hill, I could see the first cars of the morning racing up Highway One from the south. A caravan of ten roadsters zagged through the twists and turns of the road heading up to the lodge. The cars accelerated as they climbed the slight rise just before the hairpin curve, speeding around the corner and into the roadbed full of nails before anyone could warn them.

At the speed they were going, they may have crashed even without the flattened tires caused by the screws and nails. The first spun around after blasting into the truck tangled in the guardrail cables. The second crashed broadside into the first with a terrible crunch, creating a chain reaction of torn metal and broken parts ripping from both cars. The third car rear-ended the second with an equally impressive burst, its front torn apart as if hit by some explosive. Luggage strapped to the backs or tied to rooftops broke off upon impact, sprinkling the whole accident site with suit jackets, pleated pants, fair isle sweaters, fedoras, and straw boater hats. Engines smoked, gasoline leaked, and axels laid broken. Yet the real horrors were the sights and sounds of drivers and passengers pitched against dashboards, doors, and steering wheels. Attendants carried the injured men past the crashes, nails, and screws, to lay them on a clean stretch of roadbed.

I fell flat onto my belly, subconsciously making myself as invisible as possible. Hugging the hill overlooking the nail patch, emotions trampled over me—a flood of disbelief, an instinct to help rescue, a compulsion to flee, and a self-delusion that things might not be as bad as they seemed or that I wasn't really responsible. With my head in my hands, I tried to process, trying my best to avoid the guilt and remorse. Regrets would cloud my mind as long as the images of the injured men lingered.

The fourth car in line had been conservative enough to slow down before hitting the curve. Its tires still flattened, but the driver stopped before crashing. After him, the remaining six cars stopped without incident, filling both north and southbound lanes in an orderly fashion.

A cloud of gloom descended among the young millionaire guests. The jabbering, joking, and wagering came to a halt. Solemnity replaced the fun and frolic, now that their own wealthy compatriots were the ones injured. Having fetched supplies from the main building, attendants returned with makeshift stretchers and first-aid kits. Those who needed help were carried to the lodge, while the rest received treatment along the road for cuts and bruises with compresses, ointments, and bandages. Some guests helped. Most just left, no longer entertained, and formed a melancholy column slowly walking back to the lodge.

#

I never meant to hurt anyone. Not the broken bone, dripping blood kind of hurt. I wanted justice. I sought atonement for the burning of the village, Hans's death, and unfair evictions. I'd convinced myself that my motives were noble, yet deep down, I knew the act of sabotage came from a darker place—from the festering aloneness of Stygg Havn, the humiliations caused by Gates, and the abandonment by the villagers. It came from rage, borne from my own pain and degradation. I'd lashed out against the indignities that had ruined my life for all those years since the war. I struck out against Jenny, my ex-wife, and Fred, her new rich husband. Against the overprivileged young millionaires and the acerbic sensibilities of Polly. And, of course, I had completely lost control with my hatred of Gates.

Franklin made it all sound so glorified, his bold encouragement for me to fight back, to act with dignity, pursue worthy causes, and take heroic actions. Now young men were severely injured in the roadway because of my actions—acts of good or evil, depending on your point of view. Heroism or terrorism, two sides of the same coin, separated only by perspective. Sinners against saints and saints against sinners. All one and the same. Now I was both. For me, revenge didn't satisfy as I'd hoped it would. Things had become too complicated, with heavy doses of remorse and second-guessing. Someday, Gunnar and I might sit around a campfire telling the next generation how we saved the village. For the moment, it didn't feel like anything to be proud of.

The damage had a trajectory of its own. They carried the injured up to the lodge. The young millionaires, who only minutes ago had placed bets over the cleanup of the truck accidents, now gathered in small, somber groups, fretting over the troubling turn of events. The fun and frolic of Stony Fest were squashed, now considered frivolous and irreverent. Boat rides, games, buffets, and drinks were all on hold, so as not to inflame the growing sense of unease among the guests.

I'd done more than enough. Now I needed to escape—after a visit to the lighthouse to check the cottage one last time for the ledger—just to make sure nothing would be left behind in my haste to escape. A final check for the documents that held the legal proof required for destroying all of Gates's operations and justifying my actions.

I walked through the woods, away from the crowds, to avoid being seen. The harbor now sat abandoned. The Hacker-Craft, still covered, rocked back and forth against the pier. Sailboats and rowboats remained up along the shore, the shoreline devoid of all its changing tents and beach umbrellas. One solitary guest sat with his two trunks in the middle of the pier, awaiting the arrival of the steamer, due in about an hour.

On the near side of the harbor, the superintendent's steel-hulled lighthouse ship dominated the dock. She blew smoke from her coal-fired boilers, the large stack towering over the relatively small pilothouse. Both the dock and the ship appeared unattended.

The lighthouse was a sorry mess. Cephas worked alone,

slowly pouring a large stockpot full of boiling water onto the befouled walkway to remove the offal. The steam rose with the thick smell of rotting fish.

"Superintendent arrived last night," Cephas said, setting down the empty stockpot. "He says I need to fire you." Cephas grabbed the broom to sweep the now-greasy water off the walkway, over the rock face.

"Least of my worries," I replied.

"Doesn't matter much. Just look at this place. I'll be fired too, whenever they get around to it."

Cephas had likely been scrubbing, rinsing, and sweeping all night. Still, he had hardly made a dent in the slimy mess. I followed him as he walked back to the main cottage to boil more water. On a bench next to the door lay a collection of screwdrivers, putty knives, and ice picks, each of them covered with slime having been used to clean the guts and carcass parts from cracks and crevices around the lighthouse.

Inside, Cephas refilled the stockpot with water and put it on the stove to heat, then wiped his hands with a dishrag before sitting at the table. He pulled the tobacco pouch from his pocket and filled the pipe, lit it, rotating the match around the bowl.

"I know you've never been a sailor, but can't you see how someone might fear a Jonah? How a Jonah might be bad luck?" Cephas didn't sound angry or blaming. Just matter of fact.

"What else could explain all this? Fish guts, ransacks, nails, road closures, accidents . . . And I just know those guests are bound to panic. Just wait and see. First sign of trouble and they'll all go crazy."

"I'll pack up and leave," I said. "That should improve your luck."

"Better hurry," he said, pointing out the window with the stem of his pipe. "That steamer's bound to fill up quickly."

Moments ago, there were only two trunks on the lodge pier. Now, a large pile of them spread from the tip of the Hacker-Craft all the way to the shore, an unhappy crowd milling about.

"Rumors," Cephas said. "I bet there's some rumor about reporters or revenuers on their way to the lodge. They're panicking, thinking they'll get caught. Those boys are about to run like rabbits."

#

Other than the large pot of water simmering on the stove, the cottage was quiet. Cephas smoked his pipe, watching the lodge guests from the window as they pushed their way onto the pier. I climbed the stairs to search one last time for the ledger. My room was as I'd left it the night before, the broken bottom drawer thrown against the wall, all my belongings strewn about from the ransacking. I checked common hiding places like underneath mattresses or behind furniture, finding nothing but dust bunnies and cobwebs. I kicked through the rubbish on the floor, then looked underneath the rug. Still nothing.

I came to the realization that by now, my bedroom would be the least likely of places to find the ledger. With my steamer trunk on the bed, I loaded it with clothes picked from the mess on the floor. Once filled, I kicked a path through the rummage and dragged the heavy trunk out of the room and down the stairs. I didn't even notice Gates until I reached the bottom stair.

"Hey, fella. Going somewhere?" Gates stood next to the table, still in his dungarees and Henley collared shirt, now pit-stained and covered with grime. Being the most important day of Stony Fest and knowing his guests were about to stampede the steamer, I assumed he'd have matters more pressing than me to deal with. Cephas stood in the kitchen with his back to us, suddenly preoccupied with putting all the kitchenware back in the cabinets. Gates stepped in front of me as I dragged my trunk toward the door, blocking my progress. He pulled a letter from his pocket and threw it on the table in front of me—the same letter I had assumed was mailed to Franklin, telling him of the ledger's successful decoding.

"Look familiar?" Gates asked. "It's all about my coded ledger book and how you cracked the secret code. Says that the information would be ruinous for the guests and damning for me. It says I'll be locked up for good. You really think I'd let that happen?"

I tried to push past, but Gates pushed harder, backing me up against my steamer trunk and the table.

"Pretty stupid for you to send such a subversive communication from here. I go through all the lighthouse mail. I even wrote Franklin's reply, telling you to meet him today with the ledger when the steamer arrives."

I'd never seen Gates so disheveled. He wore unwashed dirty work clothes, rings of sweat circled under his arms, his oiled hair flopped down over his eyes. No boutonniere, no cream-colored suit, no pretense of high society.

The trunk leaned against my leg, putting me off balance as I reached over the table to grab the letter. If not for the trunk, my reactions might have been different. I watched as Gates's hand rose high above the table, then came down straight over mine, with a sharp pain like nothing I'd ever experienced. Not like smashed or broken bones. This was different. Unnatural. Terribly wrong. When I tried to pull away, a sharp jabbing pain halted even the slightest movement. Blood pooled underneath my hand, sticky on my thumb and fingers.

Gates stared, focusing on our two hands, his directly above mine. As he slowly removed his, I could see the ice pick handle standing straight, the pick jabbed through the back of my hand, an inch above my wrist between the metacarpals of my middle and ring finger. Gates had my hand impaled, nailed to the pine tabletop with the pick. I gasped, as much from the gruesome sight as the pain.

My natural instinct was to pull the pick out. As I reached for the handle, Gates grabbed the coat sleeve of my skewered hand, jerking my arm back and forth. Pain radiated through my whole arm as the wound stretched and ripped against the pick's thin metal shaft. I stood, grabbing him with my free hand to make him stop, but had neither the leverage nor the strength to stop the sickening pain. By now, a sloppy ring of torn flesh circled the shank of the pick, the white tendons standing out against the crimson-red blood. I screamed with an anguished bellow that I'd only heard once before: the time I lost my eye during the war.

"Don't ever touch that pick again," Gates said with controlled tension. He pounded the pick farther into the tabletop with a stoneware mug from the table. After five blows, the mug shattered. He grabbed a second one and continued pounding until the bottom of the pick handle came within an inch from the top of my hand.

"That should hold you for a while. Don't go anywhere."

Cephas stood motionless in the kitchen, facing away as if too mortified to either watch or move. The big pot started to boil, but Cephas left it on the fire. Gates turned his attention from my torture to my steamer trunk.

"What have you been hiding from me?" he asked. "Something you planned to give to Franklin? Something that belongs to me?"

He popped the latches on the trunk and flung the top open. After reaching in through the clothes and not finding what he was looking for, he dumped the contents and threw the trunk against the wall. He kicked through the pile of clothes, sifted through my belongings, then dropped hard into the chair across from me, his steel-blue eyes fixed in a glare, scanning for the slightest of reactions, emotions, or reflexes. He took my eye patch off and threw it on the floor before wrapping his fingers tight around the cuff of my jacket sleeve, next to my impaled hand.

"Let go," I begged. "Just tell me what you need."

"Where's my ledger?"

"I don't know," I answered honestly. I stood, leaning hard against the top of my arm, using my weight to keep the impaled hand as motionless as possible.

"Wrong answer."

Gates pushed me away while yanking the jacket sleeve back and forth, tearing the flesh of my impaled hand against the ice pick. My screams turned to yelps as I became short of breath and lost the energy to respond. From the corner of my eye, I watched Cephas flinch with each of my outcries.

"Steamer's here, Gates! Steamer just arrived!" Cephas remained frozen but began yelling frantically, as if his nonsensical gibberish might somehow pull Gates away from the gruesome torture.

"In the harbor! Steamer's here to pick up all those guests." His voice screeched an octave higher than normal, and he pointed with both hands at the same time.

"Steamer's stopped. Right in the middle of the harbor. Just stopped."

Gates looked quickly over his shoulder, then went back to work, viciously yanking my coat sleeve.

"Where's my ledger?" Gates growled. "I read your letter. You planned to give the book to Franklin today. Where is it?"

"Not me. I don't have it." I could barely get the words out between my uncontrolled blubbering. I crouched as far over the table as I could to anchor my arm and keep my hand from tearing. The pool of blood grew to the size of a large serving platter, smeared from left to right as Gates pulled and pushed my arm back and forth. I let out a series of half-dead moans, sucking air in between, no strength to scream.

"Should've killed you weeks ago," Gates said. "Superintendent says I have to wait till he's gone. That gives us a few more minutes for you to answer my questions. Where's my ledger?"

"Steamer!" Cephas yelled. "Steamer's leaving now! Didn't even dock. Left all the passengers on the dock. Gates! The steamer's leaving!"

Gates gave a cursory glance back before returning to his work, locking his fingers even tighter around the jacket sleeve and ripping my arm back and forth. Having given up on trying to hold my hand steady, I kicked, scratched, pulled at the pick handle, and tried yanking his hand away but soon collapsed into a sobbing mess. The deep throbbing pain now radiated into my torso. My head nodded forward as I started to blackout.

"Don't you pass out on me," Gates said. "That just spoils the fun. Tell me where my ledger is!"

"Gone," I said, barely audible.

Gates stood, grabbed me by the hair, and slammed my head into the table. "What do you mean, gone?" he asked. "Gone where?"

"Ship!" Cephas yelled. "Lighthouse ship. Now the lighthouse boat's leaving!"

"Who took my ledger?" Gates yelled.

"Boat's already casting off!"

The water on the stove boiled hard, but Cephas paid no attention, moving from the kitchen to the window by the door. His yelling increased in volume with each update.

"Backing away from the dock!"

"Not much time left!" Gates shouted. "You're dead as soon as they leave. Where's my ledger?"

The lighthouse Cephas considered his eye of the Lord was my hell on earth. My head bobbed in and out of consciousness. Gates yanked and tore. Life drained with incredible pain and losses of blood. The air was too thick to breathe, the stale smell of fish guts mixing with the black smoke from the tender's steam engines.

Suddenly, everything fell quiet. We all heard it. After gunning the lighthouse ship's engines, a sickening chug and clunk resounded as if the propeller chopped through something, laboring harder and harder until the engines went silent.

Gates froze and listened. Sounds of men yelling were barely audible compared to all the screams and engine sounds just minutes ago. He listened and waited for the engines to restart but heard nothing. He gave my arm a strong tug as if to let me know I had more torture to come.

"Cephas. What happened?" Gates sounded tense but didn't yell. At the stove, the water in the pot boiled rapidly, but no one paid attention to it. Cephas stood at the window, looking out.

"Tangled," Cephas said. "Props. All tangled up."

"Tangled on what?"

"Fishnets!" Cephas said. "Looks like fishnets from the villagers' eviction the other night. Your men threw everything into the water. Props must have pulled one up from the bottom. Can you believe it?"

Cephas sounded relieved and almost pleased.

"A tangled ball about four feet wide, right where the

propellers should be. Never seen such a thing!"

"Get back over here."

Cephas walked back to the stove, still facing away from us, talking about the fouled props.

"A couple crew members leaning over the back with long poles, stabbing at it like they're fighting off a big sea serpent. Strangest thing you'd ever see."

Blood dripped from the tabletop, pooling on the floor below. Gates leaned away from me, still holding my arm with one hand. The other stretched out toward Cephas.

"That knife," Gates said. "Give me that big kitchen knife."

Cephas grabbed hot-pad holders.

"No! Give me that knife! Right next to the stove!"

Gates shook my arm back and forth on the table, his face dripping with sweat, his eyes steel blue, cold and evil. Still staring at me, he continued reaching out to Cephas with an open hand.

"The knife. Give me that knife!"

The response from Cephas was primitive. No reason, only reaction and reflex. In one smooth motion, the pot swung in a perfect arc with a speed and trajectory that must have been guided by the hands of God. A thorough dousing in boiling hot water. A room exploding with screams of agony. Screams not from me, but from another place.

They came from Gates.

8 JUST DESSERTS

Only a few feet separated Gates and me. Still, his loud, tortured screams barely registered. Even the intense pain from my hand felt detached, as if someone else's hand sat skewered on the table in front of me. My eyes closed, and my mind drifted. Fading off would've given me peace, but Cephas kept pulling me back. I groaned from the pain as he shook the ice pick from side to side to loosen it, finally freeing my hand from its impalement.

He shouted with great importance as he hurriedly wrapped my mangled hand in a dishtowel. His eyes shone bright with urgency. I watched his lips move and sensed his emotion, but none of the words made it through to my muddled brain. He slipped his shoulder under my good arm and grabbed my belt to lift me from the table, only to have my legs buckle, leaving me collapsed in a pile on the floor.

Gates fared no better. His screams were robust from the start, filled with rage. He glowed with a menace, as if possessed by an inner strength that rose above his injuries. Then suddenly, he gasped, his head reeled from left to right, and he collapsed back into his chair. All that stalwart determination drained in an instant. His fingertips fumbled across his face, gently touching the blistered, maimed skin. His screams throttled back to a weak, high-pitched moan, his outrage crumbled into fragility. He dropped to the ground, barely able to crawl as he inched his way out of the cottage door.

On his second try, Cephas pulled me to my knees, and I became more lucid. From the harbor below, the lighthouse service vessel's engine roared, laboring as it cut through layers of fishnet wrapped around the propeller. The engines raced forward and reversed. Their run times lasted progressively longer until the props finally broke into a clunky attempt at full throttle.

As the ship throttled down to an idle, there was a loud knock of a different engine—the one powering the lighthouse tram. I assumed it to be Gates, heading down to the lighthouse tender. From the squeal of the wheels rubbing against rails, I could tell the carriage was already halfway to shore.

". . . get up! . . . away . . . move!" Cephas knelt next to me, yelling with great urgency. Still, I could only understand the occasional word. I wanted to lie down. I sensed Mae in the background, calling for me. I imagined her warm smile, the shimmer of her dark eyes, and her auburn hair cascading over her shoulders. Like an angel. Another jarring tug from Cephas and my mind floated back to Barberry Creek, swimming with Mae, embracing in a weightless caress as we laughed, swam, kissed, and caressed. The smell of pine and the rushing sounds of water from the waterfalls made it feel so real and so wonderful.

Cephas abruptly pulled me back to reality. Once again, he propped his shoulder under my good arm and grabbed my belt to pull me to my feet. By now, I had enough strength to stand. We shuffled from the cottage up to the walkway railing that overlooked the harbor. Below us, the lighthouse service ship, now free from the fishnets, slowly backed its way to the lighthouse dock. The tram had reached the shore, Gates slumped over in the seat, unable to move. Crewmen jumped from the service ship to the dock, leaving the ship unmoored. Unable to coax Gates to his feet, one crewman grabbed under Gates's arms while the other took his legs, and the two of them carried him back to the vessel. Within minutes the ship motored out of the harbor below us, heading southeast past Tollefson Island.

The harbor now sat empty except for a pile of abandoned trunks left behind when the steamer avoided the hysterical mob of guests by refusing to dock. Even the lodge stood silent, its lawns deserted on what should have been the busiest day of Stony Fest. The air hung thick and still, thunderheads forming off to the south. I felt weak but now more alert than I'd been all day. Cephas helped me back into the cottage, sat me on the sofa, and then fetched supplies from the kitchen—a first-aid kit, dishtowels, a pitcher of water, and a washbasin.

"Where's Mae?" I asked.

"Haven't seen any villagers since the eviction. Maybe they found some other fishing village to join."

"I need to find her."

Cephas coarsely patted my hand through the bloody dishrag that wrapped around it. Pain shot to my arm as if he'd opened a vein from my wrist to my shoulder.

"Just to remind you," he said. "You're not going anywhere with this mangled hunk of flesh."

"We plan to get married. Did you know that? We're engaged. I need to go find her." Even to myself, my voice sounded childish and innocent, as if the torture had drained me of all my manhood. I tried to stand, but Cephas pushed me back onto the sofa, causing enough pain to end my resistance.

"It's all that matters now," I said. "She's all I have."

"Tell you what," Cephas said. "You just take it easy. When your hand gets better, we'll go look for her."

I couldn't get Mae out of my mind. It sickened me to be separated from her. I missed her and worried about her, wondering if she still cared about me. I had a knot in my stomach—the same painful, unsettling cramp as when I learned Jenny wanted to divorce me, unwilling or unable to deal with my disfigurement.

"Where'd the lodge guests go?" I asked without really caring, still thinking of Mae.

"Scattered," he said. "Like cockroaches ahead of the broom.

221

Hell-bent on protecting their precious reputations. Trying to find a way back to young wives and girlfriends, hoping to be long gone before the newsmen and revenuers arrive."

He sat in a chair next to the couch, holding my hand over the washbasin. After removing the blood-soaked dishrag, he gently dabbed around the edges of the wound, cleaning the blood off the back of my hand, the palm area, and the fingers. Now with the excitement over and the danger abated, Cephas wasn't panicked, mad, or despondent. He looked old, just going about his business with a cool resignation. He showed no remorse for the damage done to Gates, nor any worry about his job, pension, or retirement.

"Why'd ya do it?" I asked. "Why the boiling water? You could've just walked away."

Cephas stopped as if in deep thought, the rag dripping bloody red splotches onto the floor. He had a straight-away stare as if pulling insights from the ether.

"The real question is why I waited so long, why I didn't stop him weeks ago."

Seeing the puddle of bloody water on the floor, Cephas wiped it up, wrung the rag into the basin, and then inspected my hand.

"It was so easy to hold you responsible," he said. "To blame you and your damaged eye for all this evil. Even the scriptures condemn you. If your eye is healthy, your whole body will be full of light, but if your eye is bad, your whole body will be full of darkness. Sure enough, darkness descended the day you arrived. You fought with the guests and almost drowned on your very first night. In the first week alone, you fought with Polly and knocked Gates out in the boxing ring. Then the village burned, and Hans died."

"Sorry I asked." I kicked my shoes off before lifting my feet up onto the couch.

"Blaming you meant I didn't have to accept my own responsibilities. I didn't have to stand up to Gates."

As he spoke, he fetched my eye patch from the floor, brushed the hair out of my face, and then fitted the patch over my missing eye.

"My pension was all I cared about. It made me blind to all Gates had done. The corruption grew like a cancer, starting with little things, like all the liquor, Polly's partying every night, or the harm they did to the villagers. I never believed it would escalate into something as horrible as fires, death, and tortures. I couldn't just stand there and let Gates kill you."

He pulled a handkerchief from his pocket and wiped the sweat from his face.

"Somewhere along the way, I lost all my religion, blind to my own sins. Gates was my demon. I should have stopped him weeks ago. I kept myself busy saving my pension and didn't even see how I was losing my soul. I can now see it was never your eye that was cursed. It was mine."

Cephas bowed his head and moved slowly, as if the simplest task required great concentration. By now, most of the blood was clotted and cleaned. The skin torn around the wound made a jagged hole the size of a quarter. Inside, I could see little bits of white, likely tendons or bone. He inspected my wound before fetching two medicine bottles from the cupboard. I'd seen similar bottles of antiseptic at the army field hospital. My teeth clenched as I recalled the pain they inflicted. He grabbed my thumb tight in his fist, holding my mangled hand over the basin.

"This'll hurt like hell," he said. He poured the bleachy Dakin's solution straight from the bottle into the wound. I had no chance to react. As I screamed, I tried to pull myself from the sofa but didn't have the strength. I struggled to pull my mangled hand away, grabbing at the bottle with my free hand to make him stop. I was too weak to accomplish anything other than knocking the basin onto the floor. I laid back, limp, completely powerless, blubbering like a little boy all cried out.

"Halfway there."

Cephas's words were hardly reassuring. He turned my hand over and poured the rest of the bottle slowly over the hole in my palm. I faded in and out as he dried my hand with a clean towel, dabbed the fleshy wound with iodine, and covered the whole hand with rolls of bandages. My last recollection was the sight of a big white gauze ball the size of a softball at the end of my arm.

#

The thunder rumbled off in the distance, waking me at 3:30 a.m. The pain from the wound felt less localized, having developed into a dull throb from my shoulder to my fingertips. I went to the bathroom to pee, finding it more complicated than I'd imagined with only one usable hand. In the kitchen, I ate a stale biscuit from the breadbox and drank a cup of cold day-old coffee before heading up to the lighthouse. In spite of all that had happened, I'd never lost my love and appreciation for the majestic watchtower. I hoped to work at least one more shift.

The air was hot, thick, humid, and still, as it often is before an approaching storm. Counting four seconds between the lightning's flash and the thunder's boom, I calculated the downpour to be less than a mile away, closing in from the south.

Hail the size of acorns pelted me on my short run from the cottage to the lighthouse. The ice balls hammering the metal roof of the lantern room sounded like gunfire as I climbed the circular stairs. Cephas was short and to the point as we met in the watch room.

"Mind the lantern," he said. "I'll get the foghorn."

No pleasantries. No concern over how my arm felt or if I was up to the task. No thanks for my willingness to help, in spite of my injuries. I might have been offended. Instead, I was grateful that he trusted my sense of duty, rightly recognizing my commitment, regardless of all that had happened.

The storm hit with a fury, unlike anything I'd ever experienced. The wind swirled first from the west, then circled around from the southeast. Mountains of sea and foam battered the giant granite promontory with a force that reverberated to the tip of the lantern room. Columns of water peeled from the waves, scaling the cliff beyond the lighthouse railing before sheering off in the wind and slamming into the buildings. Moments later, the next wave crashed with the same fury as the one before.

Cephas fired up the diesel engines from the fog signal building, conjuring the deep bass, ear-splitting, diaphonic, beeee-ohh sound that roared across the water with a booming grunt, to be repeated every eight seconds. I tended the lantern, though the light hardly carried past the glass windows, immediately dissipating with the rain and spray.

The rat-a-tatt of hailstones, the flashes of lightning, and the booming fog signal conjured up all the terrors and shell shock from the war. I laid on the floor, struggling against the jitters and shortness of breath. Each loud clap of thunder and flash of lightning reawakened the ghostly terror of mortar rounds. The lack of visibility made an already cramped room excruciatingly claustrophobic. Anxiety turned to panic with all the sights and sounds so similar to war. Still, I forced myself to crawl through the main chores of winding the clockwork that turned the lantern, pressurizing the kerosene tank, and mopping up the puddles of water from the leaks. Whether or not it was needed, I cycled through my chores over and over again, if only to hold my anxiety in check.

I sang as I worked, belting out old army songs from my time at boot camp. I sang at the top of my lungs, fighting against the deafening noises of the foghorn and thunder. After a number of renditions, the pounding hail gave way to a softer, steadier rain against the metal roof. The thunder faded as the leading edge of the storm moved north into the forested wilderness. The foghorn kept booming well past the final raindrops, but by then, my singing and working had taken the edge off my anxiety.

The wind mellowed to a gentle breeze by daybreak, and the waves calmed to a light surf. The bright morning sun illuminated the golden brick and cream-colored trim of the tower. All traces of fish guts and carcasses were gone, the walls and walkways blasted clean by the rain and waves. Cephas considered the storm a message from God.

"A baptism," he said. "A promise of forgiveness and new beginnings. A burial of the old. Our first steps into the newness of life."

#

An expectant pause filled the harbor, as if at any moment an army of attendants might begin setting up buffets, launching boats, and planting beach umbrellas. The armies never came. Everything stayed quiet. I felt the peace I had originally expected from Stony Point before learning of the lodge and its young millionaire guests. Now, I was finally experiencing the sweetness of solitude.

Shortly after sunrise, Cephas started cleaning, working his way through each of the buildings, putting everything back in place from the most recent ransacking. It was still his lighthouse. For over fifteen years, it had been his body of work, his devotion and his legacy, not to be abandoned.

While he worked, I slept, half lying, half sitting on the couch with my throbbing hand perched high up on the back cushion. I dreamed of a steamer in gale-force winds just off Stygg Havn. The ship headed for Duluth, its decks filled with desperate men. The boat pitched wildly, adrift with a flooded engine compartment. The steamer crew worked below deck, pumping water and trying to restart the engines. The passengers grew impatient, arguing among themselves. The winds blew from the southeast—the worst possible direction, and the steamer drifted perilously close to the rocky reefs off Gull Point.

Every ten seconds, the beam from the lighthouse swept across the ship with an intensity that shocked the eyes, making it impossible to see in the ten seconds of darkness that followed. While Cephas considered the lighthouse his eye of the Lord, the beam was nothing but a curse for everyone on the ship, adding to the panic and desperation, making everything all the more hellish on board.

Half blinded, the passengers crowded onto the starboard side, the ship listing dangerously to port. Some had life jackets, but any sane man would have known that the vests wouldn't save their lives in the ice-cold water. They'd just make the bodies easier to recover.

I held the ladder leading up to the pilothouse. Men grabbed at me, pulling me loose. No one laughed or bullied. Everyone went about their business with an eerie silence and a lack of emotion. All the exertion focused on hauling me away from the ladder and to the railing along the gunwale. Rumors had spread about me being the cause of the raging storm. The crowd watched in silence as four men lifted me over the rail, dropping me into the stormy waters below. I came up for one last gasp, to see the sky clearing, the waves settling, the wind subsiding, and the ship's crew chanting my name. I awoke from the horrible dream, jerking straight up from the sofa, causing a shooting pain in my bandaged hand.

"Stop that. Lie down!" The harsh voice caused me as much fear and confusion as my dream had. The scratchy tenor voice was unmistakably Polly's. He sat on the edge of the sofa. Franklin was behind him in his wheelchair. If you'd forced me to guess which two people I might wake up to, I never would have guessed that combination.

"You made quite a mess up here," Polly said. "Nails and screws all over the roadway, pulling the whole lodge down the crapper."

"Makes me proud as hell," Franklin said. "Wish we could've all been here to see it." He grabbed my leg above the knee, hard enough to draw a squeal of pain from me. The two acted as familiar as cousins. I wouldn't have been any less surprised if Gunnar walked in arm-in-arm with my ex-wife, Jenny.

"How do you two know each other?"

"He's my houseguest," Franklin said. "His whole family's at the estate. Elsie, Elsie's mom, and little John. Mum just loves having a newborn in the house again."

Franklin and Polly each had a content smile on their faces, as if this tidbit of improbable information explained everything. I gingerly pulled myself up into a sitting position, waited in patient silence, hoping either one of them might shed more light. Polly finally filled in a few blanks.

"Remember last Monday when John was born? How the whole harbor was twisted up in knots, ready to explode? You pulled off those fishing excursions to stop Gates from evicting the villagers. The lodge was overcome with a plague of flies and rotten smells, and Gates was obsessed about a ledger he was missing. Unbeknownst to you, that was the night Gates intercepted the letter intended for Franklin, which talked about the ledger and decryption key, and how you planned to have Gates locked up for good."

"I bet that pissed him off," I said.

"Sure did. He asked me what I knew about it. Luckily, I could honestly plead ignorance."

Polly stuffed a pillow behind my back, making it more comfortable for me to sit. It was a kind gesture that I never would have expected from him.

"That's when Elsie and I decided to leave. I sent a note to Franklin to tell him what happened and asked him to meet us at the pier in Duluth."

"But how'd you know where the ledger, the encryption key, and the books were hidden?" I asked.

"Oh, please," Polly said. "You call that a hiding place? The false bottom drawer was old and useless back when I was a teenager. Lucky for you, I found the books before the ransacking started."

Polly poured me a cup of coffee from the pot on the stove, then sat back down on the edge of the sofa.

"You can see why I wanted to leave so badly. I only wish you'd come with us. Would have saved you from all that torment."

"Then he never would have made such a glorious, wonderful mess," Franklin said.

"So, you took the books and matrix key to Duluth?"

"Yeah. Met Gus and Franklin at the pier," Polly said, putting the pot back on the stove.

"Our driver had already picked up Elsie's mom," Franklin said. "He drove Elsie, her mom, and Little John back to the estate. Gus drove the other car, taking Polly and me to the Superior Telegraph newspaper. I know the publisher from my school days. Polly told them everything that happened, weaving a story with the intrigue and suspense of a Sherlock Holmes novel."

"They read through your decryption of the ledger as soon as we arrived," Polly said. "Took them no time at all to validate your code-breaking. After that, there was nothing but pages turning and pencils flying. By the time we left, they knew this would be the biggest story Duluth has ever seen. They had three boats rented for this morning, to bring us, reporters, and photographers up to Stony Point, intending to scoop the whole story ahead of the other papers."

"They're up here now?" I asked.

"Covering every inch of the lodge, the harbor, and the highway," Franklin said. "Rumors were just beginning to fly in Duluth as we left. Stories about angry mobs trying to leave Stony Point and the big accident on Highway One. We didn't know about the bootleg trucks, the whisky all over the road, or the long line of young millionaires trying to escape to Beaver Creek, like refugees leaving a war zone."

"I promised them a good story," Polly said. "That was before I knew about the god-awful mess you made of this place. They're finding more scandal than they ever could've hoped for."

"Where's everybody else?"

"Gus and Cephas took one of the motorboats up the coast to look for the villagers," Franklin said.

Polly went to the kitchen to make sandwiches. He cut a few thin slices of meat for each and topped them off with dollops of mustard before wrapping them in wax paper. Franklin and I stepped out onto the walkway overlooking the harbor. The whole shoreline appeared frozen in time—no buffets, beach umbrellas, or lodge guests. The party sounds that had filled the air for so many days were now gone. Gates's Hacker-Craft remained tied up at the end of the marina's pier. I began to tremble like I had a bad case of the chills. I noticed it in my limbs first, then through my torso.

"You ok?" Franklin asked. "Something wrong?"

"I dunno," I answered, hanging on to the rail, trembling.

"Don't know if there's any good that comes out of this or if it's all just pain and misery. The eviction of the villagers, the injuries from the car crashes, the ice pick through my hand, the boiling water in Gates's face. Hardly seems like anything is worth all that trouble."

I stomped my feet, thinking it might stop the chills and the trembling. It only made me feel more incapacitated. Franklin reached out to help, but I pushed his hand away.

"I'm no prohibitionist," I said. "I had nothing against those men. I didn't care if they drank whisky or warm milk. I only cared about the treatment of the villagers."

I stuffed my hands under my armpits to stop the trembling, thinking how it was something Cephas might do.

"So, now what?" I asked. "The young millionaires are still all young millionaires, and the villagers are off somewhere, still homeless. Me, I have no job and no prospects."

I kicked at the gravel, sending small stones ricocheting down to the boulders below.

"Is this the dignity and heroism you promised me?" I asked. "Feels pretty shitty if you ask me."

Franklin grabbed my arm, pointing to the lodge.

"Those reporters and photographers are having a field day up there. They'll be writing headlines that'll sell more papers than the Armistice. Tomorrow's paper will be thick with stories of greed. There'll be scandals uncovered at the highest levels among councilmen, judges, and police."

A group of men congregating on the big lawn jotted in their notebooks and took photographs before heading into the lodge.

"There'll be pictures of warehouses filled with whisky," Franklin said. "They'll show the bootleg vehicles disguised as lumber delivery trucks with those clever compartments to conceal the booze. The stories will be about corruption and hypocrisy. You won't be the villain. You'll be the hero."

Only days ago, Gates was in complete control, with an army of men and women ready to make Stony Fest unforgettable for its hundreds of attendees. Now the lodge and the harbor were deserted on what was to be the first full day of the celebration.

"You'll see," he said. "By tomorrow morning, all of Duluth will be buzzing about a brave assistant lighthouse keeper who stood up to all those powerful people from Duluth—and won. I bet your parents and that heartless ex-wife of yours will read about it in the local Aitkin papers."

Franklin reached into his coat pocket and pulled out a neatly folded folio of papers, about the size and thickness of Cephas's tobacco pouch.

"Maybe this will make it worthwhile," he said. "The villagers won't be homeless, after all. I'm working on the legal documents for Stony Point. Some of the paperwork is missing and needs to be updated, but once I'm finished, Stony Point will belong to Mae. It should have passed from Knute's dad to Knute, and then to Mae after Knute passed away. Once she signs all these documents and I properly file them, she'll own everything."

"The fishing village?"

"No. The whole harbor. Even the lodge. It's all built on what will be her property. Best part of it is, Gates won't be around to contest her ownership. He could've tied things up in court for years, but now he's running from the law, not corrupting the law. Maybe the villagers will give up fishing altogether and run their own high-class resort. A place packed all summer long, not with wealthy drunks, but with happy families."

"Still feels pretty shitty," I said.

In truth, I was feeling much better.

#

Polly popped out of the cottage, eating his second sandwich.

"Got something here that I found while showing the reporters around," he said. "Might be yours. I found it at Barberry Creek."

It surprised me that Polly would bother going to Barberry Creek. Then again, it wasn't far from the hairpin curve with all the accidents.

"Probably the carving I left there," I said. "It's nothing. It doesn't matter anymore. Mae's probably miles away by now."

Polly handed both Franklin and me a sandwich. After a quick inspection, Franklin frowned and gave his sandwich to me.

"Found it on a pile of wood shavings," Polly said. "That's why he thought it might be yours."

I ate my first sandwich and put the second in my pocket to eat later.

"Has some initials on it. J+M. Any idea what that means?"

"Jilted misery?" I joked. "Jobless man? Jumbled memories?"

Polly reached into the pocket of his coat and pulled out the surprise. He held it out as I turned around, then put it into my good hand. Not the carved wooden heart that I expected. It was made of leather. The same black leather used to make my eye patch. A black leather sheath for my carving knife, with vertical slits at the top to slide my belt through. My carving knife fit perfectly into the little pouch, held snugly by a flap that snapped down in front.

On the back, I found the initials J+M. On the front flap, the name Askeladden.

# # #

ACKNOWLEDGEMENTS

Many thanks to the talented group of writers at the Minneapolis Western Suburbs Writing Group for their insights, expertise, and support. Thanks to Greg Kagan who generously contributed his time and expertise, helping to put the polish on this novel.

Such a project would never have been possible without the help of friends and family - particularly my wonderful wife Sandy.

ABOUT THE AUTHOR

Bruce is a Minnesota based freelance writer, with an insatiable thirst for books that bring interesting points of history to life. He did much of his research for Stygg Havn along the north shore of Lake Superior, studying the history of the communities, landscapes, lodges, and lighthouses in the area.